"Anything that might develop between us has to be strictly casual. No strings or expectations— and no involving our families."

Whoa. Was she suggesting—?

Jade smiled, and Trevor felt his throat close. "Just in case something should happen," she murmured.

"Something...like this?" With a grin and a rare surrender to impulse, he reached out with his right hand to snag the back of her neck. She made no effort to draw back when he lowered his head—and he would have stopped immediately if she had. Instead, she met him halfway, seemingly as curious as he.

The kiss was light, carefully restrained. Just an exploratory meeting of lips, a brief, testing sample. Jade tasted exactly as he'd expected: sweet, with just a touch of spice beneath. Had it not been for the resented crutches, he'd have moved closer to prove that the rest of her felt as good against him.

Dear Reader,

Coming from a large family with many distinguished veterans among the generations, I married the son of a career army/air force veteran who served in two wars, and we live near the US Air Force base in central Arkansas. I have a great regard for those who have served in the military. I've seen the scars, both physical and emotional, that remain after that service ends, and I was intrigued by the idea of writing a series of romances with veteran heroes, each with his own issues to overcome before finding his happily-ever-after destiny. I've also seen the dedication required by the loved ones who keep the home fires burning while their warriors are away.

The Soldiers and Single Moms trilogy came from that initial idea. And, as a mother of three now-grown "kids" and grandmother of two little boys, I always enjoy writing about the rewards and challenges of parenthood. I've loved spending time with the characters I've grown to know during their journeys in these three books—and I hope you've enjoyed meeting them along the way!

Happy reading!

Gina

GINA
WILKINS

—

The Soldier's Legacy

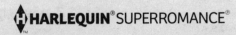

HARLEQUIN®SUPERROMANCE®

Recycling programs
for this product may
not exist in your area.

ISBN-13: 978-1-335-44912-2

The Soldier's Legacy

Printed in U.S.A.

www.Harlequin.com

Before she even learned to read, **Gina Wilkins** announced that she wanted to be a writer. That dream never wavered, though she worked briefly in advertising and human resources. Influenced by her mother's love of classic Harlequin romances, she knew she wanted her stories to always have happy endings. She met her husband in her first college English class and they've been married for more than thirty-five years, blessed with two daughters and a son. They also have two delightful grandchildren. After more than one hundred books with Harlequin, she will always be a fan of romance and a believer in happy endings.

Books by Gina Wilkins

HARLEQUIN SUPERROMANCE

Soldiers and Single Moms

The Soldier's Forever Family
The Way to a Soldier's Heart

HARLEQUIN SPECIAL EDITION

Proposals & Promises

The Boss's Marriage Plan

A Reunion and a Ring
The Bachelor's Little Bonus

Bride Mountain

Healed with a Kiss
A Proposal at the Wedding
Matched by Moonlight

A Match for the Single Dad
The Texan's Surprise Baby
The Right Twin
His Best Friend's Wife
Husband for a Weekend

Visit the Author Profile page at Harlequin.com for more titles.

As always, for John, who has been with me through forty years of marriage, raising a family and more than a hundred books. I couldn't have done any of it without him!

CHAPTER ONE

ALWAYS-PRACTICAL SINGLE MOM Jade Evans had made detailed plans for the coming weeks for herself and her three children. A fire ignited by a careless construction worker had sent that carefully-crafted schedule up in smoke along with the kitchen of their new home, only days before they were to have moved in. Their furniture and most of their belongings had already been delivered before the fire, though fortunately most of the damage had been confined to the kitchen and roof.

"Wow." Twelve-year-old Caleb stood with his mother and two sisters in a soaring entryway with a dining room on the left side and a front parlor on the right. Glass sliders at the back of the big den ahead looked out over a spacious deck, a glistening pool and a beautifully landscaped lawn that sloped gracefully down to a private dock on the Intracoastal Waterway. His brown eyes wide, Caleb pushed his floppy brown hair off the top of his glasses. "Nice place, huh, Mom?"

"Yes, it's lovely."

Jade could understand why her son was impressed. It was hard to imagine that this spacious house was home to only one man—Trevor Farrell, the son of her mother's closest friend. An army veteran and now-successful resort owner, Trevor had been tragically widowed at just twenty-eight—almost a decade ago while he was deployed overseas. Jade didn't think he'd owned this place when he was married. So, he'd bought it after his wife's death, either as a private escape or as an investment. Perhaps he had plans to remarry eventually. His mother hadn't given up hope for grandchildren to enjoy as much as Jade's mom. Linda McGill relished being Nanna to Jade's children.

Mary Pat Rayburn, the short, pleasantly rounded woman who'd opened the door and ushered them inside waved a hand toward the staircase in a warm welcome. "Let me show you up to your rooms."

"We're going to live here?" six-year-old Bella asked, slipping her hand into Jade's. With her golden curls and huge amber eyes, Bella was the youngest and most skittish of the children, the one Jade thought of as her "loving little worrier."

Notoriously impatient, ten-year-old Erin sighed as she pushed back her darker blond hair to focus on her sister. "We talked about this, Bella. This is Ms. Hester's son's house. We're only staying here until our new house is fixed so we can move in. Right, Mama?"

"Yes, that's right." Jade agreed rather reluctantly. She was still finding it hard to believe that she and her children would be sharing Trevor's home for the next couple of weeks.

Having accepted a job here in Shorty's Landing, Jade had recently sold the house she'd owned, close to her mother's home in Columbia, South Carolina.

She and the children could have stayed with her mother until the repairs on their new house here were completed, but school would begin in less than a week. It would've been difficult to get the kids back and forth with a ninety-minute drive each way, especially with Jade starting her new job. It was hard enough for them that they'd be in new schools, and now they had to deal with their home in upheaval, as well.

When she'd learned Jade needed temporary lodgings in the area, Hester Farrell had railroaded Jade into occupying Trevor's rarely used second floor until the repairs were completed. Suspicious about Hester's motives, Jade had initially resisted the offer. When it came to Jade and Trevor, Hester was no more subtle a matchmaker than Jade's own mom.

Jade had been forced to inform her mother more than once that she wasn't interested in being pushed into a romance with Hester's handsome and successful son—despite hints that grew more pointed each time Jade's path crossed Trevor's. As if both being widowed early and having mothers who were close friends formed the basis for a lasting relationship between her and Trevor, Jade often thought in exasperation.

She didn't want to do anything that would throw more fuel on that particular fire. And accepting charity was difficult for someone who'd become accustomed to relying on no one but herself.

Still, the intimidatingly efficient Hester had forged on with her proposition. Both Hester and Jade's mother had implied that it would be ungrateful of Jade to refuse the generous offer. So now here they were, being welcomed into Trevor's home by his housekeeper less than two full days after Hester had extended the invitation on her son's behalf. Jade couldn't help wondering if Trevor was any more enthused about the situation than she was.

She and Trevor had been introduced for the first time only three years ago during a party at his parents' house to celebrate Jade's mother's sixtieth birthday. Coincidentally in town for a class reunion, Trevor had dropped in to give his regards. Jade and Trevor had interacted on only a few occasions since, most recently when he'd accompanied his parents to Jade's father's funeral last year. Jade couldn't claim to know Trevor well, but when she thought of him, she always recalled his impeccable manners and his charming, but unrevealing, smile. Despite his deeply ingrained courtesy, she'd had the sense that wherever he was at the time, he felt as though he should be somewhere else—a busy man with divided loyalties pulling him in many directions.

Having been wed to a man whose attention was always somewhere else, Jade recognized the type all too well. Stephen hadn't been home much during their tragically shortened marriage, but when he was, she knew he'd been thinking of his responsibilities to the military. As much as he'd loved her and the kids, and she'd never had reason to doubt that he had loved them, he'd never seemed totally comfortable changing diapers or grilling burgers in the backyard or unclogging drains. The battlefield had called to him. She'd always wondered if he'd felt the pull of home when he was deployed or if a war zone was where he truly felt most himself.

She'd learned to be independent and almost completely self-sufficient during her somewhat unconventional but still happy marriage. She was chagrined to be in the position of having to accept Trevor's help now, but she hadn't had many other options. Finding a temporary place to rent for a family of four would have been difficult. She had to admit this was a convenient, if awkward, solution to her crisis.

With a resigned shake of her head, she motioned toward the stairs. "Everyone follow Mrs. Rayburn now."

"Oh, y'all can just call me Mary Pat," the housekeeper insisted with a musical chime of a laugh as she started up the stairs. "I've never cared much for formality, as Trevor would tell you."

Reaching the second-floor landing, they faced a wall arranged with framed photographs of gorgeous landscapes, an intriguing mix of coastal and inland shots. Jade wondered if Trevor had taken them; she'd been told he was a talented photographer. If these photos were his, his talent hadn't been exaggerated, she mused, studying an image of ocean spray blasting up from behind a boulder on which a heron posed with proudly spread wings. An aerial view of a wooded mountaintop was breathtaking both in theme and in the implied risk involved in taking the shot. Jade had heard Trevor's mother bemoan her son's proclivity for risky activities like riding fast motorcycles, mountain climbing and paragliding. As the widow of an adrenaline junkie, Jade didn't fault Hester for wishing her son would pursue less risky hobbies.

"I like that one," Bella whispered, pointing to a tableau of two brown horses standing nose to nose in a rolling green pasture as if sharing a secret from the photographer they side-eyed.

"I like it, too," Jade said, smiling down at her youngest.

"There are three guest bedrooms up here and one downstairs, all with baths attached," Mary Pat announced with a wave of a hand. "This door ahead of us leads into the bigger bedroom. I figured you'd want that one, Ms. Evans. The other two bedrooms are on either side of the hallway. Maybe the girls would like to share one and Caleb can have the third. Unless you'd prefer to use the downstairs guest suite, Ms. Evans?"

"No, we'll all bunk up here, thank you. The girls will share. And please call me Jade. I'm not really the formal type, either."

"Where does Ms. Hester's son sleep?" Erin asked, peering into one of the open doors.

"Oh, his suite is downstairs," Mary Pat replied. "He hardly ever comes up here, to be honest."

"Then why does he have all these rooms?" Erin asked with typical blunt curiosity.

"He calls it an investment. But I think his mama talked him into buying the place," Mary Pat added with a wink at Jade. "If you know her, you're aware she's a force to be reckoned with.

Fine woman, but you don't want to be getting on her bad side."

Jade believed Mary Pat had just concisely summed up Hester's personality. Jade's mom insisted Hester was simply a well-intentioned meddler, but Jade had always been secretly intimidated by the woman. "Where do you sleep, Ms. Mary Pat?" Erin asked.

"Did you see that cottage off to one side of the property? Trevor had it built for me when my husband passed away three years ago. I was never blessed with children, and Trevor is like the son I always wanted. His mama is gracious enough to share him with me—probably because it takes both of us to keep him in line," the housekeeper added with another of her musical laughs.

Jade was getting the distinct impression that while the likable Mary Pat adored her employer, she didn't hesitate to speak her mind to or about him.

"There's one other room up here y'all need to see." Mary Pat turned to her left and walked to the end of the hallway. She opened a door and stepped back to invite them in with another wave of her expressive hands.

Jade heard the kids gasp in delight, and she sighed in surrender as she looked into a spacious rec room equipped with a large-screen TV with leather theater seating, a pool table and a foosball table. Tall, leather-covered stools drew up to a built-in bar on which rested a wooden bowl filled with assorted fruits. Two game tables sat in front of shelves stocked with books, games—both video and tabletop—and an impressive selection of movies. A smaller table had been tucked into a dormer nook, surrounded by inviting beanbag hassocks and topped with a nubbed baseplate for use with a big bin of brightly colored plastic building blocks.

Erin was already being drawn to the bookshelves while Caleb studied the video games. Bella, overwhelmed, clung to Jade's hand, though she looked longingly at the blocks table. Considering this room and the pool in the backyard, Jade figured the kids were never going to want to leave this house for the more modest home she had purchased in a less-expensive neighborhood a few miles away. It was a nice place, but not like this one. No private pool. No extravagant entertainment room.

Still, she thought they'd be quite happy in their new house, once it was fire-damage free and habitable again, of course. The kids had examined and approved every inch of it before the purchase papers were signed. They'd miss their previous home and friends in Columbia, but Jade thought she'd prepared them well for their adventure here.

She'd been considering this move for more

than a year, since her physician cousin had first approached her about taking a nursing job in a medical clinic in Shorty's Landing. With all the children in school, Jade could put her nursing training to full use, having worked only part-time for Bella's first six years. And frankly, it would be nice to start fresh in a new town with new acquaintances. As kind as everyone in her hometown had been to them after her husband's death, there were times when it had become difficult for all of them to be always seen as the tragically bereaved survivors of a larger-than-life military hero.

"Mr. Farrell really never comes up here?" Caleb shook his head in disbelief. "If I had a room like this, I'd stay in it all the time."

"This floor is set up for his guests. He has a big TV, a reading nook, and a home office in his private suite downstairs," Mary Pat explained. "When he's home, he's usually there."

"Although I have been known to sneak up here late at night to work on my pool-shooting skills," a man drawled from the doorway. "I figure if I keep practicing, I'll beat Mary Pat someday. Don't ever bet against her, by the way. She's a hustler."

"Not a hustler," Mary Pat said with a grin as everyone turned to watch Trevor Farrell enter the room. "Just better than you'll ever be, practice or no."

Trevor laughed, the sound deep and rumbly. Jade swallowed. He was even better looking than she'd remembered—tall and slim, with light brown hair, very blue eyes and a smile that could have come straight from a toothpaste ad. His posture was straight and he looked poised, a man accustomed to being in charge. His expression was warm as he approached her. "It's nice to see you again, Jade."

She tucked a strand of blond hair behind one ear. "Trevor, it was so generous of you to take us in while our house is being repaired. We appreciate it very much."

"As you can see, there's plenty of room. You aren't putting me out at all. I'm only sorry the accident at your new house delayed your move-in. That must have been disappointing for you all."

"Oh, I think everything's working out just fine," Erin proclaimed, running a hand admiringly along the back of a leather theater chair. "I'm Erin, by the way."

"Yes, I recall meeting you at your grandmother's sixtieth birthday party—what? Three years ago? You've grown quite a bit since then."

Erin nodded. "I was just seven then. I'm ten now."

"I remember you." Caleb looked around from

the video game selection as he spoke, pushing his glasses up on his nose. "Is it okay if I play *Dougie the Donkey* on your system later? I'll be really careful."

"Of course you can play the game, Caleb, if your mom approves. Maybe you could even show me a trick or two. I've never gotten past the Gator Boss fight on level nine."

"Seriously? I took him out in like three tries."

Trevor chuckled. "So far my skills at both pool and video games have been questioned. What about you, Little Bit?" he asked casually of Bella, who was peeking out at him from behind her mother. "Do you have a special talent you could embarrass me with?"

Jade half-expected her shy youngest to mumble an answer and hide again, which was Bella's usual response when spoken to by strangers. Instead, after a moment's thought, the child replied, "I can do cartwheels. Three in a row."

Trevor threw up his hands. "Well, there you go. I can't do one cartwheel without falling right on my…er…face."

Bella giggled, then crowded behind Jade again as if she'd surprised even herself.

"In case you forgot, her name is Bella," Erin said in a long-suffering tone. "She's kind of a scaredy-cat."

"Am not," Bella muttered, her voice muffled by Jade's shirt.

"I wouldn't call anyone who can do three cartwheels in a row a scaredy-cat," Trevor said solemnly, giving Jade a wink that made her catch her breath. She blinked a couple of times, as surprised by her own automatic response to this charismatic man as by Bella's. They'd always been surrounded by crowds in their earlier meetings. Maybe that had somewhat diluted the effect of his substantial charm.

"Anyway," Trevor said. "I have a dull business dinner tonight and I need to change first. I just wanted to welcome you and tell you that if there's anything you need while you're our guests here, please let us know."

Erin opened her mouth to speak, but closed it again quickly when Jade frowned at her. Heaven only knew what her outspoken middle child had been on the verge of requesting.

Mary Pat moved toward the door. "I'm going down to start dinner for the rest of us. I'll let you know when it's ready, Jade."

"Oh, you don't have to cook for us," Jade felt compelled to protest. "I can…"

"Are you kidding? I'm always delighted to have an excuse to cook for a group. And I'm planning to eat with y'all, so I'm looking forward to that, too." Mary Pat punched Trevor's arm lightly as she passed him. "This one's hardly ever home at mealtime."

"You know I'd rather have your cooking than anyone else's," Trevor shot back, patting her cheek. "Just have to work most evenings."

"And by work, he means schmoozing with guests at the resort or having dinner with travel writers or vendors," Mary Pat explained in an aside as she left the room. "Most of which he could cut back on significantly without affecting his business in the least. The man is a workaholic, but nothing his mama or I say can make him change his ways."

Smiling, Trevor spoke to Jade. "Mary Pat is one of a kind. I tell her all the time I'm not sure if it's a benefit to the world or a shame there are no more like her."

Amused by the relationship between Mary Pat and Trevor, Jade returned his smile. "Looks to me as if you're lucky to have her."

Casting an exaggeratedly wary look toward the doorway, Trevor placed a finger to his lips as he stage-whispered, "Don't tell her I said this, but you're right."

Dropping his hand, he took a step backward toward the hall. "Again, if there's anything you need, just let us know. There are bottled waters and assorted soft drinks in the bar fridge along with some yogurts and other snacks, and

of course the fruit in the bowl. Help yourself…
uh…with your mom's permission, of course, kids.
And, Jade, there's a coffeemaker and an assortment of coffees and teas."

"Wait up a second, Trevor." Releasing Bella's
hand, Jade moved to follow him. "You kids stay
in here and play with the blocks or something for
a few minutes while I speak with Mr. Farrell."

The girls were already headed toward the
blocks table when Jade stepped out of the room
and into the hallway with Trevor.

He paused at the top of the stairs. "Is there
something I can do for you, Jade?"

"I wanted to thank you again for your hospitality," she said quietly. "I have a feeling your
mother pressured you into this, but it was still
very kind of you. And I want to assure you that
I was as surprised by the offer as you probably
were. It never would have occurred to me to ask
you to open your home to us this way."

He started to speak, and she sensed he was
going to respond with the practiced, professional-
host courtesy he'd displayed before. But then he
dropped the act, giving her a glimpse of the man
behind the admittedly attractive polish. "Knowing my mother, I have no doubt whose idea this
was. And, yeah, Mom did let me know after she'd
set it up that you and your family would be staying with me for a couple of weeks. But don't take

that to mean I regret having you here. I'd have made the same offer had I heard about your situation on my own. If the resort weren't full to capacity this week, I'd have arranged a suite for you there to give the kids more options for entertainment."

"More options?" Jade glanced toward the rec room where her children were happily entertained at that moment. "I think they have more than enough here to occupy them, thank you."

"My mom told me you're moving to Shorty's Landing to start a new job," Trevor said.

She nodded. "I'll be working for my cousin. She's opening a family practice clinic with a partner, and I'll be her nurse. The clinic opens a week from Monday."

Obviously, none of this was news to Trevor, who'd probably heard all the details from his mother. "I look forward to meeting your cousin, Dr....?"

"Amy Ford. You might have met her at my dad's funeral last year. She's an excellent doctor. Very compassionate and thorough. Dr. Lincoln Brindle is her partner, and he's wonderful, too."

"I'm sure they'll be an asset to the community," Trevor said, slipping smoothly back into his rather formal manner.

"They will be."

He would know all about being a community

asset, of course. Even as a newcomer to the town where Trevor had made his home for the past eight or nine years, Jade had already heard his praises from the few locals she'd encountered. He was considered one of the most prestigious community leaders. The daughter of a successful attorney and a human resources manager, Jade came from a comfortable background, herself, but the Farrells were wealthy. Very wealthy. And everyone in their hometown—nearly everyone in this state, for that matter—knew that Trevor had done quite well for himself with the rapidly expanding Wind Shadow Resort chain he'd started a few years earlier.

"Anyway, thank you again for your generosity. We'll try not to be any trouble for you while we're here."

"And again, it's no trouble. You saw how happy Mary Pat is to have you and the kids here. She's going to have so much fun with them."

Jade didn't know what else to say. She nodded and forced a smile. "I'll let you get ready for your evening now. Enjoy your dinner."

"I have a feeling Mary Pat will enjoy hers more," he said with a flash of those pearly whites. "Good night, Jade."

"Good night, Trevor."

Seeing the slight limp when he put his weight on his right leg as he descended the stairs, she recalled that he'd been in a serious motorcycle accident just over a year ago. Her mother had called to tell her about it the night it happened, when Trevor's family had worried he might not even survive his injuries. She'd been told he'd undergone at least two surgeries since to repair injuries to that leg.

She shuddered at the thought. Motorcycles terrified her. Her late husband had loved them, and had barely escaped serious injury more than once with his escapades on them. She hated to think there would come a day when her son would express interest in one of the machines.

She only hoped Trevor had gotten rid of his, if it was still drivable, for his own mother's sake. Had this particular daredevil learned caution from his misadventure—or was he still hooked on defying danger? None of her business, of course, but she knew his parents hoped for the former.

TREVOR WAS ACCUSTOMED to returning to a dark, quiet house at the end of a long workday, usually well after his housekeeper had retired to her cottage for the evening. Sometimes he slept in the small suite connected to his office at the resort, but most nights he came home so he'd at least feel like he'd left work for a few hours, even though he often spent a couple hours more catching up on paperwork in his home office.

It wasn't as if he had to rush home, he replied whenever he was chided for his long workdays. Mary Pat liked to watch TV in her cottage in the evenings, and he didn't even have a pet waiting for him. So who really cared whether he came home at seven or midnight?

Tonight four extra people were staying in his house, not that he expected to see any of them at this hour. It was after ten. He'd noted when he'd turned into the driveway that the upstairs lights were out. The kids were probably asleep, and Jade was likely tired after a busy day of getting settled in.

Jade. He pictured his houseguest as he walked up the stairs from the lower-level garage into the kitchen and hung his keys on a hook. Blond hair, amber eyes, high cheekbones and a stubborn chin. He knew Jade was only thirty-two—young to have a twelve-year-old son, even younger to be widowed for five years. But then, he'd been widowed for almost ten years, himself. He'd been just twenty-eight when Lindsey was killed in a car accident.

As hard as the loss had been for him, he couldn't even imagine how difficult it must have been for a mother of three young children.

Her kids were cute. He liked children—from

a safe distance. His Wind Shadow Resort here in South Carolina was a family-friendly destination with mini golf, arcades, a water park and a kids' day program, and he always interacted well with the younger guests. He expected to get along just fine with Jade's trio, though he probably wouldn't see much of them during the next two weeks.

Despite his mother's frequent and unsubtle hints, he wasn't in any hurry for his own off-spring. They required entirely too much emotional investment. Too much time, too much energy, too much anxiety—particularly for someone who'd already experienced loss and didn't want to live in constant worry about other vulnerable innocents. Did that make him a coward? Okay, maybe. But a contented one, nonetheless, he assured himself.

He was walking through the den toward his suite when a movement outside the big glass sliders caught his attention. Only the minimum of security lights were turned on, rather than the full range of lighting available for nighttime entertaining. With a frown, he stepped closer to make sure no one was out there in the gloom who shouldn't be.

Seeing a dark form seated near the edge of the pool, he reached quickly for the slider handle. Had one of the kids sneaked out this late? He didn't even want to think about a child falling into his pool in the middle of the night. The pool was fenced off from outsiders but accessible from the patio, a situation he hadn't needed to reconsider until tonight.

That was exactly the kind of dread he'd just told himself he didn't want in his life.

He was relieved when he walked down the steps from the deck and saw Jade seated cross-legged on the tile. She'd turned her head when he opened the door. He felt all his senses leap to attention in response to the impact of her dark eyes and soft mouth glistening in the low light. He pushed those responses down, reminding himself that she was a guest in his home.

He motioned toward the glittering pool. "Thinking about taking a dip?"

"Well, not in a shirt and jeans," she answered with a laugh. "I was just enjoying the nice night. I like to sit under the stars to unwind after a long day. This is a beautiful back lawn, Trevor. And this pool is fantastic."

"Thanks." He was rather proud of the pool, which he'd designed to resemble a natural element surrounded by realistic-looking rocks. A tall waterfall anchored the far end, with a curving slide built around it into the water. A low diving board jutted out from another side. When had he last taken time to enjoy any of those features?

An outdoor barbecue kitchen, along with tables, benches and inviting lounge chairs, made the backyard ideal for entertaining, and yet he made use of it all too rarely. It had been at least three months since he'd hosted a barbecue, and that had been a business function for visiting investors.

He glanced toward the various comfortable seating areas, then gave a shrug and sat beside Jade on the cool, night-damp tile. "Did you have a nice dinner?"

"Very nice, thank you. Mary Pat kept us laughing all through the meal. I practically had to twist her arm to let us help her clear away afterward."

"Mary Pat loves nothing more than fussing over people. There are times I feel sort of guilty for not giving her more to do around here," he said with a sheepish chuckle. "I try to come home at least once a week for dinner just so she can cook for me—and yes, I'm aware of how that sounds."

"After seeing her beaming at the dinner table while the kids were scarfing down their food, I totally believe you."

They smiled at each other, and then Jade looked away, her gaze turning upward toward the night sky. Leaning back on his hands, Trevor followed her example. The stars were beautiful, like flawless diamonds scattered carelessly over black velvet. He couldn't remember the last time he'd simply sat and looked up at them. A breeze rustled the fronds of the palmettos planted around the patio and played in the leaves of the old live oak trees bordering his property. The rock waterfall, glittering in the illumination of built-in canister lights, provided a soothing, almost musical accompaniment.

He'd owned this house for four years, yet he could count on one hand the number of times he'd simply sat by the pool and completely relaxed. It felt good. He glanced at the attractive woman sitting quietly beside him and realized it was even nicer to have someone to share the peaceful interlude with. Jade looked perfectly comfortable with the companionable silence.

It had been a long while since he'd enjoyed one-on-one time with an appealing woman. He'd tried to convince himself he was too busy with new work projects, but the truth was he'd simply gotten tired of dealing with conventions and expectations.

He heard Jade draw a deep breath, as if taking in a long taste of the night before she asked, "How was your business dinner?"

Grateful to be distracted by a topic that was much more comfortable for him, he shrugged and replied, "It was fine. Nothing out of the ordinary."

"Mary Pat told us during dinner that you'll be traveling to your resort in Texas tomorrow."

He nodded. "I'm planning to spend the weekend there. I'll be back Sunday evening. In the meantime, I hope you and the kids make yourselves completely at home here. The pool and the rec room are at your disposal as much as you like. And if there's anything else you need, please don't hesitate to let Mary Pat know."

"Thank you. Caleb and Erin are already looking forward to getting in this pool. They love to swim."

"Any time. Mary Pat knows where all the switches are for the pool features. It has lights for night swimming, too."

"I'll keep that in mind."

Trevor found himself fantasizing for a moment about seeing Jade in the pool under the twinkling stars. He'd bet she looked damned good wet.

What was wrong with him tonight? Telling himself to stop being such a guy, he looked back up at the sky.

After a moment, Jade pushed herself to her feet, stretching as she rose with a grace that reminded him of a sleek cat. "I should check on the kids. And then I'll turn in. Good night, Trevor."

Shifting his weight on the tile, he cleared his throat. "Yeah, um, good night, Jade. I think I'll stay out here a few more minutes."

He watched her walk away. Had she taken ballet lessons? Something about her posture and the way she moved brought the question to his mind. Well, that and a few other things a good host probably shouldn't think about in regards to his guest.

MARY PAT HAD a hearty breakfast ready by the time Jade and the kids came downstairs Friday morning. As much as she enjoyed the pampering, Jade still felt uncomfortable about being waited on this way. She'd hired babysitters and once-a-week maid service when the children were little and she was in nursing school, but she'd never had a live-in housekeeper and cook. It felt too decadent.

Trevor joined them for breakfast before leaving to spend the weekend at his second resort on the Texas Gulf Coast. Erin and Caleb chattered at him throughout the half hour he sat with them. Jade was impressed with his patience in answering their questions and responding to their random comments, even though it was obvious to her that he was keeping a close eye on the time, preparing for his departure. He went out of his way to include shy Bella in the freewheeling conversation, eliciting a few smiles and even a couple of soft laughs from the child in response. Jade was content for the most part just to listen while she enjoyed her waffles, contributing only when she was directly addressed. Mary Pat bustled around the table like a proud Southern grandma blissfully feeding her brood, settling only occasionally into her own chair.

Trevor made his excuses before the others were finished with their meals, explaining that he had to get to the airport. He encouraged Jade and the children again to use the pool and other amenities, adding he was sure Mary Pat would take good care of them. Jade noted that he squeezed his housekeeper's shoulder lightly on his way out and Mary Pat patted his hand in response, an affectionate exchange that demonstrated their mutual fondness.

She and the kids had several errands scheduled for that very warm day. When they returned to the house, Jade, Caleb and Erin made good use of the swimming pool. Bella, who was afraid of water, sat on the side and entertained herself with toys while the others laughed and swam and played on the tall, curving waterslide.

Jade climbed out of the pool first, telling Caleb and Erin they could play awhile longer before getting ready for dinner. Toweling her hair, she divided her attention between her older two, who swam like playful dolphins, and her daydreaming youngest nearby. Jade realized she was sitting in the same spot she'd shared briefly with Trevor the night before. She couldn't help thinking again that he seemed like a genuinely nice guy. It was a wonder such a handsome, successful and charming man lived alone in this lovely home.

Was he still grieving the young wife he'd lost in a traffic accident? She remembered hearing about it at the time from her mother. Saddened by Trevor's loss, Jade had been unaware, of course, that she would be widowed herself within a few short years.

She could understand if Trevor found it hard to allow anyone new into his heart. She wasn't sure she would ever take that leap again herself. She'd been so deeply in love with Stephen during their somewhat unconventional but passionate marriage, and the grief of that devastating loss had been grueling to get through. She'd managed somehow for her children's sakes, but it had been a tough time for them all.

"Mom, Mom, watch this!" Erin called from the top of the slide. "Headfirst!"

Pulling her attention back to her maternal duties, Jade called out to her daredevil daughter to be careful, then settled back to watch, putting both the past and Trevor Farrell out of her mind for now.

CHAPTER TWO

"MARY PAT, STOP HOVERING. I'm fine, okay?" Trevor hated sounding cross and ungrateful, but he disliked even more being dependent on anyone. He'd spent the latter half of last year recuperating from the motorcycle accident that had come too close to ending him, and he'd only been off crutches for a couple of months since his last knee surgery. Now damned if he hadn't injured the knee again, though fortunately not nearly as badly this time. But that didn't keep it from hurting like hell.

Though his original injury had been due to a distracted driver crashing into his motorcycle, this time it was entirely his own fault. He'd thought his knee was recovered enough for some energetic kitesurfing, a sport he loved, with friends in Texas. He'd been wrong.

He'd felt the damned knee pop when he'd made an awkward landing, and the pain had been instant and excruciating. His friends had insisted on taking him straight to an emergency room. Now he was back on crutches for a week or so, under doctor's orders to keep the leg elevated as much as possible and to take it easy for a while. Considering how busy he was with work at the moment, that wasn't going to be easy.

Tonight he planned on relaxing with a hot shower, a cold beer and a baseball game on the TV while propping his leg on an ottoman. He hoped he wouldn't feel obliged to entertain the guests staying on his second floor that night. Every once in a while, being the gracious host, at work and now even in his home, became utterly exhausting.

"I'd hardly call it hovering for me to just do my job," his housekeeper muttered. With an emphatic thump, she deposited a tray on the low table in front of the easy chair in Trevor's suite.

The driver he'd arranged to collect him at the airport had dropped him off at home an hour ago, and Mary Pat hadn't left him alone since. She'd turned down his bed, fluffed his pillows and made sure he had water, pain meds, crutches, his cell phone and the TV remote within easy reach. As she'd said, it was her job. He just wished she wouldn't be quite so conscientious for an hour or two while he sulked in private.

He hadn't seen Jade or the kids since he'd returned. It was after nine, so maybe Jade was putting the kids to bed. Or maybe they were just thoughtfully staying out of his way.

Hands on her ample hips, Mary Pat displayed her frequent uncanny ability to know what he was thinking. "I advised Jade and the kids to give you some space this evening. I knew what kind of mood you'd be in. Jade told me to be sure and let you know she's right upstairs if you need anything tonight. She's a nurse, you know."

"I don't need a nurse. And I'm not in a mood." He had to suppress a wince when he heard his own grumpy tone.

His housekeeper rolled her eyes expressively. "Oh, no, of course you're not. Now, do you need anything else or are you going to snarl at me just for asking?"

"I don't need anything else. Thank you, Mary Pat," he added, apologetic.

"You're welcome, hon." She patted him on the shoulder, letting him know she understood his grouchiness was spurred by pain and frustration. Which made him feel even guiltier about taking it out on her. "And notice that I'm not saying a word about how you shouldn't have been on that surfboard thing at all."

Trevor grunted, knowing the lectures would come, both from his housekeeper and his mother. Maybe even from assorted friends and staff.

Mary Pat continued, "You shoot me a text or call me if you need anything at all later, you got it? Even if it's in the middle of the night."

"I'll be fine, but thanks."

Giving him a final pat, she bade him good-night and let herself out of his suite. As soon as the door closed behind her, he allowed himself one low moan when he shifted his throbbing leg on the ottoman, adjusting the ice pack covering his knee. He wore shorts and a T-shirt, baring his scarred leg for the treatment, and still the cold wasn't helping much. The pain meds he'd been given at the hospital were wearing off, but he didn't want to take more unless it became absolutely necessary.

He was aware that his disposition was growing darker by the moment. His business trip hadn't gone particularly well, he'd foolishly reinjured his leg, he'd snapped unfairly at Mary Pat and there were guests in his home, so he had to be on his best behavior until he was back on his feet, regardless of his mood. The whole point of owning a house fifteen miles from the resort was to have a refuge where he could get away for a few hours from polite small talk, incessant smiles and perpetual hosting.

A quiet tap on his door deepened his scowl. It didn't sound like Mary Pat's usual firm rap. Had Jade come down to check on him? If so, it was thoughtful of her but not the greatest timing. Still, it would be rude to ignore her. Forcing himself into his usual practiced-host demeanor, he said, "Come in."

The door opened slowly, but he had to lower his gaze to identify the visitor, who was much shorter than he'd expected. "Bella? Are you lost?"

The child stepped fully into the room, her expression tentative, one hand behind her back. He noted that she was dressed in blue pajamas decorated with leaping dolphins, and he wondered if she was supposed to be in bed.

"Is there something I can do for you?" he asked, though he wasn't sure how much assistance he could provide at the moment.

"Mommy said you got hurt," she said, her voice so soft he had to strain to listen. She pointed to his elevated right leg. "Does it hurt bad?"

"It's felt better," he answered candidly, "but I'll be okay."

Her brown eyes looked huge as she gazed at him with sympathy. "Were you trying to do a cartwheel?"

Reminded of their conversation the day they'd met, he smiled. "No, I wasn't trying a cartwheel. But perhaps you can show me how you do them sometime."

"Mommy says I have to do cartwheels outside unless I'm at gymnastics class," she informed him solemnly.

"Then you can show me outside when we get

the chance." He studied her more closely. "What do have behind your back?" he asked in a casual tone.

Keeping her eyes focused hard on his face, as if to judge his reaction, she brought her hand around to show him a stuffed brown bear. "I brought this for you," she replied in little more than a whisper.

Confused, he looked more closely at the bear. Looking well-loved, it was dressed in a pink T-shirt bearing the words Get Well Soon.

"GamGam gave me this when I had tonslisus," Bella added earnestly. "It made me feel better. Maybe it will help your leg not hurt so much."

Mentally translating *tonslisus* to *tonsillitis*, Trevor swallowed hard as he tried to come up with the proper response to her touching gesture. "That's very kind of you, Bella. Thank you. Um—does your mother know you're down here?"

Stepping closer to his chair, she set the bear carefully on his ottoman, next to his ice-pack-covered knee. "I don't know."

Which meant no, he decided. With a sigh, he reached for the crutches lying beside his chair. "I'll take you back upstairs."

"That won't be necessary." Jade stood in the doorway to his suite. Her arms crossed over her chest, Jade eyed her youngest in disapproval.

"Bella, I've been looking all over for you! What on earth are you doing down here? Didn't I tell you we have to leave Mr. Farrell alone?"

"You said he was hurt," Bella argued. "So I brought Dr. Bear to make him feel better."

"Oh. Well. You still shouldn't have come down without telling me." Jade shot a quick glance at Trevor, then motioned toward the door. "Back to bed, young lady. I'll be up in a few minutes to make sure you're tucked in."

Bella took off without another word, leaving Trevor grinning despite himself. He stifled the smile when Jade looked around at him again.

"I'm sorry. I thought Bella was in bed until Erin let me know she was missing. I was in the rec room watching a TV show with Caleb."

He leaned forward to pick up the toy. "She thought this would make me feel better. I'd hate to see her get in trouble for that."

"She's in trouble for sneaking downstairs without asking. I have to be able to trust her to follow my rules." Jade tucked her hair behind one ear as she glanced down at his leg. He was sure she saw every scar he'd accumulated through the accident last year and the follow-up surgical repairs. They weren't pretty. "Is there anything I can do for you?"

"I'm good, thanks." Setting the stuffed bear on the table beside him, he shifted his weight in his chair. The movement dislodged the ice pack from his knee. He made a grab for it, but it fell to the floor. Jade rushed forward to scoop it up.

"This isn't very cold," she said with a frown. "Do you have another in the freezer?"

"I do, but I can probably leave it off for a while. I've had it on for almost half an hour."

"The usual recommendation is twenty minutes, so you should be good for now. Would you like me to put this back in the freezer for later?"

"Sure." He motioned toward the opposite wall in the sitting area of his bedroom suite. His deep leather chair and a matching one, both with ottomans, faced a fireplace above which hung a large-screen TV. Flanking the fireplace on either side were well-filled bookshelves. A French door to his right led out to the patio, and his bedroom and bath were on his left. His home office opened off the bedroom, so that his private sanctuary was entirely separate from the guest quarters.

Well, for the most part, he thought with a glance toward the teddy bear. "There's a mini-fridge with a freezer behind the door on the right side of the fireplace. You can just stick the pack in there, thanks."

Jade followed his directions, then closed the cabinet again and glanced around. "This is a lovely space."

"Thanks. I enjoy it. Is everything okay upstairs

for you and the kids? Anything you need?" he felt compelled to ask, despite his discomfort.

"No, it's perfect for us, thank you."

"Did you and the kids have a nice weekend?"

"Very nice, thank you. We spent Saturday at the beach. Caleb and Erin swam while Bella built sand castles and looked for shells. They're going to love living so close to the ocean. But I'm sorry your trip ended so badly."

He wasn't sure if she'd heard the details of how he'd reinjured himself, but if so, at least she didn't seem inclined to lecture him. He replied offhandedly, "Just a minor setback. I'll be back on my feet in a few days."

"Speaking of which…" She reached for a throw pillow on the other chair and carried it toward him. Gesturing toward his elevated leg, she asked, "Do you mind? Your leg really should be higher to make the edema go down faster."

"You're the nurse," he said with a slight shrug.

Her hands were cool and obviously skilled as she lifted his calf to slide the extra pillow beneath. She resettled the leg carefully, then pressed lightly against the visible swelling. "Is there much pain here?"

Both her tone and her touch were briskly professional, yet still he had to clear his throat before answering lightly. "It's felt better."

"You have pain meds?"

"I have them." He didn't promise that he would take them. Not unless absolutely necessary.

Obviously not fooled, she smiled dryly and started to take a step back. "Okay, macho man, that's your call. You have my cell number. Call if you need anything during the night, please. It's the least I can do in return for your hospitality."

On impulse, he caught her wrist. He really disliked appearing weak and injured in front of her, sitting here with his leg on pillows while she stood there looking...well, looking so damned good. "I told you before, you don't owe me anything."

She looked down at his hand, then raised her gaze to his. "And I told you that you have my gratitude, whether you want it or not."

He didn't want her gratitude. Because he couldn't say what he did want from her, he released her. "You should probably make sure Bella got back to bed safely."

"Yes." But she didn't move away. He noted that she rubbed her wrist absently, though his clasp had been gentle. "I can tell you're hurting," she said quietly. "I understand you want to be cautious with the prescription meds, but can I at least get you an over-the-counter pain reliever?"

He nodded toward the tray on the side table between the chairs. "Mary Pat left snacks, a carafe of hot herbal tea, meds—both prescription and OTC—and some sort of healing crystal. I'm good, thanks."

He saw her smile as she glanced at the tray. "I'll say again, you have a treasure in her."

"Yes. I do." Feeling guilty all over again about having snapped at his housekeeper earlier, he promised himself he'd be on his best behavior during the remainder of his recovery. Or at least he'd try, he amended more realistically.

He didn't try to detain Jade this time when she moved toward the door.

She didn't look back as she left. He watched her until she closed the door behind her, cutting off his very nice view of her backside. Telling himself pain and exhaustion must be messing with his mind, he closed his eyes and put his head back against the chair with a low, frustrated groan.

TREVOR WASN'T AT the breakfast table Monday morning.

"He said he wasn't hungry," Mary Pat explained to Jade and the kids. "When I went in to tell him it was ready, he was already on the phone with his assistant. I'm sure he'll be at his desk all day, working harder than ever and pouting because he's supposed to be off his feet for a few days."

Erin giggled. "Grown-up men don't pout."

"Oh, honey." Mary Pat exchanged a laughing look with Jade. "Don't you believe that for a second."

Reminding herself that it was impolite to laugh at their host, even good-naturedly, Jade looked down at her plate where a flaky homemade biscuit was topped with a thick sausage gravy. It was hardly a health-conscious meal, despite the fresh fruit compote served on the side, but she had to admit it was tasty. And it was very kind of Mary Pat to cook for them. Still, maybe she could drop a few hints later that oatmeal or fruit and yogurt would suffice for a few days.

"So, what's on your schedule for today?" Mary Pat asked, including the whole family in the question. "Any big plans?"

"Back-to-school shopping," Jade replied. "Backpacks, lunchboxes, school supplies, that sort of thing."

"I need new shoes," Erin reminded her. "My old ones are gross."

"I want new shoes, too," Bella piped in. "And a Hello Kitty backpack."

"I need some new jeans," Caleb grumbled. "Mine are all getting too short."

"Okay, everyone, I know what we need." Jade shook her head ruefully. She'd already done most of the shopping for the new school year, but her children still had their lists of "necessities." It was going to be a long day.

"Why don't you come with us, Ms. Mary Pat?" Erin asked, her face lighting up. "We're going to have lunch out. And maybe get ice cream!"

"I never promised ice cream," Jade challenged with a lifted eyebrow.

"I said maybe." Undiscouraged, Erin forged on, "Anyway, it'll be fun. So, want to come?"

"Thank you, Erin, but I really shouldn't. I have work to do here, and I hate to leave Trevor while he's recuperating." Still, Mary Pat looked pleased by the invitation. "Maybe I'll shop with you another time."

"We'll give you a rain check." Erin had only recently learned the term, and she used it confidently.

Mary Pat chuckled. "I'll gladly take it."

When they'd finished eating, Jade sent the kids upstairs to brush their teeth and find their shoes for the outing. "Let me help you clean up, Mary Pat," she said after they scampered away. She reached for the gravy bowl, which was still more than half-full, even though everyone had eaten heartily.

"Oh, I've got this. But you can do me another favor, if you don't mind."

"Name it."

"Will you take a tray in to Trevor while I put

away the rest of the food? I told him he'd be getting breakfast in his room so he's expecting it, even if the grouch won't admit he's hungry."

Jade wished fleetingly that Mary Pat had just asked her to scrub the kitchen floor, instead. She told herself that was a silly thought. She was hardly intimidated by Trevor. There was no reason for her to avoid being alone with him. She knew how to deal with grumpy men, so she could handle Trevor even if he was in a bad mood—though she doubted that his habitual courtesy would allow him to be anything but polite to a guest. From her own few observations and everything she'd heard from mutual acquaintances, he had elevated hosting to an art form, which was part of what made his resorts so successful and his investors so willing to gamble on him. "Yes, I'll take it."

"Thanks, hon." Mary Pat gathered the gravy bowl and biscuit plate. "I'd hate for these good leftovers to go to waste."

Five minutes later, Jade juggled a heavily loaded tray so she could rap lightly on the door of Trevor's suite. Judging by the weight of the tray, Mary Pat hadn't believed Trevor's claims that he wasn't hungry. Though the food was beneath covers, it felt like enough to feed two or three men.

She couldn't help thinking of her brief visit

with him last night. Even disheveled in shorts and T-shirt, grumpy and hurting, he'd been undeniably all virile male. Disconcerting so. Perhaps she'd been too strongly reminded of all the times she'd tended her husband after he'd injured himself in one of his daredevil sports.

She'd loved Stephen madly, but she'd never fully understood why he'd been so willing to risk breaking his neck just to challenge himself, to the worry of everyone who loved him. For a moment, she almost pitied any woman who'd let herself fall for charming, often reckless Trevor. But then again, she suspected he'd be a hard man to resist for any woman who hadn't already lived through that constant anxiety.

Hearing muffled words she interpreted as "Come in," she balanced the tray with one arm as she opened the door. The sitting area was empty, so she followed sounds to the attached office, a sunny room equipped with what appeared to be state-of-the-art technology. The office door was open and she could see Trevor sitting at his desk, his back to her as he worked a keyboard, making spreadsheets and other forms flash across the monitor in front of him.

"I told you I'm not hungry, Mary Pat. My damn leg is killing me and I have a hundred things to do. I'll eat in a while."

He was definitely cranky, Jade thought with

raised eyebrows. It was the first time she'd ever heard him snap. And it said even more about his close relationship with his housekeeper that he allowed himself to be less than proper and professional in front of her.

"I'm not Mary Pat, but I suspect she'll be in shortly to make sure you've eaten despite your objections."

He spun his chair in response to her voice, then grimaced when the sudden movement obviously caused him pain. He schooled his expression immediately, settling his features into what she'd come to think of as his "gracious host face." She rather regretted that he felt the need to hide behind it with her when she'd begun to think of them as friends.

"Jade. I'm sorry, I didn't mean to sound so rude. Thanks for bringing a tray. You can just set it there. I'll eat when I've finished reading this report."

The table he pointed to sat in front of a small sofa positioned between two bookcases. Like the cases in his sitting area, this one was also filled almost to capacity with books that looked well-read, she noted as she set down the tray with care. She always appreciated a fellow book lover.

Absently rubbing his right knee, he tilted his head toward her, still in apologetic mode. "I told Mary Pat I'd just have an apple or something for breakfast, but she's determined to stuff me with food every chance she gets. I guess I shouldn't be surprised she recruited you to make the delivery."

"I didn't mind. How's your leg this morning?"

"It's better, thanks."

Jade placed her hands on her hips and merely looked at him.

After a moment, he sighed faintly, sounding just perceptibly cross again when he conceded, "Okay, it hurts. And before you go all Nurse Jade on me, I had it propped up earlier. Just put it down for a while so I could get some work done."

"I didn't come in to nag you," she assured him. "I just brought your breakfast. You're a grown-ass man. Whether you eat—or elevate your leg— it's entirely up to you."

Her pointed retort seemed to catch him by surprise. After a brief pause, he laughed sheepishly. "Sorry. Believe it or not, I'm usually much more gracious to my guests than that. I have no excuse."

"This is your home, Trevor, not your resort," she reminded him. "And I'm a friend, not a guest. So, don't feel that you have to pretend for me that everything is just hunky-dory."

"Hunky-dory?" He chuckled. "Haven't heard that term in a while."

She smiled. "Something my grandmother

said frequently. I find myself quoting her a lot these days."

"I know the feeling. I hear myself sounding a lot like my dad at times, even though I've spent most of my life trying to be different."

Maybe he realized suddenly how that could be interpreted. "My dad's a great guy, of course," he added. "I've always just wanted to explore my own paths, rather than follow in the family footsteps."

His family's fortune came from three or four generations of hotels and other real estate dealings, she mused. Did he really think establishing a chain of resorts was such a different path? Rather amused by what seemed to be his idea of rebellion, she spoke lightly. "I suppose we're all influenced by family ultimately. Heaven only knows what my kids will pick up from me."

She thought he relaxed with the quip, as though relieved by the redirection. "Nothing to worry about there, I'm sure."

"Well, I have been known to let the S-word slip out in front of them when I get mad," she said solemnly. "'Oh, sheesh!'"

"Sheesh?" he repeated. "Who'd have guessed you had such a potty mouth, Jade Evans?"

His spontaneous laugh pleased her. It made her feel good to think she'd distracted him from his pain, if only briefly. She smiled back at him. "What can I say? I'm unpredictable."

She'd been joking, of course, yet something in his expression looked a bit speculative when he murmured, "I'm beginning to realize that."

Their gazes held for a moment, and then she cleared her throat and took a step toward the doorway. "Yes, well, this rebel has to take her kids to buy notebooks and backpacks for the first day of school. Is there anything I can pick up for you while I'm out?"

He was already turning back to his computer. "Thank you, but I'm good. Enjoy your outing."

"Better eat some of that breakfast before Mary Pat comes in to check," she advised over her shoulder as she left.

She heard him chuckle quietly, though he didn't reply. He was likely already totally immersed in those "hundred things" he needed to do.

She could only imagine how much responsibility he held for his growing enterprise with its widespread properties and many employees, investors and guests. From what little she'd observed so far, she suspected delegation was not one of Trevor's strengths.

It was no wonder he was in no hurry to add even more obligations to his plate. He would probably be relieved when the repairs were completed at her house, and so would she. The last thing she wanted to do was to become a burden on Trevor—or on anyone else, for that matter. She took care of herself and her own, and she liked it that way.

CALEB AND ERIN begged to run straight to the pool after the exhausting shopping trip, and Jade agreed. They'd been cooperative during the outing—for the most part—and hadn't squabbled—much—so she figured they'd earned a swim.

They'd explored most of Shorty's Landing, scouting out shops and parks to visit later. They'd been greeted warmly by the small town's tourist-oriented business community. Rather than ice cream, they'd decided to stop in to a coffee-and-doughnut shop, The Perkery. Located on the main thoroughfare, nestled among a variety of shops, the colorful place had caught their eye and drawn them in.

The kids had been mesmerized by the glass display case filled with pastries, cakes and cookies. The shop's owner, Elle O'Meara, had introduced herself and insisted on giving each of the kids a free treat to welcome them to town. She'd invited them to come back soon, and assured Jade she was available to answer any questions she might have about the community.

The kids were still on the sugar high from their doughnuts when they dashed out into Trevor's backyard to play and swim. Jade had hesitated about putting on her own swimsuit to join them. Knowing Trevor was home made her self-conscious, for some reason. But telling herself that was foolish, she'd changed into a tankini and flip-flops and accompanied her children out to the pool.

Trevor probably wouldn't come outside, anyway. And even if he did, she wasn't bothered by being seen in a bathing suit. Considering she'd borne three children, she was content with her curves. School started the day after tomorrow, and she'd start working full-time on Monday, so she should take advantage of every opportunity to spend time with the kids.

Jade, Caleb and Erin had barely gotten in the water when Mary Pat came out with a tray holding iced lemonades. She set the tray on a patio table, and Bella settled into one of the chairs with a tumbler. Once again, Bella had donned her swimsuit, but it wasn't even wet. She'd dipped her feet into the pool, but had resisted Jade's attempts to entice her farther into the water.

Caleb and Erin scrambled up the stairs built into the manmade rocks of the waterfall, then descended noisily into the pool on the curving slide. "Mom, come play," Erin called out, climbing the steps again. "It's fun."

"Maybe in a bit." Tired from herding her trio

from store to store, Jade was enjoying floating lazily in the cool, rippling water. The late-afternoon sun slanted across the surface and warmed her cheeks. All she wanted to do was close her eyes and float…

"Hi, Mr. Trevor!"

Jade's eyes opened instantly in response to Erin's cheery greeting, followed by a noisy splash as the girl sped down the slide into the pool. Seeing that Trevor had come outside on crutches and was making his way carefully across the tile, Jade swam to the side of the pool, pushing back her wet hair.

She frowned as she watched Trevor balance himself on the crutches, placing them carefully on the tiles while keeping his weight off his right leg. He wore navy board shorts and a gray T-shirt. Was he planning to come into the pool?

Echoing the thought, Erin called out, "Can you swim with us, Mr. Trevor, or is your leg too hurt?"

Standing at the top of the steps into the pool, he smiled. The sunlight slanted over his face, making his blue eyes glitter and bringing out the hints of gold in his light brown hair. The shorts revealed the scars on his right leg, and a few on his left, yet somehow he managed to look strong and self-assured even on crutches. Not to mention downright sexy, Jade thought, privately acknowledging her hormones were still fully functional.

Shaking her head, as much to clear it as to express disapproval, she said, "It's Mr. Farrell, Erin."

"Mr. Trevor is fine with me." He set his crutches aside, slipped out of his sandals, and lowered himself carefully to the side of the pool, letting his feet dangle into the water. Smiling at Jade, he added, "I'm sure Mary Pat has told you we're very informal here."

Caleb swam up to paddle nearby, peering at Trevor's legs as if assessing the damage to them. Jade knew that without his glasses, Caleb's vision was somewhat fuzzy, but he was only mildly nearsighted, fortunately.

"How are you feeling, Mr. Trevor?" he asked with the careful manners Jade had tried to instill in him.

"I'm better, thank you, Caleb. How's the water?"

"It's a great pool," the boy answered enthusiastically. "I like the slide. And the waterfall."

"Did you check out the grotto behind the waterfall?"

Momentary silence followed Trevor's question. And then Caleb asked, "There's a grotto?"

"What's a grotto?" Erin demanded.

"It's like a cave, right, Mr. Trevor?"

Trevor chuckled. "That's right, Caleb. And

having watched you two swim, I'm sure you can find it, if your mom says it's okay."

He glanced at Jade then to add, "It's safe as long as we're here to watch them."

She gave a nod to Caleb, who started swimming toward the waterfall with Erin right behind him. During their one previous swim, they'd been too entertained by the slide and the diving board to pay more than cursory attention to the waterfall itself. Now Jade watched as they peered behind the falling water and grinned in delight at what they discovered.

"Can we go in, Mr. Trevor?" Caleb called out.

"Of course."

Seeing them disappear through the fall, Jade looked up at Trevor with a lifted eyebrow.

"It's a small cave room," he explained. "There's a curved rock bench and colored lights embedded in the walls. Mary Pat turned those on when the swimming started. You can swim in, hoist yourself onto the bench and relax while you watch the waterfall in front of you."

"Sounds lovely. Did you design it?"

"With help from a pool architect," he admitted.

Tilting her wet head, she asked, "And how many times have you been in there just to relax?"

He cleared his throat. "A couple, maybe."

"That's what I thought." Everything she'd heard about Trevor from his family and his housekeeper—not to mention her own observations during the past few days—led her to believe he was quite the workaholic. His idea of relaxing with strenuous sports was significantly different from her own more languid pursuits. She shook her head, her wet hair tickling the back of her neck with the movement. "How's your leg?"

"It really does feel better. Ice and anti-inflammatories have been helpful. Thought I'd get some water exercise while everyone else is out here."

"Swimming is an excellent way to keep you active while you recover," she agreed, sliding automatically into nurse mode. "The water helps support your weight so you don't stress your knee. Just be careful not to twist it."

"Yes, ma'am." His tone was good-naturedly teasing, his mood obviously much improved. "I won't do any flip turns off the ends of the pool."

"Wise decision."

They shared a laugh as Trevor gave a light kick to ripple the water around her. Smiling up at him, she resisted the impulse to splash him back, though his grin let her know he was aware of her temptation.

"Do you want a lemonade, Mr. Trevor?" Bella asked, interrupting the cozy exchange as she approached with a glass she carried carefully in both hands for him.

Drawing his gaze from Jade, he turned to accept the glass with thanks, probably more to be nice to Bella than because he wanted the lemonade. And then he patted the tile beside him as he smiled up at the child. "Want to sit here beside me and put your feet in the water?"

Bella backed a half step away. "I don't like to swim."

"I wasn't suggesting you put your whole body in," he countered. "Just your feet. Like this."

Holding his injured right leg still, he kicked lightly with his left foot, making the water splash. "Feels good."

He took a sip of his drink then, looking unconcerned about whether Bella chose to accept his invitation. Seemingly emboldened by the lack of pressure, the child settled cautiously at his left side and let her feet dangle into the water. Trevor kicked up another spray, making her giggle softly and imitate him. He kicked again, and some of the water splashed on Jade this time, which led to both Trevor and Bella kicking more enthusiastically to make sure they showered her.

Laughing, she swung a hand to splatter them back, making sure most of the spray hit Trevor. Bella blinked, as if trying to decide whether to protest, then grinned and kicked more vigorously with Trevor's encouragement. Jade noted in satisfaction that Bella seemed hardly aware that she was getting liberally splashed now. In fact, the child squealed in delight.

"Mom, you should come see this. It's so cool!"

Looking around in response to the hail, Jade saw Erin sticking her head out from behind the waterfall. "On my way," she called back. "Bella, do you want to go with me to see the grotto? We can put your floaties on, if you want, so you won't go under the water."

Bella looked tempted for a moment as she gazed toward the waterfall, but then she shook her head. "No, thank you."

"How about if your mom and I both take you?" Trevor suggested. "Between the two of us, you'd barely be in the water. The grotto's worth the trip, I promise. One of my young visitors told me it was like a fairy cave."

Bella's lower lip quivered. She wanted to see the cave, Jade interpreted, but was afraid.

Trevor slid into the pool and held out his arms to the child. "C'mon, Little Bit. Anyone who can do three cartwheels surely isn't afraid of a little water."

Bella scooted back rapidly, looking very close to tears now. "No. I don't want to."

"It's okay, Bella, you don't have to this time," Jade said quickly. She needed to make it clear to Trevor that she didn't want Bella pressured or embarrassed by her fear. "Maybe another day before we move into our house. But only if you want to."

Catching on quickly, Trevor smiled at the child, though Jade wondered if she detected just a touch of disapproval in his expression. Did he think she should have pushed the child harder to overcome her fear—or was Jade merely being overly defensive? Either way, decisions like that were hers to make, she told herself firmly. She'd been doing just fine on her own, and she needed no advice from an overconfident bachelor.

"It's fine, kiddo," Trevor said, and there were no such thoughts mirrored in his tone. "Maybe you'd like to play in that patch of grass over there? You can practice your cartwheels or look for ladybugs."

Looking relieved, Bella jumped to her feet and rushed away from the pool.

Jade had probably overreacted to the very brief exchange. Was she a little worried that Bella seemed so enamored with Trevor? She didn't think that was an unfounded concern. Bella had recently seemed very aware of the lack of a father in her life, maybe from observations of friends who lived with two parents. Jade didn't want her most emotionally vulnerable child to weave unrealistic fantasies that would only leave her disappointed.

Trevor looked at Jade, his expression somber. "She's really afraid of the water, huh?"

Trying to put her possibly overblown misgivings from her mind, Jade nodded. "She is. I considered enrolling her in swim classes, thinking it might help, but the very suggestion upset her so much I didn't have the heart to make her go. I thought maybe I'd try again next summer."

"Your other two certainly aren't afraid," he observed, watching Caleb and Erin frolicking in the waterfall. "They swim like dolphins."

"Yes, well, that's because their father had them in the water as soon as they could walk." Jade pushed a drying strand of hair from her eyes and glanced around at the kids. "Both of them could swim well before they were Bella's age. She wasn't quite a year old when he died, so he never got to spend time with her. I guess I fell down on the swimming training with her. Stephen was the athlete in the family, while I'm more the bookworm. It's been a challenge to fill both roles since."

"As busy as you are now, I'm sure you had your hands even more full for a while after he died," Trevor replied.

"Three kids under eight," she agreed quietly. "One not even walking yet."

"I have a feeling swim lessons were low on your priority list."

Which didn't make her feel any less guilty that Caleb and Erin were having so much fun in the water while Bella played in the grass. That latent guilt also probably explained, at least in part, her reaction to Trevor's attempted intervention.

"Mom, are you coming or not?" Erin demanded from the grotto entrance.

With a nod to Trevor, Jade kicked off from the pool wall and stroked toward the waterfall. By the time she came back out a short while later, Trevor was swimming laps from one side of the pool to the other, letting his arms pull him through the water rather than putting extra stress on his injured leg. And despite herself, she couldn't help watching for a moment as the water rippled off his bare back and the waning sunlight glinted off his long arms. The man was well toned, there was no denying that. Not in the bulging-muscled, über-warrior physique Stephen had tried to maintain, but with the sleek body of a swimmer or a runner. Nice.

Shaking her head with a shower of glittering droplets, she climbed the steps out of the pool and called for her children.

"Time to get ready for dinner," she said, motioning for Bella to join them. "That's enough swimming for today."

She expected a chorus of protests from her older two, but they gave only token sighs before following her out of the pool—a sign that the busy day had left even them tired.

She looked back from the doorway into the house to find that Trevor had paused in his swimming and was paddling lazily in the center of the deepest part of the pool. He was watching her again. He smiled when their eyes met, and she smiled back.

CHAPTER THREE

THEY WOKE TO rain Tuesday morning, a condition predicted to last most of the day. Jade had breakfast with the children and Mary Pat, who told them she'd taken coffee and a muffin to Trevor in his home office. He was preparing for a business visit from his administrative assistant later that day, she added.

"He wanted to call a driver to take him to his resort office today, but Tamar, his assistant, insisted on bringing the work to him. I'm sure she knew she'd never be able to keep him seated with his leg up if he were there. He'd be out hobbling around on his crutches, making sure everything was running smoothly—as if he didn't have a crackerjack staff taking care of that. The place runs just fine when he's off visiting his other properties."

Jade had no doubt Trevor was anxious to get back to work. While they'd been gathered around the dinner table last night, she'd seen signs of his struggle to hide his frustration with being home-bound, especially when the kids had chattered about their outing.

"What's on your agenda today, Jade?" Adding another spoonful of brown sugar to the bowl in front of her, Mary Pat brought Jade's thoughts back from last night's dinner. The housekeeper had served a somewhat healthier breakfast this morning of steel-cut oatmeal, blueberries and whole-grain toast with her homemade peach jam. Everything was delicious.

Jade set down her coffee cup. She had a busy schedule with the academic year starting tomorrow. The mid-week kick-off was reportedly traditional for their new schools, a way to ease students back into routine with a shortened first week. "This morning I plan to help the kids get their school supplies sorted so they'll be ready to go tomorrow. After lunch, I have to go over to our house to meet with the contractor and make some decisions. I just hope they have the roof adequately covered against this rain."

"Are the children going with you? Because they're welcome to stay here with me, if they'd rather."

"Can we, Mom?" Erin asked hastily. "It's so boring when you're talking to the contractors, and we can't even go outside because it's raining."

"We can play upstairs in the rec room here,"

Caleb proposed. "It's our last day for video games and movies and stuff before school starts tomorrow."

"Mary Pat said I can help her make cookies today, like we talked about at dinner yesterday," Bella piped in. "We could do that while you're gone, right, Ms. Mary Pat?"

"Absolutely." The housekeeper's face practically lit up at the prospect. "Any kind of cookies you like, sweetie pie. I have cutters and frosting and sprinkles so you can decorate them and make them pretty."

"Okay, Mommy?" Bella asked eagerly, though Jade had approved the cookie making lesson when they'd first discussed the idea.

Jade's nod included them all. "You can stay here," she told her children, "but you'd better be on your best behavior while I'm gone."

A chorus of crossed-heart promises followed, assuring her that her trio would be perfect angels. Deciding she could count on that—to an extent—she thanked Mary Pat for agreeing to watch over them and finished her breakfast. She wasn't particularly looking forward to going out into the heavy rain to wrangle with her laconic contractor, but she was ready for the repairs to her home to be completed. They needed to settle into their life, and not as guests in this luxurious house.

She was gone longer than she expected that afternoon. She'd arrived at her house dripping from the dash from the car. She'd had to park on the street because the driveway was blocked by pickup trucks, and had entered to find the workers frantically trying to contain leaks pouring into the kitchen. Apparently the roof tarp hadn't been well secured, which was inexcusable in an area well practiced in dealing with the aftermath of natural disasters like hurricanes.

Seeing the fresh damage made Jade's rare temper snap, and she had a few words for the contractor in charge of this team. Finally satisfied that the situation was under control—and that the contractor was now aware that his client was not a meek woman willing to simply accept whatever mansplaining jargon he threw at her—she spent the next two hours discussing options with him. Afterward, she had to stop by a home improvement store to make final choices on paint and trim colors. She could never resist browsing in that store, and the time slipped away from her while she admired appliances and fixtures, flooring and accessories. Having made her purchases, she slogged through the driving rain again and drove back to Trevor's house.

She was going to look like a drowned rat when she entered, but maybe she'd have time to freshen up before he saw her. Not that it mattered, of course, she assured herself quickly. She simply had a normal amount of feminine vanity.

Sadly for the sake of her ego, she walked into the kitchen only to come almost face-to-face with Trevor on his crutches and a tall, striking caramel-skinned woman with shrewd dark eyes and impeccably styled black hair. The woman wore crisp, lightweight gray slacks and a fuchsia silk blouse, and Jade couldn't help being aware of her own tousled damp hair, wrinkled clothing and rain-washed face.

Holding her head high, she pasted on a bright smile. "It's really pouring down out there."

"Much to the disappointment of our guests at the resort," Trevor responded wryly, glancing at the window over the sink. "Fortunately, the rain's supposed to end in a couple of hours."

He motioned toward the tall woman then. "Jade, this is Tamar Jones, my administrative assistant. Tamar, this is Jade Evans. You've already met her kids."

"I did, yes." Tamar shook Jade's hand warmly. "They're delightful. So bright and polite."

"Thank you." Jade glanced at Trevor. "Where are they?"

"Upstairs, playing board games with Mary Pat—who's been having the time of her life today, by the way. She and Bella made cookies, and Mary Pat's been teaching Caleb and Erin some trick shots at billiards."

Jade could smell the aroma of fresh-baked cookies permeating the kitchen. Several covered plates on the counter probably held the results of the cooking lesson.

"How's the progress on your house coming along?"

She rolled her eyes in response to Trevor's question. "Does the term *three-ring circus* give you a clue?"

"Ouch."

Tamar shifted the large, thickly stuffed tote bag in her hands. "I should be getting back to the office. I have a long list of things to do—even longer now that the boss has had time to come up with some new ideas," she added with an indulgent smile toward Trevor.

Like his housekeeper, Trevor's assistant seemed totally devoted to her employer, which said quite a bit about how well he treated them. Jade and Tamar exchanged polite goodbyes and then Tamar pulled a small umbrella from her bag and went out to brave the elements to her car. Jade suspected the woman would look beautifully put-together even if caught in a hurricane.

"Tamar seems nice," she said to Trevor when they were alone.

"She's my rock at the office," he replied simply. "I'd hate to think of trying to handle my workload without her."

She nodded. "I've heard the best business leaders always surround themselves with the best employees."

"I will concede that my employees are absolutely the best," he said with modest expression.

She laughed. "Nice dodge."

He grinned, balancing on one crutch as he reached out to brush a still-damp strand of hair from her cheek. "Thanks."

Whoa. She felt the impact of that unexpected touch jolt her all the way to her toes. Perhaps he sensed her reaction, or maybe read it on her face. His smile faded, and his blue eyes glinted in a way that made her wonder what he was thinking.

He cleared his throat and took a step back. "So, about the issues at your house? Is there anything I can do to help? I know most of the contractors around here. Maybe I should have a word with yours?"

That suggestion straightened her spine again. "I'm handling it, thank you," she said firmly. She'd never needed a man to step in and help her deal with her personal business, and she didn't need it now from this man who'd already done more for her and her children than she was comfortable accepting.

Trevor seemed to realize he'd accidentally

stepped on her pride. "I'm sure you are. Just letting you know I'm available if you need anything."

And…she'd overreacted again, Jade thought with a smothered sigh. What was it about Trevor that made her do that? "Thank you," she said again, more sincerely this time.

"Mommy, Mommy!" Bella dashed into the kitchen, bringing a welcome end to the unexpected tension in the room. "We made cookies! And I put the icing and sprinkles on some of them all by myself!"

Jade turned to her daughter with a tone that sounded too bright even to her. "Did you? That sounds like fun."

"It was. And they're good, too. Do you want one?"

"I'm sure they're delicious, but I'll wait until later. I'd like to shower and put on fresh clothes after being out in the rain all morning."

Bella turned toward the doorway. "Ms. Mary Pat said she'd build a block house with me when she finishes the game she's playing with Caleb and Erin. I just wanted to see if you're home yet."

Jade had an impulse to remind her daughter that this wasn't actually "home," but she let it go. She didn't look back as she left the kitchen with Bella holding her hand, but she had the feeling that Trevor was watching. And that made her swallow hard.

TREVOR WASN'T SURE if Jade would come outside that night, considering her earlier dousing, but he made his way to the patio, anyway. His cabin fever was strong tonight, and he needed to be out of the house, if only a few feet away.

The rain had stopped a few hours earlier, leaving the night air comfortable, if not quite cool. Most of the furniture had dried enough for sitting, though a bit of damp soaked through his pants when he settled into a chair. Darker than the night sky, a few clouds lingered overhead, pinpoint stars and a watery moon floating peacefully among them.

Settling back into the lounge chair, he wondered why he hadn't done this more often, simply sat outside and let the peace surround him. If he closed his eyes, he could smell the flowers in the professionally maintained beds around the house, the not unpleasant scent of chemicals from the pool and the faintly fuel-tinged aroma of the Intracoastal Waterway behind his property. Even at this late hour, he could hear the occasional passing car from the street and cruising craft on the waterway, but for the most part, the area was quiet. A breeze rustled through the palmetto fronds and fanned his cheeks, lulling him into a state that was somewhere between sleep and fantasies.

He wasn't sure if it was a noise or the tingle at the back of his neck that made him open his eyes to see Jade standing nearby, looking as though she wasn't sure whether to announce her presence or turn and slip back into the house. "Hey," he said to let her know he was awake—and open to company.

"Hey," she replied quietly. "How wet is that chair?"

Noting that she wore shorts and a T-shirt now, he motioned toward the chair beside him. "Dry enough."

Her hesitation was so brief that he wondered if he only imagined it. He thought back to that moment in the kitchen when he'd blurted out an offer to speak with her contractor, a suggestion she obviously hadn't taken well. They'd been perfectly civil ever since, but maybe she'd taken more offense than he'd realized; had she interpreted his offer as a lack of confidence in her abilities to deal with the repairs herself? He hadn't intended it that way. He was simply in the habit of active, hands-on problem solving, both in his business and personal affairs—and often on behalf of friends and family, many of whom had come to expect it from him.

He wasn't comfortable with the hint of arrogance implied in his assumption that he was always the best-qualified arbitrator. Perhaps he should have paid attention to recent suggestions that he place more faith in his trusted associates—and in his friends, apparently.

Still, Jade looked quite comfortable as she settled into the chair and turned her face up to the sky with her eyes closed in much the same manner as when he'd found her out here that first time. She truly did seem to draw tranquility from the night. He needed to follow her example more often.

The two older kids had been wound up during dinner, babbling with a combination of nerves and excitement about the first day at their new school tomorrow. The adults had barely been able to get a word in edgewise, so they'd simply abandoned all attempt at carrying on any conversation that didn't include Caleb and Erin. Bella had contributed occasionally, mostly when asked direct questions, but she'd been visibly subdued. Trevor suspected she was the most anxious of the trio about the next day. As seemed to be typical for them.

"Kids all asleep?" he asked.

Jade turned her head to nod at him. "Bella and Erin are. Caleb has a later bedtime, so he usually reads for an hour before turning in. He was reading in bed when I checked, but he said he was getting sleepy."

"Is Bella doing okay?"

Jade answered after a faint sigh. "She's a bundle of nerves. I gave her a warm bath with lavender oils to calm her, then read two of her favorite bedtime stories before she finally fell asleep. She's always anxious before going into a new situation, even though she met her teacher at the open house yesterday. Her teacher seemed very nice. Bella thinks she's going to like her."

"I hope she's right. And I understand how Bella feels. I was always a wreck the night before a new school year started. For me, it got worse every year rather than better. I hope Bella doesn't go through that."

Jade looked surprised by the confession. "Why did it get harder for you? Didn't you like school?"

Just what had his tone unintentionally revealed in his off-the-cuff comment? He tried to lighten it when he replied, "School was fine. Just a lot of pressure. That happens when you come from a family of overachievers with only one child to focus on."

She was quiet for several long moments before saying, "Something tells me you were valedictorian of your class."

"Covaledictorian," he corrected her. "One of

the other students had exactly the same grade point average I did."

"And how did your parents respond to that?"

He chuckled, keeping his reply candid but casual. "They congratulated me. Bought me a car for graduation. And mentioned a few times that if I'd worked just a smidge harder, I could have come out ahead of that girl."

After digesting that for a moment, she asked, "Did you feel the same pressure in college?"

Realizing he'd brought this shift in focus on himself, Trevor answered succinctly. "I got the degrees—that was all that really mattered."

"MBA, right?"

"Right."

"Followed by military service."

"Four years."

He'd enlisted at twenty-five, an idealistic newlywed eager to serve and determined to do at least one thing his father had never considered and didn't entirely approve of. It was something he'd discussed with Lindsey before they'd married, and while his young bride had been impatient to begin their lives as prominent members of the Southern social scene, she'd supported his wishes—if reluctantly—and had done her best to be a committed army wife.

Lindsey had been his most fervent cheerleader, he mused, calling a time-dimmed picture of his pretty bride to mind. She'd believed without a doubt that he would be successful in business, and she'd eagerly described her dream future. A big house in which she would be renowned as the popular hostess for a whirl of social and charitable events. Long weekends in New York or Paris or London. Household staff and competent nannies for a child or two, if she and Trevor reached a point when both wanted to make that further commitment. It had been a rosy, perhaps overly idealized, image that Trevor had indulged even as he pursued his own whim of having the word *veteran* added to his public résumé.

He'd left the military as a twenty-eight-year-old widower. Not only had Lindsey been denied the future of her fantasies, the husband she'd championed so gamely hadn't even been in the country when she'd died.

He needed to change the subject. "So, tell me more about what's going on at your house," he said, choosing his words more carefully this time. "It sounds as though you've been dealing with quite a lot there."

He was grateful that Jade went along with the redirection apparently without any hard feelings about his earlier clumsiness. She gave him a quick rundown of what she'd found at her house, making him wince in sympathy. His lips tilted upward when she added a summary of the chewing out she'd given the contractor. The indignation lingering in her voice let him know she hadn't been gentle about it.

So his guest had a core of fire behind that cool and composed exterior. He rather liked that.

"Something tells me the guy's on notice now that he'd better make sure the rest of the job goes smoothly," he commented.

Jade shrugged. "I stayed calm, but firm. As a single woman, it's a skill I've had to learn when dealing with certain contractors, mechanics, sales people and claims adjusters. My dad once said I don't actually bite if anyone even figuratively pats me on the head and calls me little lady, but I make them believe I'm going to."

Trevor chuckled. "I didn't know your dad well, but he always seemed like a nice guy."

"He was."

"You were close." It wasn't a question; he'd seen her grief at her father's funeral.

"We were. He taught me to be strong and independent, to change a tire and my oil, to drive a nail and tighten a pipe fitting—and somehow I was still Daddy's girl."

Her description made him smile. Which was followed by a ripple of regret that her children wouldn't be able to tell similar stories someday about their own father. That wasn't fair—but then, he'd just been thinking about his own evidence that life wasn't always fair.

Trevor had never met Jade's late husband, Stephen, who, while growing up in the same area as Trevor, had been a few years his junior. Still, Trevor had heard quite a bit about him, both from his parents and through local legend. A career marine, Stephen had been deployed numerous times and had proved himself a fearless hero over and over again. The news reports had detailed how he'd died while saving three of his fellow marines.

Trevor would never compare his own brief stint in the military, mostly sitting behind a desk, to Stephen's service. Considering that he'd served only one hitch and had emerged relatively unscathed—though guilt ridden for being away when Lindsey died—he hardly even thought of himself as a veteran.

Stephen Evans would be a hard act to follow for any man who pictured himself fitting into Jade's tight little family. A guy could find himself intimidated at the thought of trying to step into those heroic shoes; not that he had any such aspirations, himself.

Still, as noble and selfless as Stephen had been, it had hardly been fair for him to leave a wife and three children to grieve him, to cope without him.

Trevor had his own reasons for staying single since losing Lindsey, though he didn't like to take them out and examine them often. But what about Jade? As fiercely independent as she came across, wouldn't it be convenient for her to have a partner in raising her children, even if it couldn't be their own father? Or was it that Jade had never found anyone who could measure up to the larger-than-life hero she'd loved and lost?

He and Jade fell into silence for a while. It struck him again how comfortable he was sitting quietly in the dark with her. Sliding a sideways glance at her, he couldn't help noticing her long, bare legs as she relaxed on the patio lounger, the soft swell of her breasts as she breathed in the crisp night air. Okay, so maybe not entirely comfortable, he thought with a rueful shift in his seat. And that underlying discomfort was the part that gave him pause.

She must have sensed him looking her way. She turned her head again. "How's your leg?"

He cleared his throat. "Better, thanks."

"You've been up on it a lot today."

"I've been using the crutches. Keeping my weight off the knee."

"That's good."

"I'm going in to the office for a few hours tomorrow. I've got a couple meetings that are fairly important, and I told Tamar there was no need to reschedule them."

"You're planning to drive?"

"I'm calling for a ride. It's probably best if I give it another couple days before I get behind the wheel."

"I won't advise you not to overdo it," she said with a soft laugh. "I'm sure Mary Pat and Tamar will take care of that."

He heaved a heavy sigh. "Very likely. And thanks for the vote of confidence in my ability to take care of myself."

"Well, as I mentioned before—"

He grinned and completed the sentence for her. "I'm a grown-ass man."

Laughing again, she nodded. "Exactly."

He couldn't help it. He had to touch her, if only lightly. He reached out to brush her cheek with the backs of his fingers. Her skin was soft, smooth, cool. His mind flooded with a variety of ways to warm her, making his entire body tighten in response to the images. "I've enjoyed having you here, Jade."

He felt her go still, making him question if he'd overstepped. But then she reached up and touched his hand. "I've enjoyed being here."

He had intended the contact to be brief. Casual. Friendly, nothing more.

Instead, his hand lingered. His thumb traced

the firm line of her surprisingly stubborn jaw, slipped around to touch her full lower lip. As nice as it felt, he could only imagine how sweet it would taste.

Abruptly recalled to his sense of time, place and appropriateness, he dropped his hand. He had no business making overtures that could cause her discomfort while she was a guest in his home. Even if she weren't reluctantly dependent on his hospitality for now, he wasn't the type of guy who made uninvited advances.

"It's getting late," he said, aware as he spoke that it was a lame comment.

He heard Jade release a breath that might have been a sigh.

"Yes, it is. And I have to get the kids up early in the morning for school."

"You know Mary Pat will happily help you with anything you need."

"That's very thoughtful, but we'll be fine. I've been handling first days of school on my own for quite a while now."

The hint of stubborn independence in her deliberately cordial tone was becoming very familiar to him. He was getting to know her better with each conversation.

He swung his legs off his chair and reached down for his crutches. He moved toward the house as Jade fell into step beside him. She reached out to steady him when the tip of one crutch slid on a damp spot on the tile. "Okay?"

"Yeah, I've got it, thanks," he said, frustrated by his renewed dependence on the crutches he'd hoped he wouldn't need again. Okay, so maybe Jade wasn't the only one who took a bit too much pride in self-sufficiency.

Her hand still rested on his left arm when he reached with his right hand to open the slider, his crutch balanced against him. He paused with his fingers on the door handle, looking down at her to see if there was something else she wanted to say before they went inside.

She met his eyes squarely. "I assume you're aware that our mothers have decided to try their hands at matchmaking between us. My mom has gone beyond hinting to outright nudging, and every time I've seen her lately, your mother has mentioned that you're an eligible bachelor in need of a suitable mate. She's made it clear that she's decided I'm appropriately suitable."

Where was she going with this? "Uh, yeah, I've been on the receiving end of a few of those hints," Trevor admitted warily, caught off guard again by Jade's unexpected frankness.

"Just so you know, I'm not a party to that scheme. It has all been concocted by our mothers— probably over wine and cookies," she added with a wry smile. "I was concerned that us sharing a house, even temporarily and in extenuating circumstances, would get them all wound up about it again, but I let myself be persuaded in a moment of panic."

She shook her head and continued, "So, anyway, let's just be clear that I'm not looking for anything more than friendship from you. Or from anyone else for that matter. To be honest, I'm not sure I want to marry again, despite my mom's encouragement. My kids and I are content with the life we have, and I don't want to take gambles with their happiness—or my own. Though my marriage was a very happy one, I've grown accustomed to being fully independent and I'm in no hurry to change that."

Trevor didn't know if her clarifications were a result of his touch or something she'd read in his face, but the last thing he wanted was for her to be uncomfortable with him. He'd keep his hands to himself from now on. And maybe he should avoid being alone with her like this again, as pleasant as it had been. He had to admit he'd miss these starlit interludes, though.

"I never considered that you were party to our moms' plotting," he assured her. "Nor am I, by the way. I don't really see myself as either husband or father material these days. It's not something I've even considered much since Lindsey died," he added awkwardly. He saw no need to go into his frequent musings about the cruel vagaries of fate—or his cowardice in not wanting to open himself up to loss again. "And your logic makes perfect sense. I can see where it would be complicated for you, bringing someone into the kids' lives who might only be there a short time, just long enough to disrupt the obviously happy home you've created for them."

Especially if, as he suspected, Jade couldn't help measuring every man she met against her late husband.

She looked pleased that he understood. "We're agreed, then."

"Agreed."

"We wouldn't want to do anything to whip our mothers into even more of a frenzy when neither you nor I are interested in their schemes."

He laughed softly at her wording. "True."

Something about the way she smiled then made his throat close. "So don't take this the wrong way…" She rose on tiptoes to speak softly against his lips, "Let's just call it curiosity."

After a startled moment, he responded eagerly.

The kiss was light, carefully restrained. Just an exploratory meeting of lips, a brief, testing sample. Jade tasted exactly as he'd expected—sweet, with just a touch of spice beneath. Had it not been for the resented crutches, he'd have moved closer to prove that the rest of her felt as good against him.

His right crutch fell with a clatter when he reached out almost unconsciously to follow through on that impulse. The sound jolted him to his senses. Sighing, Trevor lifted his head, reluctantly breaking off the kiss.

"Okay, now that we have that out of the way," Jade murmured, and though her tone was teasing, she looked slightly shaky. She reached down to scoop up his crutch before he could bend for it, then handed it to him. "Good night, Trevor. Thank you again for all you've done for us."

That changed his smile into a frown. Gratitude was not something he wanted from Jade, though he wasn't prepared to carry that line of thinking any further.

She went inside without looking back at him. After a moment, he followed. As he locked up and turned off the lights, he wondered how much sleep he'd get that night. Something told him he'd be all too aware of the intriguingly unpredictable woman sleeping only one floor above him. Why *had* she kissed him? She'd made it clear she wasn't interested in a relationship with him, and he believed her. He didn't think the gesture had been out of gratitude—at least, he sincerely hoped not. Had it truly been just an impulse?

He supposed he should stop overthinking it. It had been nothing more than a light kiss in the moonlight—perhaps, as Jade had hinted, fueled by little more than curiosity. And it had been nice. Very nice, indeed.

JADE HAD BEEN PREPARED for some chaos Wednesday morning as she made sure the kids were fed, dressed and had everything they needed for school. Fortunately, it was less stressful than she'd expected, partially because she'd been so well organized the night before, but also because of the luxury of having breakfast prepared for them by the so-efficient Mary Pat. The housekeeper had even helped pack lunches, having sandwiches, fresh raw veggies and homemade cookies ready to stash in the insulated bags. Jade told herself she shouldn't get spoiled by this type of household help…but she couldn't deny it was nice today.

Possibly to allay nerves and amuse the children, Trevor made a point of conducting an "inspection" before they headed out to the car. Grinning, Caleb and Erin submitted themselves for review.

"Backpacks packed?" Trevor barked in a fake-stern tone.

"Aye, aye, Cap'n." Erin turned to show off the Wonder-Woman-themed pack dangling from her shoulders. Caleb presented his solid blue pack, and Bella turned more slowly to display her pink-and-white Hello Kitty backpack.

"Teeth brushed?"

Caleb and Erin dutifully flashed theirs. Watching indulgently from nearby, Jade noted that Bella's smile was notably less genuine, though the nervous child tried to play along.

"Homework done?" Trevor inquired.

"Aye, aye, Cap—hey! We don't have any homework," Erin protested, planting her hands on her hips. "We haven't even had a class yet."

"My mistake." Trevor grinned and chucked her lightly under the chin. "You're going to take that school by storm, Erin."

Erin's brows knit with a slight frown. "Is that a good thing?"

"Yes. Yes, it is."

Her face lit up. "Then, thanks."

"You're welcome."

Trevor turned to extend his right hand to Caleb. "Good luck with your classes, Caleb. I'm sure you'll do just fine."

With a pang, Jade realized that her growing son didn't have to look up very far to meet their six-foot-tall host eye to eye when they shook hands. When had her boy grown so tall? And would he really be a teenager in only a few months? How had the time passed so quickly?

With a slight shake of her head to clear the momentary sadness, she moved forward, rattling the keys in her hand for attention. "It's time to go, guys. Thank you again for breakfast, Mary Pat."

"You're very welcome. Have a wonderful day at school, kids. I'll have a special treat waiting for you when you get home."

Jade had to swallow a sigh. She and her children would all be spoiled by the time they moved out of this house.

Trevor turned to Bella. "You'll have a great day, too, Little Bit. I have no doubt."

Trying very hard to look as brave as her brother and sister, Bella nodded, though her lower lip quivered. "My teacher is nice," she whispered as if giving herself an encouraging reminder.

"That's what your mom said. And I'm sure you'll make some new friends in your class."

"I already met a girl named Jovie at the open house."

"There you go. Your first new friend."

"Let's go, Bella." Jade held out her hand to her youngest.

The child took a step toward Jade, then paused and turned to wrap her arms around Trevor's legs. Balanced on his crutches, he appeared to brace himself, but he remained steady. He freed one hand to stroke Bella's hair.

"It'll be fine, Bella," he assured her quietly. "I want you to tell me all about it when you get home tonight, okay? Remember all the best parts of the day, because those make the best stories."

"Bella," Jade prodded gently.

The child drew a deep breath and released Trevor, stepping back with a heaved sigh. "Okay, I'm ready. And I'll remember all the good things to tell you, Mr. Trevor."

"I'll look forward to it."

Bella slipped her hand into Jade's then. Jade glanced at Trevor, who watched them without moving. Their eyes met, and memories of last night's kiss hovered in the air between them. It wasn't the first time she'd recalled the embrace this morning, though she was sure no one would have noticed any difference in the way she and Trevor had interacted during breakfast.

She'd mentally replayed that kiss quite a few times during the night. She'd been well aware that she had been the instigator. And that she probably should, but didn't, regret it. It had been impulse, pure and simple. A magic moment in the moonlight with a sexy man who seemed to share her inconvenient attraction, as well as her resistance to it. And she'd wondered how foolish she would be to let it happen again.

"Bella's such a scaredy-cat," Erin muttered with an exaggerated sigh of exasperation, drawing Jade's attention back to her primary responsibility—her children.

"Am not! You're a poopy face."

"Bella, Erin." Dragging her attention from Trevor, Jade turned them both toward the door. "That's enough. Let's go."

CHAPTER FOUR

JADE WAS BECOMING all too familiar with the smells of fresh-cut plywood and newly applied paint. After the school drop-offs Wednesday morning, she stopped by her house, where repairs seemed to be going much more efficiently today. Afterward, she drove to the medical clinic where she would begin work on Monday. Seeing her cousin's car in the lot alongside the work crew's pickup trucks, she parked and went inside. The sawdust and paint smells again assailed her, along with the sounds of power tools and hammers.

Over all the chaos, she heard her cousin's cheery voice and distinctive laugh. Threading through the tarp-draped furnishings in the reception area, which was being painted a soothing sage, she found Amy in her office, trying to decide where to hang all the framed awards and artwork now propped against the walls.

"Jade." Tall, curvy, thirty-five-year-old Amy swept an arm around her to indicate the newly painted walls of her office. "Looking good, right?"

"Very nice. I glanced into the exam rooms. They're all finished?"

"They are. We saved the reception area and offices for last."

It wasn't a new building, having housed another practice before, but it had been gutted and upgraded for the new clinic. Jade thought their future patients would be quite pleased with the result.

"It looks great," she said sincerely.

"I think so, too. Want to help me decide where to hang this stuff? Lincoln's taking care of some business at city hall."

"Sure, I can hang around and help for a while. The kids are in school today."

"Oh, that's right. First day, right?"

"Yes."

"How'd they handle it?"

"So far, so good. Nervous, of course, about starting new schools, but excited about making new friends."

"And Bella? How'd she do?"

"I walked into her classroom with her. The teacher had everything decorated in bright colors and cute posters and each desk had a gift bag holding pencils and stickers. She's one of those perky young women with a smile that lights up the room, and the kids were obviously drawn to her right off. And a girl Bella met at the open house rushed up to greet her, so I think she's already made her first friend."

"Oh, that's good." Plucking a frame from the floor, Amy held it up on the wall and studied the placement appraisingly as she said, "I was afraid Bella would be a nervous wreck this morning."

"She was a little anxious." Jade didn't add that Bella had been reassured by Trevor, then spent the drive to school bravely vowing that she would make sure good things happened that day so she'd have something to tell him over dinner. "She'll be fine."

"Of course she will. Do you like this better on this wall or that one over there?"

"It looks good there. Needs to be a couple inches lower, though."

They focused on decorating then, interrupted a couple of times by questions from workers. Deciding the first wall was complete, Amy turned her attention to the one opposite. "How much longer until the reno is finished at your place?" she asked, dragging the stepstool across the room.

"Another week, maybe. A lot more was getting done today."

"Good. And things are still working out for you and the kids at Trevor's house?" They'd talked a few times during the past week, so Amy had already heard some of the details.

"We're pretty much living in a mansion," Jade

reminded her dryly, picking up the level and hammer. "I'd say things are working out fine. The hard part is going to be dragging the kids out of there and into our own house."

"And what about you? Will it be hard for you to leave a mansion complete with a full-time cook and housekeeper—not to mention a drop-dead-gorgeous millionaire host?"

Amy had met Trevor only in passing at her uncle's funeral, and had said she wasn't even sure he'd remember her, but he'd definitely made an impression on Amy. Every time she mentioned him, she raved about how charming and good-looking he was. If Jade didn't completely believe that Amy was deeply, unreservedly committed to her medical partner and longtime lover, Lincoln Brindle, she might wonder if Amy had a crush on Trevor.

Jade couldn't deny, if only privately, that she had a bit of a crush, herself. And while it was nice to be reminded of how it felt to be so physically and intellectually aware of an intriguing man, that would be the extent of it for the reasons she'd succinctly outlined to Trevor.

"I think I'll learn to get by again without the mansion and the housekeeper," she said with a smile.

"And the drop-dead-gorgeous millionaire?"

"He'll be back to being a family friend rather

than our host. Frankly, that'll be much more comfortable for both of us."

Amy held up a framed certificate, studied it against the wall, then set it aside to try another in its place. "Are you aware that your mother hopes you and Trevor will grow closer while you're staying with him? I heard her speculating about it with my mom last weekend."

"Trust me—I'm well aware of my mother's silly daydreams. For some reason, she's decided I need a husband and the kids need a stepdad. Frankly, I find that a little annoying, considering how well we've been getting along on our own."

Amy shook her head slowly. "You've always been fine on your own. No one questions that. Heaven knows you've been almost wholly responsible for yourself and your kids since Caleb was born."

As close as the cousins had been since childhood, Amy had never quite understood Jade's life as a military wife. The frequent moves, the long deployments, the customs and politics. The constant, if usually suppressed, dread—which, for Jade and several others she knew, had proved justified. Granted, Jade hadn't been totally prepared for what awaited her when she'd married as a naive, starry-eyed young bride, but she'd come through it with love, determination, and dedication to her children. Having chosen to put off marriage and children to pursue her medical career, Amy had always been supportive of Jade's choices, but somewhat bemused by them.

"Do you think your mom's sudden urge to marry you off might have something to do with her missing your dad? Maybe she's projecting her own loneliness onto you."

Just what she didn't need to hear, Jade thought with a wince. Now she felt guilty again for moving away from her mom, even though it wasn't really all that far and even though her mother had encouraged her to take the job with Amy. Her mom had promised she stayed too busy with her own pursuits to be lonely. She had her friend Hester and her sister, Loretta—Amy's mother—to spend time with whenever she wanted companionship.

"I suppose that's possible. But I still wish she and Hester would stop with the matchmaking. It's getting really awkward."

Amy lowered the frame again to study her. "Trevor seems like a great guy."

"Oh, he is. But seriously, Amy, even if I were looking to get married again, what do Trevor and I really have in common other than growing up in the same hometown and losing our spouses in our twenties? He's always wheeling and dealing, on the road or in the air or at one of his properties, or risking life and limb in some grueling hobby, while I'm perfectly happy to be at home with the kids when I'm not working. Besides, Trevor told me himself that he doesn't consider himself husband or father materials."

"Really? That seems rather odd. Did he say why? Do you think he's still grieving his late wife?"

"I...um...didn't ask." Because she hadn't considered it any of her business, or because the subject had made her uncomfortable? But she'd also wondered if Amy's suggested explanation was Trevor's real reason for avoiding current entanglements. "Anyway, I assume he should be taken at his word word that he prefers being unattached."

"Still," Amy added, pushing her tousled light brown hair away from her face with both hands, "you're a healthy woman. You deserve your share of adult fun while you're young enough to enjoy it. How long has it been since you've even been out on a date, much less—you know?"

"Too long," Jade acknowledged with a shrug, unoffended by the question. She and her cousin had shared too much over the years to play coy with each other now. "But I'm not looking for anything long-term, especially right now with everything else going on in my life."

"Girl, who said anything about long-term?" Amy laughed heartily. "I'm just saying if the handsome man happens to casually flirt while you're spending this brief time together, it wouldn't be so bad if you were to return the favor."

Thinking of a kiss that had tasted of moonlight and potential, Jade admitted, "Maybe I've already flirted back."

"Good for you." Grinning broadly, Amy turned back to the wall. "Now let's get to work. I'm not paying you to stand around talking about boys."

Laughing, Jade tossed her head. "You aren't paying me at all until Monday."

Amy waved a hand dismissively. "Details. Hold this and let me see if I like it here, okay?"

"Yes, boss."

Both were grinning as they got back to their decorating, though Jade was well aware that her cousin's message had been serious beneath the teasing. It wasn't the first time in the past year or so that Amy had reiterated that Jade was still young and shouldn't put her personal needs and desires completely aside for the sake of the children.

While Jade agreed with her cousin's advice on the whole, she wasn't sure a friend of the family was the best outlet, no matter how tempting he might be. If she wanted a stress-relieving affair, she'd do much better to find someone unconnected to her regular life, someone she could see discreetly on occasion for uncomplicated grown-up fun. Trevor Farrell hardly fit that description—and yet, she hadn't met anyone in a long time who'd captivated her quite so much.

Which meant she probably wasn't ready for flirtation of any sort, she assured herself. She had her kids and a career she enjoyed to focus on until—or if—the time ever arrived when she wanted more. She would be quite satisfied with those blessings.

THE DINNER MARY PAT served Wednesday evening was tailored specifically for the Evans children in honor of completing their first day at their new schools. She'd prepared fried chicken to please Caleb, roasted sweet potatoes topped with brown sugar and pecans for Erin and Bella's favorite fruit compote, proving Mary Pat had gotten to know them well during the past week. Caleb and Erin dived into the tasty meal eagerly, though Bella was more subdued.

"I thought Mr. Trevor was going to eat with us," she said with a pout.

Understanding Bella's disappointment, Jade tried to be patient with her reminder. "Honey, Mary Pat explained that Mr. Trevor had to work this evening."

According to the housekeeper, issues had arisen with Trevor's Florida project that required his attention, and he was meeting with some of his staff to discuss strategies. To Mary Pat's disapproval, he'd added that he might be quite late getting home.

Mary Pat had expressed her hope to Jade that Tamar was at least making sure Trevor wasn't overusing his leg. Jade had responded that she assumed Trevor knew better than to further prolong his recuperation.

Honestly, was everyone so accustomed to seeing to Trevor's needs that they didn't give him credit to know what was best for himself? Jade could understand how that would be frustrating for him. While she might not personally endorse the occasionally reckless behavior she'd heard about from their disapproving mothers, she still believed he had the right to make his own choices.

"But Mr. Trevor said he wanted to hear about my first day of school," Bella whined.

"I'm sure he'll join us for breakfast tomorrow, sweetie," Mary Pat responded. "You can tell him about it then. In the meantime, why don't you tell us about your day? We'd all like to hear about it."

Erin looked prepared to make a wisecrack, but prudently chose not to when Jade shot her a look. Erin scooped up a big bite of sweet potato and crammed it in her mouth, perhaps to avoid temptation.

"You were going to report on the best parts of

your day," Jade reminded Bella. "Would you like to tell us now?"

"Not right now," Bella mumbled, poking her fork into a strawberry. "Maybe later."

Jade and Mary Pat exchanged looks down the table, and then Jade deliberately turned the attention to her son. "Tell us more about your day, Caleb. You said you think you're going to like your science class best?"

As Caleb launched into a replay of his day, around bites of crunchy coated fried chicken, Jade told herself that she really was going to have to spur on the workers at her house even more tomorrow. She glanced at Bella's brooding expression, and she worried again that her daughter was growing too attached to Trevor. The child was bound to be disappointed if she expected busy Trevor to be available whenever she wanted him.

Trevor wouldn't be the father Bella perhaps daydreamed about when her friends talked about their daddies. Even though Jade had tried her best to fill both parenting roles for her children, she knew they were aware of that lack. Especially Bella, who had not even hazy memories to fill the void. With his cheery teasing and easy affection, Trevor probably seemed like an attractive alternative to a child who had little understanding of adult complications.

Jade sighed. The sooner she and her children

were in their own home and back to their old, comfortable routines, the better it would be for all of them.

TREVOR DIDN'T EXPECT to find Mary Pat in the kitchen when he walked in at just before ten Wednesday night. She was usually long settled in her own quarters in front of her TV by this hour. "You're not waiting up for me, are you?" he asked after greeting her.

"Don't flatter yourself," she retorted, patting his arm affectionately. "I decided to make an egg casserole for breakfast, and it needs to sit in the fridge overnight before baking. I just put it in."

He moved toward the fridge. "I'm starving. With all the meetings and phone calls this evening, I barely had time to grab a bite earlier. Are there any leftovers from dinner? Sandwich meat, maybe?"

She motioned toward the kitchen table. "Sit down, Trevor. I'll fix you a snack."

Tired and hungry, he didn't bother to protest. He sat. Minutes later, Mary Pat slid a warmed-up plate in front of him—fried chicken, sweet potatoes and a roll. "There's fruit salad, too, but I figured you'd want the protein first."

"This looks great, thanks."

She plunked a glass of her fresh-squeezed lemonade beside the plate. "You want a pain pill to go with that? You're a little pale."

"No, I'm fine. Just tired," he said. The leg hurt, but not as much as it had a couple of days earlier. He took a bite of his food and swallowed gratefully. "This is good, Mary Pat."

"It was even better when I served it four hours ago."

Hearing the censure in the throwaway remark, he shrugged. "I told you, it was unavoidable that I missed dinner. All hell was about to break loose in Florida, and I had to handle some things."

"I'm not saying it wasn't important, just that you probably could have let your very capable staff take care of most of it and consulted with them by phone from here."

Because he conceded unwillingly that she had a valid argument, he took another bite of chicken rather than responding. Satisfied that she'd made her point, she sat opposite him with a glass of lemonade for herself and a narrow slice of chocolate cake, a dessert he was already eyeing.

He wiped his mouth with his napkin and reached for his lemonade. "How were the kids at dinner? Did they have a good first day at school?"

"They were fine."

He knew her much too well to miss the sudden chill in her tone. "What? Did something go wrong?"

"Bella was very disappointed that you weren't here this evening. Apparently, she spent all day looking for good things to tell you about. She was certain you'd be waiting eagerly to hear about it."

Trevor winced. "Well…she can tell me in the morning. Over breakfast. I'll make sure to ask her about it."

Mary Pat sighed and shook her head, laying down her fork to look at him somberly. "Trevor, hon, you haven't spent a great deal of time with children—outside of your hosting duties at the resort, I mean—but there's something you should understand. Children, especially shy, slightly anxious ones like Bella, take adult promises very seriously. I know, you didn't actually promise her you'd be here for dinner tonight. Still, you implied you'd be here when you made the deal with her to remember all the good things today and tell you about them tonight. It was a lovely idea, and it did seem to ease her worries about her first day at school, but she was crushed when you didn't follow through on what she interpreted as a mutual agreement."

Losing his appetite, Trevor pushed aside his almost empty plate, feeling as though he'd been thoroughly chastised. See, he wanted to say. This was why he shouldn't be responsible in any way for children. If he counted his failed attempt to get Bella into the grotto, this was twice he'd screwed up with the kid. "Damn. Should I go up and talk to her now?" Or would he only make things worse if he did? He had no clue about this sort of thing.

"I expect she's asleep. Her bedtime is eight o'clock."

He pushed a hand wearily through his hair. "Okay. Fine. I'll try to make it up to her in the morning."

"I'm sure you'll charm her into forgiving you."

Her tone made him frown. "Is there something you're trying to tell me, Mary Pat?"

She sighed and stood to cut him a piece of cake he wasn't sure he wanted now. "Just be aware, Trevor. Those kids are in a vulnerable place right now, what with the new home and new schools and all. You have to keep that in mind when you interact with them."

"I'll be more careful."

And maybe that vow should extend to their mother as well, he told himself. As he kept reminding himself, there were consequences to getting involved, even casually, with a single mom—and especially with her too-vulnerable children. While his considerable and far-reaching responsibilities to his businesses and employees were daunting at times, he'd rather face those issues any day than to risk hurting innocent little Bella, or any other child.

"It's been wonderful having them here, hasn't it?" Looking around from the dishwasher, Mary Pat sighed. "Nice to hear children's voices and laughter in this big house that's usually so quiet."

He shot her a look. Was there a message beneath that apparently innocuous remark? Or was he just too tired to think straight tonight?

Deciding the latter was true, he picked up his crutches, leaning heavily on them when he rose from the chair leaving his dessert half finished. "I'm going to turn in. Thanks for the food, Mary Pat. Sleep well."

Apparently seeing the exhaustion in his face, she switched instinctively into maternal mode. "You, too, hon. Is there anything else you need tonight? Can I bring you some water? Got your pain pills?"

"I'm good, thanks. Bottled water in my suite, and over-the-counter meds if I need them. Good night."

He would think about kids, about Florida—and about Jade—once he had gotten some sleep, he promised himself.

TREVOR COULDN'T HAVE been more charming at breakfast had he been dining with dignitaries, Jade observed the next morning. Apparently, he'd been informed—obviously by Mary Pat—that his absence last night had disappointed. That was unfair, really. As Jade had reminded her children, especially Bella, several times after dinner, Trevor was a busy man with many important things to attend to. He couldn't just walk away from his responsibilities for dinner with his unexpected house guests.

Bella was too young to fully understand, but at least she'd seemed somewhat mollified by the time she'd gone to sleep last night. And Trevor was going out of his way to make it up to the child this morning. He'd even offered a gift.

"I've been trying to clear out some of my stuff and I found this," he said, sliding a red leatherbound book across the table toward Bella. "It's a sketch book. I'm not sure where I picked it up, but it's never been used. I thought you might like it. Might I suggest that you use it like a picture journal? You can draw a picture every evening before bedtime that shows the best thing that happened to you that day. Like hugs from your mom," he added with a wink toward Jade.

To keep things fair, he reached into the bag he'd carried down to breakfast and drew out two more nice journals. "I know you guys probably prefer computers," he said as he offered them to Caleb and Erin, "but there's still something relaxing about writing or drawing by hand. I've been known to doodle for an hour or so while I'm thinking about a problem, and I find it relaxes me and helps me reach an answer."

The kids reacted as if he'd just given them new cars, Jade thought with a slight shake of her head. The man really did have a way about him. Though she hoped he wasn't trying to buy forgiveness from her brood, she approved of his choice of gifts. Each of the journals had a colorful pen attached by an elastic band. Caleb was the first to note that the pens bore the logo of Wind Shadow Resort. "I'd like to see that place sometime," he said after thanking Trevor for the gift.

"Of course. If it's okay with your mom, you can make a day of it there while you're out of school this weekend," Trevor promised. "We have a lot there for kids to do—mini golf, a small water park, an arcade and, of course, the beach."

Three sets of eyes turned imploringly to Jade, who shrugged and assured them that she accepted the offer. To be honest, she'd like to see that resort, herself.

"So, Bella, I'm very sorry I had to miss dinner with you last night because of work," Trevor continued. "I couldn't get away in time to hear about your day."

"It's okay, Mr. Trevor." Instantly sympathetic, the softhearted child smiled at him. "I remembered the best things from yesterday. It was a good day, but my two favorite things were playing with Jovie at recess and making 'struction paper decorations for the teacher to hang on the bulletin boards. I made flowers."

"Nice. Mary Pat, do we have any construction paper around here?"

His housekeeper tapped a finger on her chin in a considering gesture. "I think we have some in the art cabinet upstairs."

"Maybe you could make some flowers for me to decorate my office when you have some free time?" Trevor suggested to Bella. "It could use some extra color."

Visibly thrilled, the child agreed.

"Everyone thank Mr. Trevor for the journals and then finish your breakfast," Jade said, perhaps too abruptly. She wasn't sure why the cozy scene had made her suddenly uncomfortable, but she felt a need to bring them all back to practical concerns. "It's almost time to leave for school."

"I'll draw you a picture today, Mr. Trevor. And if you can't be at dinner tonight, I'll show it to you tomorrow."

"Thank you, Bella."

Shortly afterward, Jade asked the kids to carry their plates to the kitchen and then sent them up to get their things. She lingered to help Mary Pat clear the table. Trevor stood, using only a cane now to support his weaker leg.

Growing uncomfortable as he watched her without speaking, she cleared her throat. "That was kind of you to give the kids the journals. Thank you."

"I need to clear out some stuff, and I thought they might like them."

"Still, it was a nice gesture. I've been encouraging them to journal. It's a positive creative outlet, an escape from technology and a safe, private way to express their developing emotions. Maybe they'll take it more seriously now that you've seconded the suggestion. You know—the typical kid's reaction to someone other than mom calling something cool."

He chuckled, then asked, "You didn't mind me suggesting a visit to the resort this weekend, did you? Had I not banged up my leg, I'd have taken you all out earlier this week, before school started."

"No, of course I didn't mind. It will be a nice break for them after their first school week, even a short one."

Trevor nodded. "It's on, then. I'm afraid it will be a bit crowded this weekend, but I do have certain privileges there."

She laughed softly. "Yes, I'm sure. Have a good day, Trevor."

She reached down around him to pick up a half-empty bowl of sliced cantaloupe to save for later. The movement made her arm accidentally brush lightly against his. The touch was light, brief, but still made her skin tingle with what felt like a small electric shock. It wasn't static. It was pure chemistry.

His eyes seemed to darken, but his tone was even when he said, "See you later, Jade."

Feeling shaky now, she stepped away from him, looking down at the bowl of melons as she hurried toward the kitchen.

WIND SHADOW RESORT was as grand as the advertisements suggested. Built in a U shape to maximize views of the fountain-centered man-made lake and the ocean beyond, it featured balconied guest buildings, restaurants and bars, a spa, an amphitheater, the mini golf course Trevor had mentioned, and several other tempting attractions. An assortment of shops and an arcade were located on the lower floor of the reception building, with management offices above.

After spending several hours at the resort and being treated like VIP guests Saturday, Jade wondered if her children would ever come back down to earth. Trevor didn't join them for the entire visit, but he made sure they had everything they desired and that the staff knew they were his special guests. Though judging by the way the ultra-friendly staff interacted with the other guests, everyone who patronized this establishment was pampered, which probably explained the resort's success.

She found it particularly interesting to see how other people reacted when Trevor was around. He put on no airs, but there was something about him that drew attention and respect. It was obvious that all of his employees here were as devoted as the housekeeper and assistant she'd already met. Had he decided that was all he needed by way of family outside his parents? Were loyal employees enough to fill his emotional needs? If so, she found that a little sad, considering how important her children were to her.

Still, she noticed that there was something slightly different about Trevor here than at home. It wasn't formality, exactly. He seemed to be on first-name basis with his staff, from management to maintenance, and treated them all with the same courtesy he extended to his guests. Rather, she saw him here as she'd been greeted by him that first night at his house. The consummate host, the polite Southern gentleman, the ultimate nice guy.

Didn't it get tiring to have to wear that mask all the time? And how could anyone really know him, if he kept every thought and emotion hidden behind an admittedly charming demeanor?

Trevor caught up with them in the arcade later that afternoon, where he was promptly challenged to air hockey and Skee-Ball competitions with Caleb and Erin. Despite his continued use of the cane to support his right leg, he gave them stiff competition, amid much teasing and laughter. Afterward, he hosted them for dinner. He'd offered to treat them to a fine meal in Torchlight, the resort's most formal restaurant, but Jade had suggested a more casual venue, considering that she and the kids were all windblown, slightly sunburned and sandy. So they chose the more casual outdoor café next to the lake. Bella was particularly charmed by the festive colored lights hanging from the palmettos surrounding them, and the candles and torches already flickering into life even though the sun had not yet set.

They were joined for dinner by an old friend of Trevor's, Walt Becker. Trevor explained that Walt, who was also his attorney, had dropped by with some legal papers and Trevor had invited him to come meet Jade and the kids. "I thought he'd like the chance to welcome the new residents of our area," Trevor added after introducing Walt.

"He's just feeling sorry for me because my

fiancée is in Seattle visiting her sister's family, and I'm having to fend for myself this weekend," the solidly built, salt-and-pepper-haired attorney confided to Jade with a smile that warmed his square-jawed face. "That's why I'm working on a Saturday. Nothing better to do."

"We're glad to have you join us," Jade responded, then motioned toward her middle child. "Erin has talked about becoming an attorney when she grows up."

"I'd be a good lawyer," Erin agreed with a toss of her ponytail.

"Yeah, our grandmother said she'd argue with a signpost," Caleb quipped, earning himself what must have been a kick beneath the table from his sister. "Hey!"

Jade cleared her throat and gave her older two a look that had them focusing quickly on their menus. She heard Trevor laugh softly.

He sat at her left at the big round table, with Bella on her right, then Erin, Caleb and Walt. Bella's shyness had returned with the addition of the stranger in their midst, and she huddled close to Jade's side as if trying not to call attention to herself. Jade supposed Walt did look somewhat intimidating, though her own first impression was positive. She'd been a marine wife long enough to recognize a marine when she saw him.

They all placed their orders and were waiting for their food when Erin blurted out to Walt, "What's wrong with your hand?"

Jade couldn't quite swallow her groan. She'd already noted that Walt's left hand was a prosthetic, but she'd tried to teach her children better manners than this. Erin never meant to be rude; she simply tended to voice whatever thoughts ran through her active mind.

Before Jade could reprimand her child's tactlessness, Walt lifted his left arm and replied genially. "This one? Oh, it's fake. But it serves me well enough."

"How did—"

"Erin," Jade murmured then.

"It's okay," Walt assured her. "Kids are always curious, and that's fine with me. I lost the arm in combat, Erin. I was a marine."

"Our dad was a marine," Caleb said, pushing his glasses up on his nose in a proud gesture. "He was killed in battle."

"He was a hero," Erin added, not to be outdone.

"And I'm grateful to him," Walt replied gently. "To all of you."

"Oorah," Caleb said, his chin held high as he

repeated the marine battle cry that had been one of his first words, thanks to his father's prompting.

"Oorah," Walt repeated, nodding his approval.

"Were you a marine, too, Mr. Trevor?" Erin asked.

Jade happened to be looking at Trevor at that moment—okay, so she "happened" to look at him quite frequently—and she fancied she saw a shadow pass through his eyes before he replied lightly, "No, Erin. I served a term in the army."

"Hooah," Walt said with a grin.

Trevor's smile looked strained to Jade when he responded, "Hooah."

"Don't let him fool you with that 'just served a term' remark," Walt added, aiming the comment at Jade. "There's no one more committed to vets and their families than this guy. He's on the board of several veterans' charities, works tirelessly to raise funds for them, has a policy of hiring vets first in all his enterprises. He might have spent only one term in uniform, but he's continued to serve every day since."

"Yeah, that's enough of that, Walt," Trevor muttered with a frown, obviously uncomfortable with the glowing acclaim.

Jade thought all the adults were relieved when the food was delivered. The kids dived into their fried seafood baskets with enthusiasm, while she enjoyed a grilled shrimp plate. Conversation centered then on the activities the kids had taken part in during the day and their school experiences thus far, including their favorite subjects—science for Caleb and history for Erin.

"What about you, Little Bit?" Trevor asked Bella. "What's your favorite thing to learn in school?"

"I like story time," Bella said very softly, proving again that Trevor had a manner of drawing her out of her reticence. "I can already read some."

"I'm not at all surprised."

"I can read you a story later," she offered, her face brightening.

"I'd like that."

Bella went back to eating with renewed enthusiasm. Returning her attention to her own meal, Jade thought again of that fleeting emotion she'd thought she'd seen in Trevor's eyes a short while earlier, when he'd been asked an apparently innocent question about his military service. Something about that moment still bothered her, though there was nothing in his expression now but genial humor and consideration for his guests' pleasure.

Would she ever know the real Trevor Farrell beyond those occasional glimpses? Or should she even concern herself with that, considering she wasn't expecting to spend much time with him in the future?

CHAPTER FIVE

JADE HAD SPENT plenty of time outdoors at the resort that day, but always surrounded by people and bustle. She needed her customary dose of starry peace to relax her enough to sleep after the kids were all tucked into bed. It was something she'd done for years, even in crowded base housing when her outdoor space had been nothing more than a minuscule concrete square calling itself a patio. Stephen hadn't joined her very often when he was home. He'd tried a few times, but he'd grown restless after a few minutes of sitting quiet and motionless.

Eschewing the chairs on Trevor's patio, she settled on the cool tile in a lotus position, her face turned up to the sky. And though she hadn't been at all sure he would come out that evening, she wasn't particularly surprised when she heard Trevor open the slider and step outside. She didn't have to check to make sure it was him. She just knew.

Opening her eyes, she saw him grinning down at her, his cane in his right hand. "I'd come down there with you, but I'm not sure I'd get up again."

Returning the smile, she motioned to a nearby chair. "Don't even try. You've taxed that knee enough today."

He drew the chair closer before sinking into it. "It's still sore, but really a lot better. I think I'll be able to toss the cane by Monday."

"You know what's best for you."

He laughed softly. "I appreciate that you keep saying that."

Still smiling, she drew up her legs to wrap her arms around her knees. "The kids had a great time at the resort today. Thank you for arranging that for them."

"I was glad to. And by the way, anytime you want to bring them out to the resort for the day, just let me know. You'll be our guests there."

"That's very kind of you."

His eyes might have dimmed just a fraction— or was that only a trick of the low lighting? "It's the least we can do for your Gold Star family."

People who knew them both had always said Erin came by her outspokenness honestly—from her mother. There were times when Jade simply had to speak her mind. This was one of them.

"And we appreciate that, Trevor, but my family doesn't ask for any special treatment because of my husband's death. To be blunt, one of the reasons I wanted to move away from Columbia was so my children and I could be treated a bit more normally. Like a regular family, rather than a tragic hero's survivors. We will always be proud of Stephen and we'll always regret that we lost him so soon, but he wouldn't want our kids to be seen as poor little unfortunates. Frankly, I was becoming concerned that Caleb, especially, was being affected by that message."

Once again, her directness seemed to take him off guard. And, again, his congenial mask slipped to reveal more of his genuine response to her words. "I can understand that, Jade. Even identify with it, to an extent. After Lindsey died, I came home to so much concern and sympathy that it was hard to deal with after a while. I mean, people meant well, and I appreciated it, but after a time you wish they'd just treat you normally again."

"Right? Like when you walk in a room where everyone's laughing, and they stop and look sad for your benefit?"

"Or they start to mention your wife's name and then stammer around, afraid of invoking sad memories," he said quietly.

"And yet, when you really need to be sad, you hold back because you don't want to make others feel bad. Or hear them tell you to be strong, and time will heal and all those other clichés that are well intended, but not helpful."

"Or they tell you how brave you are, and what

an inspiration to everyone," he said with a somber nod. "You can ask Walt about that one, too. He didn't lose a spouse, but he's told me his fake arm apparently looks like a halo to some people. And trust me, Walt is no angel."

Jade heard the fondness and admiration beneath that comment and appreciated that he'd deliberately lightened the moment. "You know, I got that impression during dinner. I like him, anyway."

"He's a great guy. Best friend I ever had. And, even though he hates for anyone to say it, a true hero."

Pushing a hand through his hair, Trevor shifted in the chair. "Anyway, the open invitation to the resort for you and the kids stands. And now, how about we change the subject? Do you have plans for tomorrow?"

More than willing to go along with the redirection, she nodded. "I'm taking the kids for lunch with my mom. She wants to hear about their first week at school and there are a few things at her house I want to bring back with us. We won't be too late, since it's a school night."

"A work night, too, with the clinic opening Monday."

"Yes. I'm looking forward to it. It'll be nice to get back to the career I trained for. What about you? Plans tomorrow?"

"Back to the office," he said with a shrug. "Just the usual."

"On a Sunday? Do you work every weekend?"

"Most. Sometimes I take a day off and go out on my boat, or take the camera out looking for something interesting to shoot. Occasionally I take long weekends for climbing or parasailing with buddies. I try to make time for skydiving a few times a year—it's a hobby I took up in college and still enjoy. I used to take the bike out for long rides when I had a few hours off, but, to be honest, I haven't been in a hurry to replace it since the accident last year."

She repressed a shudder, both at his reminder of the accident and his careless list of potentially dangerous hobbies. If he was that determined to risk life and limb at every opportunity, maybe it really was best for him to remain single. But then, having spent years worrying about the worst-case scenario with her husband, and then having those fears come true, had perhaps left her a bit more wary than most when it came to gambling with fate.

"Not saying I won't buy another bike," he added. "Just haven't gotten around to it yet."

She didn't reply. Instead, she looked back up at the sky, watching a thin ribbon of cloud drift over the face of the moon. A boat passed on the waterway, its running lights reflecting on the water, the engine a low throb in the otherwise quiet night. The air was still warm, the breeze barely cooling, but it felt good against her cheeks.

Labor Day was next weekend. The year was marching on so quickly, as they seemed to do these days. Her children were getting older; she would be thirty-three soon. And suddenly she found herself thinking of her cousin's advice not to let her youth pass her by without indulging in some adult fun.

She glanced at Trevor and found him gazing at her with an expression she couldn't quite read. She studied him openly for a moment, letting her eyes linger on his firm lips. And then she released a long breath. "I should go in. It's getting late."

He stood with her, leaving his cane lying beside his chair. "I always enjoy these nighttime chats with you, Jade."

Her pulse rate jumped in response to the husky timbre of his voice. There was just something about the way he said her name...

"So do I," she replied quietly, making no effort to move toward the door. Her gaze was on his mouth again, and she didn't try to pretend otherwise.

She couldn't say who moved first. One moment they were standing there looking at each other, and the next they were entwined in an embrace, their lips meeting, softening, parting. Regardless of what lay ahead for them, the attraction now was real. Intense. Jade saw no reason to conceal her awareness of that fact any more than Trevor was doing.

His hands swept her curves and she locked her arms around his neck, letting herself melt into the kiss, though she remained just clearheaded enough to keep his sore leg in mind. This man did know how to kiss—and she definitely appreciated his skill. Just imagining how talented he must be in other areas flooded her entire body with heat.

They ended the kiss slowly. Lingeringly. Jade suspected Trevor shared her feeling that there could have been—should have been—so much more. But this was neither the time nor the place. When or if that time ever came, it wouldn't be while she was staying in his home with her children. As long as they were under his roof, she was in his debt—a dynamic that didn't go well with moonlight kisses for either of them. And, yes, she was aware of the irony that she'd initiated their first kiss.

She dropped her arms and took a step back. "Good night, Trevor."

He made no effort to stop her. Certainly he, too, was aware that this was as far as they could go. For now, at least. "Good night, Jade."

She heard him sit again as she let herself inside. Apparently, he'd be staying out for a while. As much as she'd have liked to stay with him, she knew it was best if she resisted this time. Yet she carried the taste and feel of him with her as she climbed the stairs to her empty borrowed bed.

"IT'S SO NICE to have the children here again," Jade's mother said wistfully as she looked out her kitchen window to her fenced backyard. "I've missed them."

The kids had dashed out after lunch to play with JoJo, the big, goofy, lovable mutt who "guarded" their grandmother's backyard.

"It's only been just over a week since we moved, Mom," she said, pouring herself a glass of iced tea from the never-empty pitcher in her mother's refrigerator. She knew her mother was still adjusting to recent retirement from her human resources career. Though her mom stayed very busy with her clubs and volunteer activities, Jade had no doubt it was difficult to have her grandchildren even ninety minutes away. "And we've video chatted with you twice since. I promise, you'll always be a big part of our lives."

"I know." Patting her ash blond hair in a habitual gesture, Linda McGill turned away from the window. "I still approve of your decision to move to Shorty's Landing and work for Amy. I just get selfish sometimes."

"My darling mother, there isn't a selfish bone in your body." Jade's tone was teasing, but she meant every word of it.

As if offering proof, her mother asked in concern, "You've video chatted with Lucy, also, I hope. It's hard for her to be away from her grandchildren, too."

Jade's mother-in-law had moved to Pennsylvania to be closer to her daughter's family after her son's death. She'd seen Jade and the children three or four times a year since, and Jade had made a concerted effort to keep "GamGam" involved in their lives through phone calls, letters and lots of shared photos. "Of course we have."

"Good." After looking out one more time at the noisily playing kids and dog, Linda poured tea for herself and set it on the table across from Jade. "Can I get you anything else? More pie? A cookie?"

Jade groaned. "Thanks, but after that huge lunch, I couldn't eat another bite. Between you and Mary Pat, I'm going to have to diet for a month after I move into my own house next week."

Taking a seat, her mother laughed. "Spoiling you, is she? Hester's told me about Trevor's housekeeper. Apparently, she's quite a character."

"She is that. And she's wonderful. We've all fallen in love with her."

"And Trevor?"

"Um—" Caught off guard by the timing of the question, Jade blinked before saying evenly, "He's been a very gracious host. Still, I'm sure he'll be glad to have his house back."

"I'll bet he's enjoyed having you there. It must get so lonely rattling around in that big house by himself, when it's obviously designed for a family."

Jade eyed her mother narrowly. "We talked about this, Mom. No matchmaking."

It looked as though she was going to have to make it even clearer than she already had that her love life—or lack thereof—was strictly off-limits to meddling. "Trevor and I are friends. Let's leave it at that, please."

Her mom held up both hands. "Fine. I was just pointing out that he is a very nice man and I'm surprised he hasn't remarried and started a family of his own by now. Hester says she knows he grieved his young bride but she doesn't believe that's what's holding him back. She thinks he's just waiting to fall in love again, and he hasn't yet found the right woman."

Jade thought that was only one of the reasons. "More likely he's married to his business these days. The man never stops working, even when he's supposed to be recuperating."

"Only more evidence that he needs something more in his life."

"He chooses to work as much as he does because it's what he wants. He seems to be happy."

"Yes, he always seems happy enough when I see him," her mother conceded. "Still—it's a shame. And the two of you seem to have so much in common…"

A spate of excited barking from outside, followed by peals of laughter, drew Linda to the window. "They love that silly dog. And he's so happy to have them here to play with him today."

"Now they're just going to be bugging me again to let them have a puppy," Jade replied absently.

Her thoughts lingered on their conversation, particularly the part about Trevor being lonely. Was he? It had been nice to briefly share her feelings with someone who truly understood the loss of a spouse, and Stephen's name had come up in conversations a few times, but she and Trevor hadn't really talked much about Lindsey. She wondered again if Trevor was still deeply in love with the young bride he'd lost and unable to find anyone else who measured up to his memories of her. And was she really sitting here at her mother's kitchen table trying to analyze Trevor's reasons for staying single, when she wasn't even comfortable examining her own too closely?

Shaking her head, she pushed those thoughts aside for now and focused on a good-natured argument with her mother about why adding a new puppy to the mix of a new home, new school, new job and new family schedule was probably not the brightest idea.

THE KIDS LEFT their grandmother's house tired from their play, but the ninety-minute drive back to Trevor's place gave them time to recharge their energy. They begged for a swim before bedtime, and because they'd be moving out in a few days, Jade gave permission. Mary Pat prepared a light meal of hot dogs and cold sides for them to eat at the patio tables before their swim. It wouldn't be dark for another couple of hours, but she turned on all the patio light strings, anyway, to Bella's approval.

Trevor joined them midway into the meal, looking tired but satisfied with his day's work. He'd left the cane inside and walked with little more limp now than he had the first night Jade and her children had stayed here. She felt her heart trip when he gave her a slow smile, but she was confident her expression displayed nothing more than friendly welcome when she greeted him in return. He'd changed into board shorts and a T-shirt, so he apparently planned to swim with them after the meal. She knew the kids would like that. As for her—well, any opportunity to see Trevor without his shirt was a good one, she thought, grinning as she bit into her hot dog.

After the meal, Bella settled onto the tiles with a family of dolls and their small plastic hinged dollhouse. Jade knew the child would be happily entertained for hours with the toy. She, Trevor, Caleb and Erin went into the pool, where Jade swam leisurely laps at one side while Trevor and the kids played more boisterously near the water-fall. Within minutes, he was teaching them vari-ous dives from the board. Jade sighed but didn't comment when he demonstrated a few moves, favoring but not overly protecting his injured leg. Both Caleb and Erin listened attentively to his in-structions, followed them carefully then beamed happily when he praised them.

Jade sat on the edge of the pool with her feet in the water to watch the diving lesson, calling out the occasional encouragement or compliment. After a few minutes, Bella settled beside her, kicking at the water with her bare feet. "The wa-terfall is pretty, isn't it, Mommy?"

"Yes, it is. I could sit and just watch it for hours."

"Erin said there are fairy lights inside the

grotto. All different colors. And they twinkle on the water."

"That's right. It's very pretty. Maybe I could figure out a way to get my phone in without getting it wet to take a picture for you."

"Or better yet." Trevor stood in front of them, the water lapping at the top of his glistening chest as he held out his arms invitingly to Bella. His tone was easy, but his expression cautious as he continued, "I could take you in. You can close your eyes and hide your face in my shoulder to keep the water off, pretend you're taking a shower. Then when you open your eyes, you'll be in the fairy cave."

Erin swam closer and Jade braced for a wisecrack that would only make Bella's tension worse. Instead, Erin's more naturally sweet side came out when she said, "You'll love it, Bella. It's so pretty in there. And Mr. Trevor will keep you safe."

"C'mon, Bella." Paddling to the waterfall, Caleb motioned before disappearing into the little grotto.

Jade worried that everyone was again putting too much pressure on the anxious child. "It's okay, sweetheart. You don't have to—"

She stopped in surprise when Bella drew a deep breath and held out her arms to Trevor. "Okay. But don't drop me in the water."

"I would never drop you, Little Bit."

Bella wound herself so tightly around him that Jade thought it was a miracle he could breathe. As Trevor had suggested, Bella hid her face in the curve of his neck, burrowed so deeply it was a wonder either of them could breathe. Gently encouraging the child, Trevor made his way to the grotto the older siblings had already entered.

Telling herself it would be petty to feel piqued that Bella trusted Trevor in the water more than her, Jade slid into the pool and followed. She heard Bella give a gasp when they went through the waterfall, but the child didn't cry out.

Jade found her older two children, waiting on the low bench that lined the rounded cave, their legs submerged almost to the knees. She boosted herself next to Erin and then watched Trevor peel Bella off himself to set her on the bench. Swiping at her dripping hair with both hands, Bella opened her eyes a crack and then widened them in delight. "Oh. Oh. It's so pretty!"

Seeing the grotto through a child's eyes, Jade had to agree it looked like the fairy cave Erin had described. The tiny lights nestled so cleverly in the real-looking rock walls glittered and sparkled gaily, the colored reflections dancing on the tumbling, splashing fall. Their voices echoed in the shadowed hollow, adding to the otherworldliness of the scene.

"It's great, isn't it, Bella?"

The child nodded enthusiastically in response to her sister's question. "I like it in here." She giggled at the sound of her own voice, then added, "It would be nice if it had a back door, though, so you didn't have to get wet to come in."

Erin rolled her eyes. "Oh, for—"

Jade elbowed her quickly, and Erin closed her mouth.

Trevor shot them a glance, his eyes meeting Jade's with a glimmer of a smile.

Apparently, her mind was prone to fancy that day. She had a flash of what it might be like to be alone in this cozy cave with Trevor. At night, of course, with starlit darkness outside and only the glittering fairy lights inside.

The small grotto that was naturally cooled by the fine mist from the waterfall suddenly felt warm and close. Apparently Amy was right about one thing. It really had been too long since Jade had indulged her still-healthy, naturally passionate side.

She forced herself to look away from her sexy host, glancing instead at the deepening shadows. "I hate to be a spoilsport, guys, but I'm afraid we're going to have to go in soon. By the time you all get your showers and lay out your clothes and backpacks for tomorrow, it will be time to call it a day."

The kids grumbled—mostly because it was expected of them—but she knew they were tired. They would sleep well tonight. She suspected even Caleb would be asleep before his lights-out deadline.

"Ready to take the *Good Ship Trevor* back to shore?" Trevor asked Bella, holding out his arms.

She giggled and went to him with only a slight hesitation this time. Maybe she didn't even cling to him as tightly, though Jade suspected Bella enjoyed the snuggles, anyway. And who could blame her?

Back on "dry land," Bella gazed sweetly up at Trevor. "Thank you for taking me to the fairy cave, Mr. Trevor. I'm going to draw it in my journal for today."

"That's great, Bella. I'd love to see that drawing."

"I'll show it to you tomorrow at dinner," she promised.

"I'll look forward to it."

"I'm going to draw JoJo and write about playing with him," Erin said, looking a bit jealous of the attention Bella was getting.

Trevor obligingly turned to her. "JoJo?"

"Nanna's dog. He's huge. And he loves to play with us. We want a puppy, but Mom said no," Erin added with an accusing glance at her mother.

"I said not at this time," Jade corrected her.

"Let's get settled into our new home for a few months first, and then we'll talk about a puppy."

"Not one of those little yappy dogs," Caleb piped in. "A big dog, like JoJo."

Wrapped in her soft towel, Jade grimaced. "We'll see. Everyone inside now."

As her children trooped inside, Jade looked up at Trevor. "Thank you," she said quietly.

His smile was crooked. "I don't expect her to jump into the pool and start swimming tomorrow."

"No. She's still afraid. But it was a step forward."

"You've got great kids, Jade. All three of them."

"They are. Sometimes they can be trying, but on the whole, they're amazing."

He touched her cheek, a fleeting, barely there caress. "They have an amazing mother."

She moistened her lips. "Good night, Trevor. I'll see you tomorrow."

She thought it best to skip the intimate chat tonight. She had to work in the morning.

Oh, who was she kidding? She simply didn't trust herself to be alone with him tonight, considering the direction her daydreams had wandered. This was still the wrong place. The wrong time. And probably the wrong man about whom to fantasize, especially with all of the awkward connections between them.

He dropped his arm so abruptly that she wondered if his thoughts had taken a similar turn. "Good night, Jade. Sleep well."

She wasn't at all sure that was going to happen, but she nodded and turned to walk inside.

JADE FOLLOWED HER CHILDREN into Trevor's house just before five thirty Monday afternoon. She was pleasantly tired, quite satisfied with her first full day at the clinic. She was going to love her work, and looked forward to forming relationships with her coworkers and the regular patients. She wore royal blue scrubs and comfortable shoes, with her hair pulled into a low twist. She thought she should probably change for dinner, despite the casual atmosphere around Trevor's table.

"How was your day?" Mary Pat greeted her as the kids ran upstairs to put away their backpacks.

"Very nice, thank you. We weren't terribly busy since we just opened today, but we have quite a few appointments set up in the coming week."

"Wonderful. I'll call tomorrow and make that appointment we discussed. I just never have much liked the doctor who replaced my last one when he retired. From what you've said, I'm sure I'll like Dr. Ford much better."

"I think you will. And I know she'll love you."

Mary Pat smiled brightly. "Well, aren't you sweet. Dinner will be ready in half an hour. I've made a big tossed salad and I'm baking fish filets to go with it."

"That sounds delicious, Mary Pat. I'll go freshen up first, unless there's something I can do to help you?"

"No, hon, you go on up. I've got it under control."

Moving toward the doorway, Jade asked casually, "Will Trevor be home in time to join us for dinner?"

Mary sighed heavily. "Trevor isn't here. He's gone to Florida. He said he could be there for a week, maybe more. Some kind of big kerfuffle apparently needs him to be on-site, though I wonder if he's taking on too much again rather than letting his people there handle things."

A week. Maybe more. Jade bit her lip. She and the kids would be settled in their own house by the time Trevor returned. Bella would be so disappointed.

Yeah, sure. As if Bella were the only one, she thought, heading up the stairs to wash up for dinner.

Maybe this was best. There was only so much temptation any woman could resist.

After putting the kids to bed that evening, Jade followed her habit of wandering outside to the patio. A brief rain had fallen during the evening, leaving the tiles around the pool still too wet for comfortable seating. She settled instead into one of the chairs that had been sheltered by an awning, leaving it only slightly damp. She'd be changing into sleepwear soon, anyway.

The night sky was still overcast, though slowly clearing. It didn't matter that she couldn't see the moon or stars; she still drew respite from the darkness and the quiet. She closed her eyes and laid her head back, reminding herself firmly that she actually preferred being alone at these times.

The repairs at her own home were well under way now, so they should be able to settle in by the end of the week. She'd already purchased comfortable patio chairs so she would have a place to savor the nights there in the small fenced backyard. She projected a bit further ahead and imagined a big dog sprawled out beside her. Though she still wasn't ready to make that commitment, she knew her kids would talk her into it eventually.

She'd miss the soothing sound of the waterfall. Perhaps she should look into a water feature for her backyard. A fountain, maybe. She would enjoy that during her solitary nightly contemplations.

She opened her eyes when her phone vibrated in the pocket of her jeans. It was rather late for calls, but she never ignored a ring, just in case of a family emergency. Seeing the number on the screen made her hand freeze for a moment. She drew a deep breath before answering. "Hello, Trevor."

"It's not too late for a call, I hope." His deep voice rumbled in her ear, triggering a cascade of goose bumps, though the night air wasn't particularly chilly.

"No. The kids are in bed, and I'm sitting outside."

"I thought you might be. How's the weather?"

"Rainy earlier but clearing now. Cooled things down a bit."

"I guess Mary Pat told you why I had to leave so suddenly. We've been dealing with an issue down here in Florida that still isn't resolved and I just feel like it's something I have to be here to deal with."

"I'm sorry you're having problems there. Is it getting any better?"

"It'll work out, just annoying delays. I know you understand construction frustrations."

She laughed shortly. "Do I ever."

"Speaking of which, how's the house coming along?"

"Much faster now, thanks. I'm confident we'll be able to move in before the weekend."

Was it only the connection, or did his voice sound rather hollow when he said, "Oh. Well, that's great."

"Yes. It's time for us to be back in a home of our own."

"Well, Mary Pat will miss you all. Maybe I should follow your kids' lead and get her a puppy."

Jade noted that he hadn't said he would miss them, though she focused on replying lightly to his teasing. "I'm sure if Mary Pat wants a puppy, she'll get one for herself."

"No doubt. Anyway, I just wanted the chance to tell you personally that I'm sorry I had to be such a neglectful host and take off like this again. Please convey my apologies to the kids, too."

"Yes, I will. But, really, Trevor, apologies aren't necessary."

"Jade?"

"Yes?"

"I'd much rather be sitting there with you instead of in this hotel room."

She swallowed. "That would be nice."

"Sleep well." He disconnected without giving her a chance to respond.

Though she hadn't intended to stay out long tonight, she sat there for quite a while staring up at the cloudy sky and holding the phone gripped tightly in one hand. Considering how much she wished Trevor were sitting beside her right now, perhaps it was for the best that he'd had to leave.

Her time here had been fantasy, she reminded

herself. Real life waited for her in her new house, with her old routines of school-day breakfasts, after-work errands, evenings overseeing homework and reading bedtime stories before tucking everyone in and then catching up on a few household chores before turning in herself. It was a quiet, comfortable existence that she found quite satisfying.

She would always be aware that it hadn't been quite enough to gratify her adventure-loving husband. She doubted seriously that it would be any more fulfilling for larger-than-life millionaire tycoon Trevor Farrell. And if there was one thing she didn't need now, it was a risk-taking, heart-guarded man who'd always rather be somewhere else.

FIVE DAYS AFTER being summoned to Florida, Trevor sat in his hotel suite with his phone in his hand. His day had begun before sunrise and was ending after ten. Having dealt with people and crises all day, it was nice to be alone in the quiet of his quarters, but it wasn't home. As luxurious as this suite was, he suddenly wished he were sitting in a chair by his pool relaxing to the sounds of tumbling water as he turned his face to the moon. Jade had spoiled him with that soothing ritual, he mused.

It made him uncomfortable to wonder if she'd also spoiled him with her presence.

He hadn't spoken with her after he'd called his first night in Florida. Though he'd been tempted to call since, he'd resisted. He'd been busy, and he was sure she was, too. Mary Pat had kept him up to date with what was going on at home. He knew, for example, that Jade and the kids had moved into their own house during the past two days and were spending their first night there tonight.

For some reason, he found himself picturing his own home as it must look just then. Mary Pat would have already retired to her cottage, so his place would be dark. Quiet. Empty. The house he usually envisioned as a private retreat seemed larger and less welcoming in his probably over-tired imagination. He had the unsettling feeling that his voice would echo if he spoke there. Not that there was anyone to speak to.

What did a contentedly single guy need with a place that big, anyway?

His mother had seen the house advertised and had encouraged him to consider it, convincing him it would be a wise investment and that it offered a perfect place to entertain family when they visited. Though he hadn't been convinced he even wanted to buy a house, he'd agreed to look at it. His first thought when he'd turned onto the driveway was that Lindsey would have loved that place. It would have fit her to a tee—tastefully luxurious, elegant but comfortable, fitted seamlessly into its natural surroundings. Though he'd told himself it was partially in honor of her memory that he'd bought the house, there were times when he'd wondered if living in a house he identified so strongly with her was one of the ways he dealt with the guilt he would always carry when he thought of Lindsey's unrealized dreams.

Feeling the beginnings of a dark mood he recognized too well but didn't want to indulge tonight, he impulsively lifted the phone to his ear.

"I hope I'm not calling too late," he said when Jade answered, greeting him by name.

"No. The kids are all in bed, but I'm sitting outside with a glass of wine. I figure I earned it today."

"Long day?" he asked in response to her tone. It lightened his mood just to picture her reclined gracefully in a chair beneath the stars with a glass of wine in her fingers.

"Fairly. Lots of unpacking after school and work."

"Getting settled in?"

"Yes, though we'll still have plenty to do over the weekend. There are still a few minor updates I'd like to make, but it's already starting to feel like home now that the kids have all their things around them again."

"So they like their new home?"

"I believe they do. Even though there's no pool with a grotto and no fancy rec room," she added with a laugh, "only a neighborhood pool and park and a small, fenced backyard with a swing. Bella particularly likes the backyard swing. I'm sitting on it now actually."

Trevor amended his mental image to include Jade lazily pushing herself in the swing with one long, slender leg. And he thought the unembellished little backyard she'd described was exactly where he'd like to be at that moment.

"You know you and the kids are welcome to visit my place and use the pool whenever you want," he assured her, then added quickly, "Mary Pat would love to see you all at any time."

"Thank you, Trevor," Jade replied. "I've already promised Mary Pat we'd visit. It's thoughtful of you to offer the pool."

"Any time," he repeated firmly.

"What about you?" she asked. "How's everything going there in Florida? Is the latest crisis resolved, I hope?"

"Tentatively," he replied with a weary laugh. "I'm going to Texas late tomorrow to check on things at the resort there for a few days before heading back home."

"It seems as though owning three resorts in three different states spreads you pretty thin," Jade observed. "I don't know how you keep up with everything."

"Well… I have great teams at all three sites," he admitted. "My business partners are always willing to help out when they're needed. I guess I just feel the need to stay personally involved, especially when major issues crop up."

He'd invested too much time, too much money, too much of himself in his company to handle it any other way. The company and his employees were as much his family as his parents and Mary Pat. He wouldn't let them down.

They chatted for a few minutes more about his ongoing projects, the kids, her upcoming plans, and then Trevor brought the call to an end, telling himself he really shouldn't keep her any longer. Still, he thought as he set the phone aside, it had been nice to hear Jade's voice even just over the phone. The echoes of her pleasant tone and infectious laugh put him in a much better mood than he'd been when he'd called; maybe he'd just needed to talk with a friend for a few minutes, someone who wasn't depending on him for decisions or ideas or approval.

When he closed his eyes for a moment, he realized he was still picturing her on that swing, perhaps smiling now after their call. The degree to which he wished he were sitting beside her concerned him enough that he pushed thoughts of her to the back of his mind and reached for his laptop. He had a few business matters he could tend to before he was sleepy enough to turn in without fear of lying awake with his thoughts.

CHAPTER SIX

THE PERKERY WAS rapidly becoming Jade's favorite shop in Shorty's Landing. The establishment's relaxing coastal colors and comfortable furnishings drew her in and tempted her to linger. Her children were equally enamored of the place with its tempting array of pastries and a small breakfast and lunch menu. Jade and the kids were always welcomed warmly by owner Elle O'Meara, and Elle's mother, Janet. Janet was a hoot—henna haired and caftan clad with jangling bracelets and an impish smile—and she kept the kids giggling with her teasing.

It was the third Saturday in September and Jade had brought the children in for treats to celebrate their first month of school and the excellent grades they were all receiving. The girls each had a cupcake and Caleb had chosen a cookie. Elle had allowed her three-year-old daughter, Charlotte, to come from her plastic-fenced play area behind the counter to visit with them. Bella and Erin were both entertaining the happy toddler—and vice versa. Because it was a slow time in the shop as the tourist season waned and the lunch rush dissipated, Elle was able to linger at the counter, visiting with Jade as they kept an eye on their offspring.

"You're all getting settled in well, I take it?" Elle asked, absently wiping the counter as she spoke. "Your children like it here?"

"Yes, thanks. We all love our new home, and the kids like their classes so far and are making lots of new friends."

Elle's smile lit her attractive face. "I'm glad to hear it."

The girls, particularly, seemed to be making friends quickly. Jade was somewhat more concerned about Caleb. Though his grades had been good on the few assignments he'd had so far and he said he liked his classes, there was something different about him in the past couple of weeks. She couldn't put her finger on it exactly. Perhaps it was just preteen male moodiness, a condition she'd been warned about repeatedly. Maybe he was just a bit slower to adjust to the changes than his sisters. She was sure he'd come around, though she couldn't help bracing for the teen years looming closer each day.

Jade turned her attention to the light-as-air, espresso-flavored meringue in her hand. "This cookie is absolutely delicious, Elle. I could eat a dozen of them, though I'm limiting myself to this one for now."

Elle winked at her. "Feel free to indulge. They're very low calorie."

"Tempting."

The bells over the door chimed, and Jade automatically looked that way. She almost crumbled the cookie in her tightened fingers when Trevor strolled through the door, followed by his pal Walt. It was the first time she'd seen Trevor since he'd left for Florida almost three weeks ago. He looked fit and healthy, his limp not much more now than a sexy roll of hip. Was it possible he'd gotten even better looking in less than a month? Because he made her mouth water much more than the display case full of sweets beside her.

It was obvious from his expression that he was equally surprised to see her and the kids. His gaze went straight to her, his face blank for just a moment before he smiled.

Erin spotted him then, welcoming him with a whoop and a dash toward him. "Hey, Mr. Trevor!"

He returned her greeting warmly. "Hey, there, Erin. How's it going?"

"Great. I'm going to be on the school swim team!"

"Wow, way to go. You'll be the star of the team, I'm sure."

Giggling, Erin returned his offered high five with a loud clap. "Maybe not the star—but I'm not ruling it out, either."

"Good for you."

While Erin turned to greet Walt, Trevor looked down at Bella, who studied him with her hands on her hips and an expression Jade knew too well.

"You were gone a very long time," Bella told him in her most disapproving tone.

Trevor cleared his throat, looking almost comically chastened. "I know, Little Bit. I'm afraid I had to go take care of some work."

"You didn't say goodbye."

"Well, I had to leave while you were in school—"

"You could have left a note."

Jade thought about rescuing him, but decided to let him handle this. He was the one who'd befriended her occasionally-formidable tiny worrier.

"You're absolutely right, Bella," he said somberly. "I should have left a note. I hope you'll accept my apology."

Bella gave it a moment's thought, and then her pink lips tilted up into a smile that Jade suspected could melt the heart of a bronze statue and stepped forward for a hug. "I accept."

Laughing softly, Trevor wrapped his arms around her in return. "Thank you."

Properly reprimanded, he turned then to greet

Caleb with a handshake and Charlotte with a tickle. Then, leaving the children visiting with Walt, he approached the counter where Jade and Elle stood. "Ladies."

Jade greeted him with a nod meant to look only casually friendly. "Hello, Trevor."

"Hi, Trevor. How's the Florida project coming along?" Without bothering to ask for his order, Elle set a mug on the counter for him to fill from the self-serve coffee bar. "I hear there were some issues down there."

"There were, but it's all taken care of now. The project's back on track."

"Glad to hear it." Elle glanced at Jade. "I'm not sure if you know, but Trevor's a partner in this shop. And I lease the coffee shop at his resort. The resort here in the state, I mean."

"No, I didn't know you were partners," Jade said, surprised.

"I'm a minority partner in The Perkery," Trevor explained with a self-deprecating shrug. "And a silent one, at that. Elle's the expert on coffee and pastries. My guests love her shop at Wind Shadow."

"Trevor saved my butt when my former partner bailed on me last year," Elle said more bluntly. "I wouldn't still be in business if it weren't for him."

"No need to give him the hero treatment, Elle," Walt drawled as he approached the counter. "He was just making sure he had a steady supply of your famous chocolate-filled doughnuts."

"That might have had something to do with it," Trevor agreed, giving Jade a wink that almost took her breath away. She lifted her mug to her lips quickly, in an effort to hide the reaction.

"How are the wedding plans coming along, Elle?" Walt asked after requesting a cinnamon muffin to accompany his coffee.

Jade watched as Elle's whole face lit up in a way that could only be described as blissful. "Very well, thank you, Walt. You're still coming, right?"

Walt's naturally stern face softened. "Maddie and I wouldn't miss it."

From the coffee bar, Trevor lifted his now-filled mug in a salute. "And I will definitely be there."

"You'd better. And you're still welcome to bring a guest," Elle reminded him.

Trevor took a sip of his coffee, blue eyes glinting as he neatly avoided a response.

Walt's sudden grin was roguish. "Prince Charming here never takes a date to weddings. He's afraid it'll give them ideas he's not interested in fulfilling."

So Jade wasn't the only one to whom Trevor had confided that he wasn't interested in marrying again. She wondered if he would ever meet anyone who'd change his mind about that, though she didn't dwell on the thought for long.

She saw Trevor's eyebrows dip in a quick frown that he smoothed instantly. Apparently, he hadn't cared for being mocked, even good-naturedly, for his commitment phobia. He sipped his coffee before saying quietly enough that the children couldn't hear, "Bite me, Walt."

Walt laughed and gave his friend a light shove that almost caused coffee to slosh over the top of the cup. "I'll stick with the muffin, thanks."

"Well, the plus-one invitation stands," Elle said to Trevor, having watched the interplay between the longtime friends. "Just in case."

"Mr. Trevor, are you going to come see our new house?" Bella asked, approaching the smiling adults. "We don't have a pool, but I'll show you my toys. And I got a new bookcase for my room. Mommy put it together all by herself."

"Gotta love those Swedish instructions," Jade muttered when Trevor and Walt congratulated her with smiles in response to Bella's obvious awe.

"Somehow I have the feeling there's very little you can't take care of on your own," Trevor told her.

She gave a shrug, letting her eyes meet his for a moment. "I certainly try."

Jade glanced at Elle, finding her watching the brief exchange with one eyebrow slightly lifted.

She wouldn't be surprised if Elle sensed the attraction between her and Trevor. Women tended to notice that sort of thing. She was grateful when Elle merely said, "I've been known to assemble a few shelves, myself. Who do you think put that display of coffee and tea accessories over there together?"

"Nice."

"Are you going to come see our house, Mr. Trevor?" Bella reminded him, tugging at his shirt.

"I'd love to see your house," he assured her.

Feeling the need to say something, Jade nodded. "You're always welcome, of course.

He smiled at her again, so warmly that her toes curled in her shoes.

Erin led Charlotte over by the hand then, explaining that Charlotte wanted her mother.

"We should be on our way." Dragging her attention away from sexy Trevor, Jade glanced toward her son, who'd been playing a handheld video game at one of the tables. "Caleb, have you finished your peach tea? Ready to go?"

Caleb turned off the game and stood. "I'm ready."

"I'll give you a call, Jade—to arrange to come see Bella's new bookcase." Trevor patted Bella's head as he spoke.

"Call any time." After exchanging farewells

with Walt and Elle, Jade gathered her children and herded them quickly out of the shop.

TAKING A RARE Saturday night away from dining with guests at the resort, Trevor ate dinner with Mary Pat. He'd called her and ordered her not to cook, instead bringing home a meal prepared by his renowned chef for them to share.

"I figured you'd like a night off from cooking," he told her as they sat at the table with the four-star fare spread in front of them.

She took a bite of lemon basil shrimp risotto served with grilled fish and crisp asparagus. The chef had cleverly bundled everything into an insulated carrier with warm packs so the meal still tasted freshly prepared. "It's good," Mary Pat pronounced after that first sample. "Could've used a little more salt."

Trevor had to stifle a grimace as he thought of how his good-natured but extremely proud chef would react to that assessment. He took a sip of his wine to keep from having to reply.

"It was sweet of you to bring this home tonight, hon," she assured him as if worried that she'd sounded ungrateful. "I was just going to have eggs and toast if you ate out tonight. This is much nicer."

"You deserve a treat every once in a while."

And he should see to that more often, he thought with a ripple of guilt.

She beamed fondly at him. "You spoil me plenty as it is."

"There's cheesecake for dessert."

"My favorite, as you know." She sighed happily. After a few minutes, she said, "Have you talked to your mother lately? How are they doing?"

"Talked to her this morning, and they're fine. She and Dad are leaving tomorrow for a cruise for their anniversary."

"Oh, how nice for them. I'm sure they'll enjoy it."

His mother would probably have a good time, Trevor mused, especially if she got to put on her cruise finery and mingle at the captain's table. His dad would tolerate it, though he would make running digs about the cabin, the food, the service and pretty much everything else. He'd be very civil about it, of course. Trevor's father was the master of a backhanded compliment. Trevor loved his dad, and respected his business acumen, but having been the target of those veiled digs all his life, he could empathize with the crew.

Setting down her fork, Mary Pat reached for her water glass. "There's something I need to discuss with you, Trevor."

He frowned at her uncharacteristically serious tone. He hoped nothing was wrong. Was she ill? Was she unhappy with her job? Whatever it was, he was here for her. Always. She was family. "Of course. What do you need to talk about, Mary Pat?"

"I told Jade that I'd help her with the children on school holidays and vacations when she has to work. I can either stay with them at their house, or bring them here, but I'd still take care of my responsibilities to you, of course, and I'd keep the kids out of your way."

That was all? His fingers, having momentarily white knuckled, relaxed around his fork. "I think that's a great idea, Mary Pat. It's win-win for everyone. And of course you can bring them here whenever you want. I've told Jade that both the pool and the rec room are available to them whenever they like."

Her soft face creased with her smile. "I knew you wouldn't mind."

She was right, of course. If Mary Pat wanted to babysit during her off hours, that was her prerogative, though he hoped she didn't overtax herself. Still, he realized his feelings about the situation were decidedly mixed. Did this mean he'd be seeing the kids more often than he'd expected—and Jade, too? Not that he was usually home during the hours they'd likely be visiting, but it made him a little uncomfortable to think of them playing and laughing here when he was away. For some reason, he had the fleeting thought that his house was happier when they were there than when he was—and how foolish was that fancy? It sounded more like something Bella would say than a…well…than a grown-ass man.

"I saw Jade and the kids today, by the way," he said to bring his capricious thoughts back in line with reality.

Mary Pat's face lit up. "Really? Did you go visit them?"

"No, just ran into them unexpectedly. Walt and I decided to wrap up a meeting with a coffee and doughnut at The Perkery, and Jade and the kids happened to be there. They did invite me to come see their place, though. I thought I'd run by to-morrow, if that's convenient for Jade. It seemed important to Bella that I visit their new house."

"They're very proud of it. I helped them move the bags they'd brought with them here, and I got the grand tour. It's a nice place."

"I'm sure it is."

"I bet the kids like The Perkery. Elle does make some tasty treats. Her wedding is coming up soon, isn't it?"

"Next weekend."

"You're still planning to go?"

"Of course."

"And you're still not taking anyone?"

"Planning to go stag. What with work and my leg and all the other stuff going on lately, I haven't had time to even think about the wedding. And since I'm not seeing anyone at the moment, I wouldn't know who to ask."

Mary Pat frowned. "It really would be nicer if you had a companion for the wedding. So much more fun than going alone."

"You could go as my date," he suggested, winking at her, and knowing exactly how she would respond.

She proved him right with a firm shake of her head. "Thank you, but no, dear. You know I don't care for big gatherings. Have you considered asking Jade to go with you?"

The thought had crossed his mind when talk of the wedding had come up at the coffee shop earlier, though he'd pushed it aside. He wasn't at all sure Jade would be interested in going to the wedding of a couple who were little more than strangers to her, in the company of a man whose presence beside her could possibly spark gossip about them. And though he'd been slightly irked by Walt's tactless joke about it, Trevor couldn't deny that avoiding speculation was a good part of the reason he rarely invited a date to a wedding.

"I'm sure Jade's really busy with the kids and the new house," he prevaricated.

Mary Pat waved a hand, dismissing the excuse.

"So, this would give her a chance to get out and socialize for a bit. I'll watch the kids, of course. It would be Jade's first social outing without her children since she moved here. I'm sure it would do her a lot of good, not to mention it would be nice for you to have the company."

Trevor shot his housekeeper a narrowed glance. "Mary Pat—"

The innocent look she gave him in return wouldn't have fooled Elle's three-year-old daughter. "I'm not matchmaking. It was just a suggestion." Mary Pat pushed back her chair. "Now, about that cheesecake."

TRUE TO HIS WORD to the children, Trevor called Sunday afternoon to ask Jade if it was a good time to come by and see her new house. "I'm afraid I'll get another lecture from Bella if I don't keep my promise," he added.

Laughing softly, Jade assured him he was welcome. The moment she hung up the phone, she made a mad dash through the house picking up toys and putting away the laundry she'd been folding when he called. This was only the second time company had visited here. Amy and Lincoln had come for dinner a couple of nights ago, bringing a beautiful potted ivy as a housewarming gift. They'd stayed late playing board games with the family, and the kids had loved entertaining in their new place. Amy and Lincoln had promised to come back for a cookout and s'mores when Jade bought the grill and small fire pit she had in mind for the backyard.

She'd just finished brushing her hair and touching up her light makeup—which she'd have done to prepare for any guest, she promised herself—when Trevor rang the doorbell.

There was almost no time for her to talk with him upon his arrival. The girls descended immediately when he entered the living room. Chattering and competing for his attention, they tugged him in two different directions to see the new house they were so proud of. Jade couldn't really fault them for that. She was proud of their new home, too.

Her house in Columbia had sold for a tidy profit, which she'd invested into this one. The bedrooms weren't large, but there were four so everyone had a private space. Rather than a formal dining room, the newly renovated kitchen featured a dining bay that looked out over the fenced backyard with its small wooden deck and redwood swing. Theirs wasn't a water view, but the houses surrounding them were tidy and well maintained.

Returning from the bedrooms, the girls walked Trevor around the living room, pointing out individual items displayed on the bookcases built on either side of a big window. Interspersed with books and a few treasured knickknacks, Jade had nestled frames displaying the kids' artwork and family photographs. She noted that Trevor looked for a rather long time at the last family photo taken with Stephen. In it, Jade sat in a chair with newborn Bella in her arms, very young Caleb and Erin on either side of her, and Stephen in full dress uniform behind her, his hand resting on Caleb's shoulder.

As she watched Trevor through her lashes, Jade mused that he and Stephen seemed to have little in common outwardly. Where Stephen had been solidly muscled and squarely built, Trevor was taller, sleeker, more the intellectual than the warrior. That wasn't a criticism, she assured herself. These were both good men—ethical, hardworking, responsible, dutiful. Patriotic, though they served in different ways.

Apparently, she had a type, disparate as Stephen and Trevor initially seemed. Which was only an acknowledgment that she found Trevor attractive and intriguing. She wasn't angling for another marriage to a man with decidedly mixed priorities—leaving her to always wonder exactly where she fell on the list. She had been madly, head over heels in love with Stephen when they'd married just out of their teens, and while her emotions had matured and leveled since those tumultuous years, she wasn't prepared to make herself that vulnerable again.

"That's our dad." Seeing the direction of Trevor's attention, Caleb spoke with pride in his voice and in his suddenly straightened posture. "Captain Stephen Evans. See all those medals on his uniform? Mom has them in a case upstairs. She's saving them for me."

"Daddy was a marine," Bella added, parroting what she'd been told. She was too young to understand what it meant, entirely, and would never remember the father she'd lost too soon. Jade had done her best to bring her own memories of him to life for her youngest child. "He was a hero."

"Yes, Bella, I know he was."

"Did you see much action in the army?" Caleb asked, trying a bit too hard in Jade's opinion to act worldly and grown-up.

Seeming to harbor similar thoughts, Trevor spoke in a peer-to-peer tone when he replied, "No, Caleb. Though I trained for combat, as all recruits do, I was stationed in a noncombat area."

"Oh." The boy frowned, looking unsure how to respond to that information. Jade wondered if she also saw disappointment in the boy's expression. If so, that would be unfair and something she'd have to discuss with him.

Before Jade could intercede, Trevor turned away from the bookcase. If he, too, thought Caleb was unhappy with the answer, it wasn't apparent in his expression when he held out his hand to Bella. "You were going to show me your backyard, Little Bit. Okay if I try out your swing?"

Jade watched Trevor and the girls move toward the back door, with Caleb following a bit more slowly. It occurred to her only then that she'd seen no photographs at all displayed at Trevor's house, other than the lovely landscapes hung at the top of the stairs. She'd seen no pictures of family, friends or his late wife either in the public rooms or in the parts of his private suite she'd entered. She wondered why that was, but didn't dwell on it, choosing to focus instead on being a gracious hostess.

Jade couldn't resist taking a photo of Trevor sitting on the swing between her girls a few minutes later, pushing at the ground with his feet. Caleb sat on one of the patio chairs, playing his handheld game and occasionally looking up distractedly. She took a picture of him, too, earning an eye roll.

After a time, she invited Trevor in for coffee to give him a break from the kids. They chose to stay outside to play for a while longer, though she reminded them they'd have to start their school-night routines before much longer.

"Can you stay for dinner, Mr. Trevor?" Erin asked. "Mom's making homemade veggie pizza.

She's already made the dough, so it won't take long to cook."

"As delicious as that sounds, I'll have to pass this time. I have a business dinner later this evening." Jade wasn't sure if she was relieved or disappointed by Trevor's reply, though it was apparent her girls felt the latter. As much as they all enjoyed his company, they needed this reminder that his business would always claim his time.

"You sure work a lot." Caleb didn't look up from his game as he made the obvious observation to Trevor.

"I do," Trevor conceded. "It's a particularly busy time in my company at the moment."

Ushering Trevor into the kitchen for his coffee, Jade mused that there was likely never a time when that statement didn't apply.

They sat at the table with their coffees. The bay window gave them a view of the backyard where Caleb had been persuaded to abandon his game to participate in a beanbag toss game. Jade watched as he carefully marked the throwing lines, setting Bella's a few inches closer than the one he and Erin would use. Even as moody as he'd been lately, Caleb still watched over his younger sisters.

"This really is a nice place, Jade. I know you and the kids are going to be very happy here."

She drew her gaze from the window to smile

at Trevor. "Thank you. I think so, too. The kids are pleased that we're close to a big park with a playground and soccer fields, and that we're only a short drive from the beach."

"Bella seems to be thriving. Am I wrong, or is she less shy than she was when I first met her?"

"Maybe a bit. She's still a rather anxious child, always has been, but I hope she'll get more confident with time. I'm encouraging her as much as possible."

A grin spread over Trevor's face, making his eyes glitter with amusement. "I've got to tell you, her chewing me out so sternly at The Perkery was one of the cutest things I've ever seen. Even if she did have me squirming and feeling guilty."

Jade laughed. "Bella keeps us all in line. There's definitely an iron streak behind that meek little face."

"She's a great kid. She wasn't at all rude, just honest. She hasn't learned to put on her social mask yet."

"Her social mask?" Jade lifted an eyebrow in response to the phrase.

Trevor shrugged, his own unrevealing mask firmly in place. "Yeah. That skill nearly everyone learns eventually. Speaking of social...there's something I'd like to ask you."

Jade had just taken a sip of coffee. She swallowed and touched her lips with a napkin before responding somewhat cautiously, "What is it?"

"How would you like to attend Elle's wedding with me next weekend?"

Jade's fingers tightened around the coffee cup in her hand. She set it down with exaggerated care. She couldn't help remembering Trevor's expression when he'd assured Elle that he would attend the wedding on his own; he'd looked as if he would prefer it that way. So what—or who— had changed his mind?

He spoke again before she recovered from her surprise. "I know it's ridiculously short notice, but you seemed to be getting along well with Elle yesterday. I thought you might like to meet some of her other local friends, too. It seems only logical for me to introduce you around."

She thought of Walt's teasing jab that Trevor never took dates to weddings because he didn't want to give them "ideas." Trevor was making it quite clear that this was merely a friendly invitation, which was rather amusing in light of that joke.

"It's an early evening wedding, so we wouldn't be overly late getting back," he continued. "Mary Pat has already volunteered to let the kids stay with her at my place. You know how much she'd enjoy that."

"You've mentioned this idea to Mary Pat?"

He cleared his throat and rolled his coffee cup slowly between his hands. "Um. Yeah."

Sudden comprehension hit her. Placing both hands on the table, she leaned toward him, her tone both amused and accusing. "This invitation was Mary Pat's idea, wasn't it?"

"Well...she's been after me to ask someone. I asked if she wanted to go with me, but she said I should take you. Like I said, it would let you get to know Elle and her friends better, and give Mary Pat a chance to spend the day with the kids, which she'd much rather do than attend a wedding. But I agree that it's a great idea," he added quickly. "I'm sure we'd have a good time."

Jade relaxed back into her seat. "I'm not opposed to going with you. I do like Elle and I enjoy weddings. And it's not such a hardship to spend time with you," she added teasingly. "I just hope Mary Pat's not trying her hand at matchmaking. I get enough of that from my mother and other family members, as you know."

"Trust me, I know," he said ironically. "I'm the match they're trying to make for you, remember?"

And there, she thought, was another glimpse of the real Trevor behind the "social mask." Fleeting, as always, but genuine. How many of his acquaintances saw those flashes? How many truly recognized them when they occurred?

"It's just an outing between friends, Jade.

Look at it this way—it'll give us ammunition to use against the matchmakers. When they nag us about not seeing people, each of us can point out that we just had a date for a wedding."

An intriguing suggestion. She tilted her head as she considered it. Would their mothers back off if she and Trevor appeared to be giving credence to their suggestions? Or would it only become worse? "There is that possibility. But I don't want to give them the wrong idea about us, either."

Trevor shrugged. "You and I know we've become friends and that we can appreciate that for what it is. What others think about us is their issue."

She agreed with the sentiment. It was totally no one else's business what relationship she and Trevor did—or did not—have or foresee. Because they'd each made their positions clear, there should be few awkward pitfalls ahead between them. Risky—but maybe worth it? She had to admit it sounded like fun to attend the wedding.

"Okay," she said with a nod. "I'd be delighted to go with you. I'll get in touch with Mary Pat to make arrangements for the children."

"I'll look forward to it."

His deep tone reverberated through her, making her second-guess the decision for a moment, but she told herself not to be silly. They had simply agreed to attend a wedding together. What could go wrong?

TREVOR HADN'T FULLY REALIZED how quiet his house had been for the past month until the Evans crew rushed in the following Saturday afternoon with chatter and giggles, to be greeted by Mary Pat's booming laugh. The children dashed up the stairs to deposit their bags. Mary Pat had wheedled Jade into letting them stay overnight. That way Trevor and Jade could stay out as long as they wanted, she'd reasoned.

Mary Pat had been thrilled when Jade reported that the children were all in favor of the plan. She'd spent the past couple of days cleaning, polishing, baking, stocking the game room with a couple of new options. Humming the entire time.

"I think they're excited to be here," Jade said to him when the pounding of feet up the stairs had abated momentarily. "They've been looking forward to this all week. They adore Mary Pat—and they're very fond of the pool and the rec room."

He chuckled. "They should take full advantage of all of the above while they're here."

Jade laughed and tucked back her pale hair, which she'd left loose and softly curled around her pretty face. Her deep purple dress was simple but formfitting, with a V-neckline that emphasized her slender neck and nicely rounded bust. Her only jewelry was a pair of dangling earrings with purple stones and a thin bracelet on her right wrist.

"You look very nice," he told her, an understatement.

"Thank you." She smoothed the dress absently. "The girls helped me pick it out. Purple is Erin's favorite color."

Trevor wore suit pants and a crisp white shirt, but he'd rolled up the sleeves and would don his jacket and tie when they arrived at the wedding. He gathered his things while Jade gave the kids the behave-yourselves lecture, then passed out hugs and kisses before leaving.

Ten minutes later they were on the road. He told himself he was going to have to pay attention to his driving. It was too tempting to look away from the road and admire the woman beside him. She'd stretched her legs out for comfort, her skirt draping just above her knees. Great legs.

She spoke, making him turn his attention to the pavement ahead. "Do you know, I've been so busy the past few days I haven't had a chance to find out anything about this wedding. I just showed up at your house at the time you suggested and expected you to get us there," she added with a laugh.

"Which I will."

"So, where is the wedding?" she asked.

"Fayetteville."

She twisted in her seat, obviously startled by the answer. "Fayetteville, North Carolina?"

"Yes. I'm sorry, I thought I'd been more specific when I invited you. I guess I forgot." Probably because he'd been trying so hard to keep the invitation light and completely platonic, making sure Jade didn't read too much into it. "Elle's fiancé, Shane Scanlon, is from there. His grandmother is in poor health and can't travel, so they're having the wedding there. Quite a few people from Shorty's Landing will be there, though. Elle has a lot of friends and associates who'll gladly make the trip to share this with her."

"So, we're making a three-hour drive. Okay." She shifted and adjusted the seatbelt. "Maybe we could turn on some music?"

"Sure. But you won't hear a whole song." He turned into the parking lot of a small airport. "We're getting out here."

Jade spun to look at him again. "We're flying to Fayetteville?"

"We're taking my company plane. You're not afraid of flying, I hope." He spent so much time in the air that he'd forgotten some people had problems with leaving the ground.

Maybe he'd wanted to surprise her and—okay, fine—maybe he'd wanted to impress her a little. He wasn't one to flaunt his privileges. But, oddly enough, something about Jade had made him devolve into schoolboy strutting for this not-a-real-date.

"No, but I—well, I just didn't expect…so, we're flying."

The undertone of surprised pleasure in her voice almost made him want to strut again.

Chiding himself for regressing into teen posturing, he slanted a look at her as he parked his car in front of the hanger. "As much as I enjoy your company, six-plus hours in a car is rather much for me for one day. My leg would be screaming by the end of the evening."

He was pleased to note that she eyed the small twin-engine business-class jet with more interest than trepidation. "This is yours?"

His jacket and tie folded over his arm, he motioned with the other toward the craft's open door. "Well, technically it belongs to the company, but yeah."

"Are you flying us?"

"I can. I'm a licensed pilot." For some reason, he'd felt the need to assure her of that. Again with the schoolboy bragging, he thought wryly. "But I'm not flying us today. The company pilot was available and said she'd be happy to ferry us. Her brother lives in Fayetteville, so she said she'd take advantage of the chance to visit his family."

"Of course you're a pilot," Jade murmured, and he wasn't quite sure how to take that.

Rather than trying to decipher the comment, he waved toward the plane again. "Ready?"

She smiled up at him, still looking bemused but excited, too. "Ready."

Oh, yeah, he thought, looking down at her softly curved lips. There was definitely something about this woman…

CHAPTER SEVEN

JADE FIGURED SHE could be excused for feeling as though she'd stepped into an alternate reality. Her usual Saturdays involved cleaning, laundry, grocery shopping, chauffeuring the kids, some evening reading before bed. Sometimes she even indulged in a glass of wine while cuddled beneath the covers with a good book. Today—well, today was very different.

From flying in a small jet with a ridiculously handsome man to being met at the Fayetteville airport by a driver in a posh car, she was getting the VIP treatment. And she had to admit it was fun. Jade's late father, known for being unassuming and practical in most respects, had had a weakness for luxury cars. So she was accustomed to fine leather and purring engines. But her dad never had a private jet at his command.

"I have to admit it's convenient to have your own plane," she said to Trevor on the way to the wedding venue.

He adjusted the expensive-looking tie he'd just put on. "Well, technically, one of my silent partners shares use of it with me through a lease arrangement. It's both a convenience and a luxury, though with us splitting the expense, not much more of a splurge than booking charter flights—especially when I get called away for some crisis or another. Since we had room for another six passengers, I invited Walt and his fiancée to join us for the flight today, but they chose to drive. They're planning to stay overnight and make a weekend of it."

Jade knew Trevor owned two cars, one a sedan, the other a two-seat convertible. He'd mentioned a boat—and she suspected it was a luxury one, and she had no doubt his motorcycle had been top-of-the-line. Not to mention his elegant home. Money was hardly in short supply for Trevor, either through his inherited wealth or what he was now accumulating on his own, but she couldn't say he allowed himself to be defined by it. She had seen him with his guests and staff at the resort, and he'd mingled as comfortably and respectfully with the maintenance crew and restaurant servers as with his prominent guests.

Still, she mused, absently smoothing her dress beneath her seatbelt, she couldn't help remembering that with all his success, Trevor returned home alone each night to that big, nice house, usually after his devoted housekeeper had retired to her own cottage. She didn't feel sympathy for him, exactly. Yet she wouldn't trade one hug or kiss from her children for any amount of money.

The early evening outdoor wedding was held at a sprawling country club just outside Fayetteville. The weather couldn't have been more perfect, with a cloudless autumn sky and a very comfortable temperature. Because the event was being held in the hometown of the groom, most of the guests seemed to be connected to his family, but Jade spotted a few people she'd already met in Shorty's Landing through either work or her children's schools. Trevor knew even more, and he mingled through the early arrival crowd as easily as Jade had come to expect, introducing her simply as his good friend. She was aware of a few speculative glances, but she'd been prepared for that and didn't let them bother her. Much.

She was pleased to see Walt, and to finally meet his fiancée, Maddie Zielinski. Jade admitted to herself that Maddie wasn't at all what she'd have expected. Quite a bit younger than Walt, Maddie was eye-catching with her asymmetrical haircut dyed a purply red, her striking makeup and tastefully sexy emerald dress. Remembering that Maddie was also an attorney, Jade had to laugh at her own inaccurate preconceptions of a buttoned-down, no-nonsense type more similar to Walt himself.

Having exchanged friendly greetings, Jade

watched as Maddie and Walt joked with Trevor. It was clear that Trevor liked Maddie very much and approved her as a match for his best friend.

"Did you enjoy your visit with your sister's family?" he asked her.

Maddie's already-bright grin increased in intensity. "I had a great time with them. Seattle's a beautiful city and they love it there. Simon has made lots of friends and he's enrolled in an amazing program for exceptionally gifted kids. Joanna and Adam really like their jobs. I don't think we'll ever drag them back here to live, but that's okay as long as they're happy and we can all travel back and forth a few times a year."

"Maddie's brother-in-law worked for me for a few years before he and Joanna married and moved to Seattle with their six-year-old son," Trevor explained for Jade's benefit. "He's a good friend."

"Great guy," Walt agreed with a gruff nod. "Good soldier. Wounded vet."

Of course, Jade thought. With his stated preference for hiring vets, Trevor really did put his money where his mouth was when it came to his support for veterans.

Maddie laughed softly and lightly punched Walt's right arm. "Nice complete sentences there, Sarge. It looks like it's time for us to find seats. Come sit by me, Jade, so we can admire all the pretty wedding details the guys won't even notice."

Smiling, Jade nodded. "I'd like that."

The wedding was beautiful, and made even more fun by Maddie's low-voiced running commentary to Jade. Maddie pointed out various members of Elle's and Shane's families as they were seated, and a few Shorty's Landing residents that Jade hadn't met.

Because this was a second marriage for her, Elle had initially planned a small wedding with only a few guests, Maddie whispered, but Elle had given in when the groom's family kept expanding the party. Neither of Shane's parents were still living, but his grandmother, Dottie Scanlon, whose health had been steadily declining for the past year, had wanted all of her friends and relatives to gather for this happy occasion. No one had had the heart to disappoint the beloved matriarch.

A chorus of "awws" escaped the crowd when Charlotte toddled down the aisle created between rows of folding chairs. Holding a basket of flower petals she strewed enthusiastically, she was dressed in angelic lace and ruffles, and escorted by a woman Maddie identified as Shane's cousin Parker. Parker carried an adorable tiny ring bearer clad in a navy shorts suit and white knee-high socks—Parker's son, Milo, Maddie explained, who was just over a year old.

When the wedding party was in place, the groom waiting at the podium with the officiate, the audience stood as the bride made her entrance to the accompaniment of a string quartet. That bit of ceremony, too, was meant to please Dottie, and judging by the happiness Jade could see on the elderly woman's face Dottie was delighted by it all.

Elle looked beautiful in her shimmering, champagne-colored dress, and her attractive dark-haired groom was visibly moved when she joined him to exchange their vows. Always a sucker for a romantic moment, Jade had to swallow a lump in her throat, even though she'd not yet met Shane and was only recently acquainted with Elle. She could only imagine how touched those who loved them must be.

"That'll be us soon," she heard Walt stage-whisper to Maddie. Glancing sideways at them, Jade saw Maddie snuggle against Walt's sturdy side. Despite their apparent differences, this was a genuinely committed couple, she decided. She hoped they'd be very happy, and predicted with confidence they would be.

Vows were exchanged, and Jade braced herself for the bittersweet "'til death" part. She glanced up at Trevor, who sat on her left. He was focused on the ceremony, his expression pleasant and un-revealing. Maybe he sensed her looking at him, but the smile he directed at her was not reflected in his shuttered blue eyes.

On an impulse, she reached over to touch his hand, which rested on his knee. His smile warmed a few degrees as he covered her hand with his other for a light squeeze. For just that moment, they were completely in tune, connected in ways few others could understand.

He released her then, and she drew her hand back to her lap, feeling tingles running from her fingertips all the way up her arm. She glanced again at Maddie, and realized the sharp-eyed attorney had not missed the brief exchange. Jade made herself focus again on the ceremony now wrapping up with a kiss between the bride and groom and a burst of spontaneous applause from the approving audience. She clapped along lightly, putting all potentially troubling thoughts aside and concentrating on this happy occasion.

THE POSTWEDDING PARTY lasted well into the evening. Shane and Elle were obviously in no hurry to leave their family and friends. Dinner was served beneath a canopy lined with fairy lights, on long tables decorated with clusters of candles and fall flowers. There were speeches and toasts, along with champagne and cake, and much laughter. The younger children were taken home after dinner, and Jade watched as Shane's grandmother bade her farewells from her wheelchair, looking very tired and fragile but glowing with contentment at her grandson's good fortune.

Tables were pushed aside to make room for dancing, and more champagne was brought out for the adults who remained after the first wave departed. Jade was amused when Maddie all but dragged Walt to the dance floor, though she noted his protest was only a token. It reminded her of Bella when she felt compelled to gripe about bedtime, even when she was obviously tired and ready for sleep.

"Well?" Trevor stood and held out his hand to her. "Shall we?"

She took his hand and walked with him to the dance floor. "I don't even remember the last time I danced," she admitted with a laugh. "I hope I remember how."

Pulling her into his arms, he gazed down at her. "Just follow my lead."

When he smiled at her just like that, Jade had the dangerous thought that she might just follow him anywhere.

It was no surprise that Trevor danced as well as he did everything else. Smooth, skilled and effortlessly flawless—all words that described both his dancing and the persona he allowed most of the world to see. Had she not felt a slight tremor run through the arm that encircled her at one point, she would never have known that their closeness, the brush of their bodies affected him at all. Their eyes met and held, and she thought she read the same thought in them that was whispering in her mind. *We're two single adults. Would it really be so bad to find out where this attraction goes...privately...if only to satisfy our own curiosity?*

It didn't have to lead to anything neither of them wanted, she amended quickly. There wouldn't be any harm in a little discreet fun between friends, especially if they agreed going in that there was nothing more to it and that it would probably be short-lived.

By the time the reception ended, only a core group of friends remained. Jade found herself sitting with Elle and Maddie at one point while Trevor, Shane and Walt huddled in an apparently intense conversation nearby. It turned out that Shane, too, had a business connection to Trevor—he was a risk management consultant responsible for Wind Shadow's liability plans—and had become his friend.

"They're talking about a weekend fishing trip to the Bahamas they've been planning for months." Elle glanced indulgently at the huddled group as she explained to Jade. "They all agree they want to do it, but they've been having trouble coming up with a weekend when all three of them are free. I guess you could call them a trio of workaholics."

"I think they've narrowed the date down to sometime next spring," Maddie said with a laugh. "I wish they would go. They could all use a guys' weekend. Maybe the three of us should do something while they're gone. You two could get babysitters and we could have a wild night while our guys are away. And by wild, I mean wine and maybe a card game with some decadent desserts we let someone else prepare for us."

"Sounds like fun." Elle glanced at Jade. "As much as I love being with Charlotte, the occasional adult-only night out is welcome. How about you, Jade?"

"Oh, definitely. But, um, Trevor isn't 'my guy,'" she added. "He and I are just friends. Actually, our mothers are close friends, so Trevor has been helping me and the kids get adjusted to our new hometown. Introducing us to our new neighbors. Just being kind."

She wasn't sure why she felt compelled to explain when she'd told herself it wouldn't be necessary. Maybe it was because she liked these two women very much and hoped they could become friends. Friends were honest with each other, just as she'd always been with Trevor.

She saw Elle and Maddie share a glance before they assured her warmly, and with obvious sincerity, that she would be welcome to join them whenever she liked. "That invitation has nothing to do with Trev," Maddie added. "I'm always happy to meet new friends, and I think the three of us would have a great time any chance we get for a ladies' night, don't you, Elle?"

"Absolutely. And maybe we could meet at the park with the kids sometime, Jade," Elle suggested. "Charlotte enjoyed playing with your girls at the shop. I'm sure she and Bella would have fun at the playground."

"They would love that. Bella, especially, enjoys playing with younger children. She's always very patient with them."

"Walt and I are talking about having a kid," Maddie confided with a toss of her head that made her dangling earrings dance. "It's cute how scared Sarge is to even think about becoming a father, but I know he'd be an amazing one."

"I have no doubt," Elle concurred. "He's such a sweetheart under that gruff bulldog exterior."

Maddie laughed. "Bulldog was exactly my thought the first time I saw him. I've always had a weakness for the breed. He grumbles when I pinch his cheeks and tell him how cute he is, but I know he likes it. I started calling him 'Sarge' sort of teasingly soon after we met and I heard about his military service. Now it's my pet name for him. He knows I'm crazy about him."

"And vice versa," Elle responded with a chuckle.

"Speaking of children, I watched Shane helping Charlotte with her wedding cake," Jade said to Elle. "It's pretty clear they're crazy about each other already." From what she'd seen, she was sure Shane would be a doting stepdad to the adorable child.

Again, the other two women exchanged glances before Elle replied. "I'm not sure if you know, but Shane is actually Charlotte's uncle. Charlotte's birth mother was involved with Shane's brother, Charlie. Charlie died before Charlotte was born. Her birth mother had a falling out with the family and chose to put her child up for adoption without their involvement. Charlotte was five months old when I adopted her as a single mother. Shane was deployed overseas at the time, and when he came home, he tracked Charlotte down to reassure himself that she was in a loving home and… well…the rest is sort of obvious. I fell in love with Shane before I even knew who he was, and I love his family, too. It's worked out beautifully for all of us."

"Oh, wow." Jade shook her head in response to the succinct summary. "I hadn't heard any of this. It's a very romantic story."

She was sure Trevor knew all these details,

but he'd been prudent in leaving Elle to reveal whatever she chose to share with her new friend.

"Trevor seems to enjoy your children," Elle commented, keeping her tone light. "Bella, especially, is obviously taken with him. She was so cute with him at the shop."

Hearing someone else pointing out that her children were becoming attached to Trevor made Jade even more wary, but her attention was claimed by Maddie, who asked, "You said Trevor's a friend of your family, Jade. Did you ever meet his wife?"

"No, she died before I met him. Not quite five years before I lost my own husband. Our mothers have been friends for close to a decade, but Trevor and I first met just three years ago. We'd seen each other only a few times before I moved to Shorty's Landing to work for my cousin."

The conversation broke up when Elle and Shane were called away then to share thank-yous and goodbyes with some departing wedding guests. Trevor and Walt returned to join Jade and Maddie.

"Looks like the party's winding down, Mads," Walt commented, placing his right hand on his fiancée's shoulder with a look Jade interpreted as impatience to be alone with her. "Are you about ready to go?"

Maddie nodded happily. Watching the other

couple exchange a loving smile as they walked away, Jade suspected they would have a very nice evening, indeed. As for her and Trevor...that remained to be seen.

Some twenty minutes later, Jade and Trevor climbed into the sleek jet. "The weather looks good," the pilot reported. "Should be a smooth flight."

"Thanks, Nadia. We're in your capable hands."

Trevor's faith in his obviously appreciative employee was visible in his warm expression.

As Nadia disappeared into the cockpit, Trevor ushered Jade to the comfortable leather seats, where they both strapped in and prepared for takeoff. "Can I get you anything while we wait?" he asked.

She laughed and shook her head. "I've had more than enough champagne for one day, thank you."

"Soda, maybe? Bottled water?"

"No, I'm fine." She stretched into the soft leather, letting her head fall back against the cushioned rest. "It feels good to just relax for a while. The wedding was lovely, but meeting so many people at once was exhausting."

"I'm sure."

"You're probably more accustomed to large social gatherings than I am."

"Very likely. Doesn't make them any less tiring, though." He looked out the window beside him and she followed his gaze. The plane's engines had started, but they hadn't yet moved. She didn't see any other planes on the runway at the moment, so she wasn't sure what was holding them up.

She glanced at her watch, seeing that it was after nine. It was a good thing the kids were spending the night with Mary Pat, considering how late it would be by the time she and Trevor got back. And with that thought, the plane's engines went quiet. She looked at Trevor with a frown.

He raised his hands. "No idea."

He was just reaching to unfasten his seat belt when the cockpit door opened. Nadia looked apologetic when she appeared in the doorway. "I'm sorry, Trevor. I'm afraid we aren't going anywhere just yet. I've got a warning light. We can't take off until it's been checked out."

Trevor grimaced. "Yeah, I seriously doubt that's going to happen at this hour on a Saturday night."

Jade felt her jaw drop, and she had to deliberately close it. Well, this was unexpected.

Trevor looked almost as discomfited for a moment, but then he nodded. "Okay, thanks, Nadia. Obviously, we don't take any risks. Let me make some calls to get things in motion for first thing in the morning, and then we'll decide what the three of us are going to do tonight."

"I'm okay with staying the night here in Fayetteville," his pilot assured him quickly. "I'll be ready to fly as soon as the plane is airworthy."

"You're sure?"

"Absolutely." She patted the doorway. "You know I'd hate to leave my girl, here, sick and all alone."

Trevor laughed, though a bit distractedly. "You're a treasure, Nadia."

"Yes, sir. And don't forget that."

"No, ma'am."

Trevor turned to Jade then when the pilot disappeared back into the cockpit. "Okay, now we need to figure out what you and I are going to do. It's a little late to charter another plane, but I can hire a car, which would get us home sometime after midnight. Or—"

"Or we could spend the night here and make the trip tomorrow, after we've rested," she responded after taking a deep breath. She wasn't nervous, exactly. It was more anticipation, a confident certainty that this development was a sign and that she'd be foolish not to take advantage of it.

Trevor looked at her steadily. "We could definitely do that."

Sometimes the stars just seemed to align, she

figured with a slight shrug. "It just so happens, I'm free tonight."

"What a coincidence." Smiling slowly down at her, he touched her face. "So am I."

THERE WERE SIGNIFICANT advantages to having considerable resources at one's fingertips, Jade thought an hour later as she stood at a window looking out at the lights of the city. Somehow Trevor had procured this beautiful two-bedroom suite and had arranged a car to bring them here, making a quick stop at a department store they'd passed on the way.

Because the store would be closing in half an hour, they'd made a game of separating and grabbing a few things they needed for the night, knowing the hotel would provide basic toiletries. They'd met then at the registers where Trevor had insisted on paying for everything and Jade let him rather than causing a scene by arguing. They were laughing when they tumbled back into the car with their bags, each joking they'd shopped so quickly they weren't even sure what they'd bought. She'd confessed that she'd always wondered what it would be like to just take off for a weekend without even bothering to pack, buying what she needed when she arrived at her destination.

"I bet you've done that before, haven't you?" she'd asked him.

"Maybe a couple times," he'd admitted. "But something tells me when you daydreamed about it, your ideal destination wasn't Fayetteville, North Carolina."

Grinning, she'd assured him she had no complaints about their current location.

She had fun with Trevor, she thought now, turning away from the window to look at him on the other side of the elegant sitting room. She enjoyed his company. And there was nothing wrong with that.

He disconnected the call he'd made when they'd entered the suite and set the phone aside. "Mary Pat said the kids are all asleep, even Caleb. She told us to take our time getting back tomorrow. She'll keep them as long as she can have them."

Crossing her arms loosely in front of her, Jade smiled. "I had no doubt Mary Pat would have everything under control. I'm sure I'll have to drag the kids back home tomorrow after she's spoiled them again."

"Oh, I doubt that. They love their new house. They were quite proud of their rooms when I was there last week."

"Well, yes, they are."

But she didn't really want to talk about the

children now. She kicked off the heels she'd worn all day with a sigh of relief, letting her toes curl into the plush carpet. She wandered toward the deep sectional sofa that faced a marble-wrapped fireplace topped by a big-screen TV. Rather than sitting, she made a slow pivot. "This is a beautiful suite."

"It's nice. Not Wind Shadow level, of course."

She made a face in response to the quip. "Of course."

Standing a foot away from her, Trevor spoke more seriously. "I really am sorry about the delay getting you home tonight, Jade. It's the first time I've ever had an issue with that plane."

"It's not your fault. Stuff happens. Obviously, I'm glad it was discovered before takeoff, if there's a problem with the plane."

"Yeah, me, too. But I still could have gotten you home tonight if you wanted."

"We were both too tired to start that drive so late. Besides," she added, laying her hands on his chest, "I wasn't in any hurry to rush home."

Holding her gaze with his, he raised his hands to capture hers, holding them in place against him. "Neither was I."

Shifting closer, she murmured with a surge of boldness, "You know, there really wasn't a need for you to get two bedrooms."

Heat sparked in his eyes. She felt his heart beat

more strongly beneath her palms. "I didn't want to be presumptuous."

Moving even closer, she spoke lightly despite the ripples of electricity running through her every fiber. "Well, if you'd rather not waste it, I can…"

The rest of the teasing sentence was smothered by his hungry mouth.

Each time they kissed, it felt more familiar. More arousing. More right. Her body already molded instinctively to his, fitting curve to plane with no thought at all. With this caress, his hands grew bolder, sweeping, exploring, teasing out a cascade of delicious shivers.

After what felt like a long time, he lifted his head just far enough to look at her. "I did try to be a gentleman with the second bedroom," he admitted with a low laugh.

She twined her arms around his neck. "I don't need a gentleman tonight. Tonight, I need this. We can go back to being polite friends tomorrow."

He kissed her again, even more heatedly this time. And then groaned and let his forehead rest against hers. "As much as I'd love to sweep you up and carry you into the bedroom…"

"Your knee would buckle and we'd both crash to the floor."

He laughed ruefully. "Exactly."

Dropping her arms from around his neck, she stepped back and held out her hand to him. "I've never particularly liked being carried. We'll walk in together."

Smiling, he took her hand and moved with her to the closest bedroom.

They didn't bother with the lamps. Enough light spilled through the open doorway from the sitting room to show them the way, to softly illuminate the bare skin revealed with the removal of each piece of clothing. She'd seen Trevor shirtless before, of course, in the pool, so she already knew he was lean, sleek and ripped. Now she could feel all those firm lines she'd only admired before, and she took full advantage of the opportunity.

Her dress fell in a puddle at her feet. She stepped out of it and kicked it aside even as her hands went to Trevor's belt.

The big bed was deep, welcoming. She snuggled into it, then opened her arms to welcome Trevor to enjoy it with her. He accepted the invitation immediately. Eagerly.

It felt so good to be held. To be caressed. To explore and savor in return. Long-neglected nerve endings reacted with shivering intensity, sending heat surging through her. An answering warmth radiating from Trevor's skin as her palms slid over him.

He engaged in a leisurely survey of his own. Beginning with her mouth and moving to her throat, he strung openmouthed kisses and arousing nips that made her squirm restlessly against the sheets. She didn't worry about any imperfections he might find in his exploration. They didn't seem to bother him any more than his scars deterred her. They were who they were, with all the baggage and history that implied. And still the fire burned between them.

She rolled on top of him, letting her hair curtain their faces as she kissed him deeply. Thoroughly. He took care of birth control swiftly and matter-of-factly. She wasn't offended that one of his hasty purchases had been condoms. She appreciated a man who was prepared for any eventuality, though his arrangement for two rooms had shown his willingness to let her choose how this adventure proceeded.

His hands were on her hips then, guiding her as she sought him, his fingers tightening when she found him. After the first gasping shock of adjustment, she took him in, all of him. Her rational thoughts shattered into sheer, mindless sensation. And she reveled in it.

Somehow she found herself beneath him, wrapped around him, moving with him. Her tension built, escalated, held her in an almost unbearably pleasurable grip. When release came, it was sudden, stunning, glorious. She was pretty sure she cried out; she knew Trevor groaned deeply, hoarsely with his own climax. They were connected on a deep, visceral level. And even if it were only this one time, she was going to treasure every moment of it.

TREVOR WOULD HAVE thought he'd sleep like a log after a long day followed by mind-blowing, teeth-rattling sex the likes of which he hadn't experienced in…well, in a long time. Instead, he was awake at three in the morning, staring at the blue dot of light on the smoke alarm above him and wondering what the hell was going on with him and Jade.

He glanced at her sleeping so deeply beside him, looking sated and content in the darkened room. Whatever troubling thoughts were nagging at the back of his mind, apparently Jade wasn't having any such issues. He didn't get the impression that she was hoping this unplanned adventure would lead to anything more between them, which should be a relief.

And yet.

He supposed he should be gratified that this idyllic night wouldn't lead to awkward expectations with this woman he hoped to keep as a friend, but he couldn't help wondering why she seemed so adamant that they'd go back to being merely friends afterward. Was it really because she preferred being independent and unattached?

Or did she think that no one could ever measure up to the husband she'd lost? But then again, what man could?

He rolled carefully, silently out of the bed and padded into the bathroom. After using the facilities and washing his hands and face, he moved back into the dark bedroom and before his vision adjusted, stumbled into a chair, spilling something onto the floor. Swallowing a curse, he froze, prepared to apologize, but Jade didn't even stir against her pillows. She was a heavy sleeper— or maybe, he thought with a tug of smile, he'd simply exhausted her.

Now that his vision was better, he knelt to gather the items he'd knocked off the chair, realizing it had been Jade's bag and its contents. Using the glow of his cell phone to make sure he didn't miss anything, he quickly gathered a lipstick tube, a set of keys and a tin of mints and shoved them into the small black bag. He was just about to straighten when something he'd missed caught his eye beneath the chair. He drew it out and saw that it was her wallet, which had fallen open to reveal a photograph he recognized at a glance. It was a smaller print of the framed photo he'd seen displayed on her bookshelf. Decorated military hero Stephen Evans surrounded by his adoring family.

His self-congratulatory mood fading, Trevor closed the wallet and pushed it haphazardly into the bag, then stood and tossed it back on the chair. After a moment, he turned and slipped out of the bedroom into the sitting room, where he headed straight for the bar. Maybe a drink would help him get a couple more hours of sleep before morning—though he wasn't making any bets on it.

CHAPTER EIGHT

SUNLIGHT WAS JUST visible around the edges of the bedroom curtains when Jade awoke after a long, deeply satisfying night. She glanced blearily at the clock on the nightstand, seeing that it was just after seven. The other side of the tousled bed was empty, and she thought she heard Trevor's voice in the sitting room. On the phone, no doubt, tending to business.

Rolling to sit on the side of the bed, she stretched, then pushed her hair out of her face. At some point in the night—or early morning—she'd donned the simple nightshirt she'd picked out at the department store. Now she reached for the bag holding the remainder of her purchases and carried it into the bathroom for a quick shower. The stall was damp, as was one of the towels hanging on a bar. Apparently, Trevor had showered while she'd slept. Had he gotten any sleep at all?

The spacious marble-and-chrome bathroom was stocked with everything she needed for grooming. Toothbrush and paste, lightly scented soaps, hair care products and lotions, a hair dryer nestled into a wall-mounted holder—anything she could possibly ask for. Bathed and blow-dried, she applied a touch of makeup from the few items she carried in her purse and dressed in fresh underclothes and the simple tunic, black leggings and black canvas flats she'd picked out without trying on last night. Fortunately, everything fit as she'd hoped, so at least she didn't have to spend the day in the clothes she'd worn for the wedding yesterday.

She found Trevor in the sitting room, sipping coffee and typing into his phone, which was plugged into a charger. Like her, he wore new clothing—a blue cotton shirt rolled up on his forearms, khaki slacks and canvas boat shoes without socks. Somehow he managed to look as smoothly polished in these moderately priced garments as he had in the probably hand-tailored suit he'd worn the day before.

Seeing her enter, he set the phone aside and rose. "Good morning. Nice duds."

Laughing softly, she held out her arms and made a model's turn. "Yes, I spent hours deciding what to wear from my vast choices this morning."

"You look lovely, as always," he assured her when she stopped in front of him.

She peeled off a stick-on tag he'd missed from the front of his new shirt. "Thank you. So do you."

He chuckled. "Thanks. I think."

"It was a compliment," she assured him.

Trevor stroked her cheek lightly and she lifted her face for the expected morning kiss. Perhaps he didn't notice. He dropped his hand and stepped away, saying genially, "I've taken the liberty of ordering breakfast. It should be here—oh, there it is."

She blinked when he moved to open the door in response to the discreet knock. Was he acting a bit oddly this morning, or was she the one who'd forgotten how a morning after was supposed to feel?

A few moments later, they sat at the table at one end of the sitting room with bowls of steaming oatmeal served with a variety of topping options, whole grain toast, yogurt, juice and coffee.

"This looks wonderful," she said, scooping raisins, pecans and brown sugar onto her oatmeal. "Exactly what I like in the mornings."

He smiled. "Well, we've eaten enough breakfasts together by now that I know your preferences."

She knew it wasn't necessary for either of them to point out that this breakfast was very different from the ones they'd shared before with his housekeeper and her children.

"So, there's a crew working on the plane now,"

he said after they'd eaten in silence for a few minutes. "We should know something shortly."

With a raised eyebrow, she glanced at her watch. Barely after eight on a Sunday morning. Wealth definitely had its privileges.

"I spoke to Mary Pat, too. She said to tell you everything's going fine at the house. And, again, she told us there's no need to hurry back, though I know you don't want to be too late because of work and school tomorrow."

She nodded because that was true, not because she was in a hurry for this weekend to end.

"So, yesterday didn't turn out exactly as you'd expected, hmm?" he asked, and though he smiled, his eyes searched her face more seriously.

Had she even fleetingly imagined she'd be having breakfast with him in a fancy hotel suite this morning after a night of passion? "Hardly."

"Any regrets?"

She picked up her coffee cup. "Just one."

Peeking through her lashes, she saw his face freeze in what might have been consternation. "Um—"

"I kind of wish I'd gotten this top in red instead of purple," she continued flippantly. "I already own enough purple shirts to please even Erin."

She saw his shoulders relax as he grinned at her "gotcha" tone. "You look good in purple. But if you really want the red, we can always make a stop on the way."

"I was teasing about the shirt," she replied, meeting his gaze openly now. "I have no regrets, Trevor. About anything. I've had a wonderful time. It's been fun."

"I've had fun, too," he assured her—but was he deliberately avoiding her eyes? Why did she have the sense that Trevor had put on his "social mask" again this morning—and, if so, why did he suddenly feel the need with her?

Had last night not been quite as magical for him as it had been for her? She hadn't expected rave reviews or heartfelt promises this morning, but she'd thought they'd shared something pretty darned special.

Maybe it hadn't been quite so special for Trevor.

So maybe she needed to stop overthinking it. This brief respite had been a nice break, a way to recharge the batteries, so to speak, but it wasn't a glimpse into the future. Neither of them even wanted it to be.

Trevor's phone rang and he mouthed an apology before answering it. She waved a hand to assure him the apology wasn't necessary and turned her attention back to her breakfast.

"Okay," he said, putting down the phone again shortly afterward. "We have transportation. The plane's been checked out. After a minor repair was made, it was checked again, and is now cleared to fly. If you're at all concerned about it, I completely understand. I'll rent a car and we can still be back at my place by early afternoon."

"I'm not concerned about it. If the plane has been inspected and cleared, it's as safe as a three-plus hour trip in a car."

Trevor nodded approvingly. "Statistically safer, actually."

"And we won't even talk about motorcycles."

He cleared his throat and took a sip of his coffee to avoid answering. Jade laughed, but she didn't think she was merely imagining that something was bothering Trevor this morning. Maybe it was only that he was in a hurry to get back to work after this unexpected delay. That, she thought with a sigh, was a common state for the men she appeared to be drawn to.

JADE'S CHILDREN WELCOMED them back noisily that afternoon, the girls tumbling over each other in their haste to be the first to spill the details of everything they'd done during their sleepover with Mary Pat. Jade seemed to have no problem deciphering the breathless babbling. Trevor caught only a few disjointed words, but he got the gist that they'd had a good time, and he was glad.

He'd had a damned good time, himself, he thought with a glance at Jade's smiling face. He'd decided to remember the fun and forget the muddled, middle-of-the-night pondering that had left him strangely unsettled. Had to have been the result of sleep deprivation and the resulting weariness, he thought firmly.

"How was the wedding?" Mary Pat asked, standing with Trevor a bit to one side of the mother-children reunion.

"It was nice," Trevor replied. "For a wedding. Lots of flowers, food, dancing, socializing. They're married."

Chuckling, she patted his arm. "Thank you for that romanticized update. I'll get the details from Jade."

"Probably best. So you and the kids had fun?"

"Oh, we had the best time." She clasped her hands in front of her. "I can't tell you how fond of them I've become."

"I think that's become quite evident." He rested a hand on her shoulder. "Should I be worried that I'm losing my place as your favorite person?" he asked, only mostly teasing.

Mary Pat's response was immediate and firm. "Never. You'll always have my heart—even if you are a pain in the neck sometimes."

Laughing, he kissed her soft cheek. "Ditto."

"So, the plane is safe now?" she asked in a whisper, looking quickly at the children to make sure they didn't overhear. "I have to confess I was worried about you getting home safely after being stranded overnight by engine trouble."

"The jet is completely safe," he replied reassuringly. "And it wasn't engine trouble, just a minor electrical issue that took about twenty minutes to fix. You know neither Nadia nor I would fly a craft we didn't consider absolutely airworthy."

"Oh, I know. I'm just an old worrier sometimes. I hope you at least found a comfortable place to stay last night." Was there a touch of conjecture in the look she gave him with that offhand comment?

"We did," he assured her, keeping his expression bland. "A nice two-bedroom suite in Fayetteville."

He'd leave it up to his housekeeper to speculate on her own whether both those bedrooms had been used.

"Hey." Erin stepped back to examine her mother with her head cocked and both hands on her slender hips. "I don't remember that shirt. When did you get it?"

"I bought it in Fayetteville when we were stranded there last night," Jade replied easily.

"It's nice," Erin approved.

Bella looked up at Trevor. "I've been drawing pictures. Do you want to see them?"

"Absolutely," he assured her, holding out his hand.

He didn't look back at Jade as he was led up the stairs.

Their weekend together was officially over now. It was time to get back to reality. Back to responsibilities—for Jade, her children and her patients, for him, the many employees who depended on him for their livelihoods and the guests expecting him to provide impeccable services in return for their dollars. No pressure for either of them, right?

He shook his head in bemusement and focused his attention on the crayon-and-colored-pencil masterpiece Bella was holding up for him to admire.

JADE HAD BEEN outside for a while, later that night, but she was having trouble finding tranquility in the darkness. It wasn't as quiet here in her neighborhood as at Trevor's more sprawled estate. She heard a couple of dogs barking, the thump of bass from a passing vehicle, a car door slamming in a nearby driveway. Those sounds didn't normally bother her, usually barely penetrated her unfocused meditations. Tonight she was aware of even the slightest noise.

Maybe she still hadn't wound down from the eventful weekend. Almost nothing that had happened to her in the past thirty-six hours or so was normal for her. So it was hardly surprising that her typical method of relaxing before bedtime wasn't working as it usually did.

Her phone buzzed, and she didn't have to look at the screen to know who it was. Had she been tensed in preparation for this call she hadn't realized she expected?

"Looking at the moon?" Trevor asked in a low voice that slid like silk along her skin.

She glanced, realizing she hadn't even noticed how pretty the sliver of new moon looked against the black velvet sky. "Yes."

"So am I."

Which, of course, brought to mind an image of him lounging in one of the chairs on his patio. Maybe after a swim, leaving him wet and barechested in that very pale moonlight.

So much for relaxation.

"Mary Pat found a pair of Bella's socks this evening. They were in the dining room. Under the table. I didn't ask how they might have ended up there."

That made her smile. "You never know where

you'll find Bella's socks. I found a pair stuffed in a Christmas tree once."

He laughed softly. "That must have been surprising."

"Somewhat. She wasn't even walking yet."

Laughing again, he said, "Anyway, I've passed along the message."

"Thank you. I'll pick them up eventually. There's no rush—she has plenty."

"Mary Pat raved for an hour after you left about how much fun she had with the kids, right up to the moment I left to have dinner at the resort with the manager and some of our guests."

Why wasn't Jade surprised that Trevor had headed to work almost as soon as they'd gotten back?

"I'm glad she enjoyed the visit. The kids had a blast with her. Bella couldn't stop talking about an imagination game Mary Pat played with the girls. Apparently they pretended to go on safari."

"I guess Caleb's a bit too old for that game?"

"I'm sure he thinks so."

Maybe Trevor picked up a hint of tension in her voice. After all, he had gotten to know her fairly well lately. "There's not a problem with Caleb, is there? Mary Pat said he was perfectly polite and cooperative the whole time he was here, but a little quieter than usual. She wondered if he was just tired after a long week at school."

"I guess that's possible. He did have a busy week."

"He's okay, though?"

"He seemed fine tonight. He said he had a good time swimming and playing your video game system."

"Okay. That's good, then."

"He'll be a teenager in just over three months," she added. "I'm sure that has something to do with his moods."

"Heaven help you."

She laughed ruefully at Trevor's heartfelt response. "Exactly."

"I should let you go. I know you like your quiet time before bed."

Not always, she thought with a little shiver of memory. But she said merely, "Good night, Trevor."

"Jade?"

"Yes?"

"I had a really great time with you this weekend." His voice was deeper now. Intimate. Murmuring in her ear as he had so many times last night.

"So did I," she said softly, those shivers intensifying.

"I'm going to be pretty busy with the Florida

project. I'm sure I'll be back down there at least a couple of times in the coming month."

Translation: their idyllic weekend really was over. Which was fine. No less than she'd expected. "I'm going to be busy, too. The kids' schedules keep us all running until their bedtime."

"I can imagine. So... I guess we won't see much of each other in the coming days."

"Doesn't sound like it. I hope everything continues to go well with your Florida project. I'm sure you have it under control."

"Knock on wood. So, I'll call you sometime?"

"Sure," she said, hoping her tone conveyed that she wouldn't be sitting by the phone waiting. "You know where to reach me most evenings," she added with an airy laugh.

"Under the stars."

"Exactly."

"Sleep well, Jade."

"You, too."

And that, she thought, setting her phone aside, was that. With a long, low sigh, she let her head fall back against her chair.

THE FIRST WEEK of October brought several days of stormy weather and a rush of patients to the clinic. Jade returned home tired each evening to face three children growing cranky by being kept indoors. Caleb spent much of his time in his room, claiming he had homework and needed to study, and he didn't say a lot when he joined them for meals. He wasn't sullen, exactly, and never outwardly rude—but he was most definitely withdrawn. Naturally lively Erin was beginning to chafe at being confined inside and her extra energy made her resort to pestering her siblings for entertainment, both of whom protested to their mother.

Bella was getting whiny, which was even harder for Jade to deal with. She loved her children to distraction, but whining set her teeth on edge. She did everything she could to distract the child and was successful most of the time, but then it would start again. It didn't help that Bella pouted more than once that she missed Mr. Trevor, and wished she could show him her latest artwork. Those wistful comments had twisted Jade's heart. It had been two weeks since she'd last heard from Trevor, when he'd called her the night they'd arrived home from the wedding trip. She stayed in contact with Mary Pat, so she knew Trevor had been very busy since the wedding, but was that the only reason he hadn't called?

Bella wasn't the only one in the family to miss him, which only showed that Jade had been right to try to protect the kids from getting too attached to him.

She knew she was far from the first mother, single or otherwise, who at times felt overwhelmed by the role, but sometimes it was hard to remember that this week, too, would pass and the sun would return.

She escorted the last patient from the exam room to the checkout desk on Friday afternoon. "You be safe driving out there in this downpour, Mr. Block."

The short, stocky man chuckled and winked at her. "Ma'am, I've driven through a few hurricanes in my time. I can handle a rainstorm."

She laughed. "I'm sure you can, Mr. Block."

Closing the door behind him, she allowed her smile to fade. She sighed and pushed back her hair.

Lincoln's nurse, Verita Hardy, looked up from behind the nurses' desk in sympathy. "Heck of a week, right?"

"You can say that again."

Verita was also the mother of three—a six-year-old and two-year-old twins. Jade figured if anyone could understand mental exhaustion, it would be her coworker.

"Any plans this afternoon before school lets out?" The clinic closed at one on Fridays, a welcome shorter workday.

"Not specifically." Jade glanced upward at the ceiling, through which they could hear the rain hitting the roof. "I guess a relaxing walk on the beach is out of the question."

Her laptop tucked into the crook of one arm and her phone in her other hand, Amy passed just in time to overhear. "I'm going for a mani-pedi," she said. "Want to go with me, Jade?"

Jade wrinkled her nose. Her cousin was pretty much teasing with that invitation. Amy was fully aware that Jade wasn't the mani-pedi type. She found the process more annoying than relaxing. "Thanks, but no."

Verita looked back up from her computer. "I have a hair appointment before I pick the kids up from daycare. It's my only 'me time' for the next three days."

"Me time" sounded good, even if not at a salon, Jade thought when she drove away a short time later, the sound of falling rain and thumping windshield wipers echoing through the interior of her car. The kids were in school until three thirty, so she had a couple of hours before it was time to pick them. She thought briefly about stopping by The Perkery for coffee and a muffin, but the weather made even that seem less inviting.

Perhaps she'd go home and read for a while—though if she went home she knew she'd end up doing laundry or dusting or something equally unfun.

On a sudden impulse, she turned the car toward

Trevor's house. She was confident he wouldn't be there, so she could visit for a few minutes with Mary Pat, who had urged her to drop by whenever she liked for coffee or tea and conversation. And she never had remembered to pick up that pair of Bella's socks, she reminded herself.

She parked as close to the door as possible. The rain had let up some, so her umbrella kept her reasonably dry as she hurried to the door. She set it on the porch to drip dry, then pushed the doorbell, hearing the muted chime inside. She felt her smile waver when Trevor opened the door. Perhaps he'd noticed her pull up; he didn't look nearly as surprised to see her.

"Jade. Come in." With an encouraging nod, he stood aside so she could enter.

"Hi, Trevor." Though she was still dressed in her scrubs and her sneakers were damp, at least she wasn't dripping wet. She glanced around to see if Trevor's stylish assistant hovered in the background, as she had the last time Jade had entered Trevor's house from the pouring rain, but she saw no one in any of the rooms visible to her. Trevor was dressed in a casual shirt and jeans, definitely hanging-around-the-house clothes.

"I didn't expect you to be home this afternoon," she admitted. "I just stopped by to retrieve Bella's socks and maybe have a cup of tea with

Mary Pat before I pick up the kids. It was just an impulse, so I probably should have called first."

"You're welcome to stop by any time, and you know Mary Pat would be happy to see you if she were here."

"Oh. Um—she's not?"

"No. Her sister in Sumter had an unexpected surgery yesterday—gallbladder, I believe—and Mary Pat has gone to stay with her for the weekend. I've been working at home for a while today, to get some stuff done without being interrupted every few minutes. I'm going over to the resort a little later for dinner with a veterans motorcycle club. They're putting together a charity ride and I offered to let them hold a dinner meeting in one of the resort's private dining rooms."

"Are you considering participating in that ride?" she asked.

He shrugged. "I haven't ruled it out. I'd have to replace my bike first, though."

"So almost killing yourself once wasn't enough for you?" She regretted the words almost the minute they left her mouth. "Never mind, it's none of my business if you get on a motorcycle again."

"People who have been in car accidents tend to drive again afterward," he reminded her.

She thought that was different, but she didn't argue. Wasn't her place to do so.

"And here I am interrupting your work." She

inched back toward the door. "I can come back another time for the socks."

Trevor reached out as if to hold her in place, though he dropped his hand before he actually caught her arm. "You can certainly leave if you like," he said, smiling down at her. "Or you could stay and have that cup of tea with me, instead. I'll put on the kettle."

She couldn't help smiling to herself. She had to admit, when she thought of being alone with Trevor, drinking tea together was not the first image that came to mind.

He looked so darned cute and approachable in his casual clothes with his hair a bit mussed and his smile reflected in his blue eyes. More like the impetuous lover on an unexpected getaway than the somewhat distant, cordial businessman who'd escorted her home the next morning. And, as she had before, she found this side of him almost irresistible—at least parts of her did.

If there was any occasion tailor-made for indulgence, it was a rainy autumn afternoon with nothing pressing to do, and a sexy, handsome someone with whom to while away that free time. She was tempted to tell him to forget the kettle and suggest they heat up his bedroom, instead, but she was still stung by his perplexing behavior on their morning after in Fayetteville. While she'd decided she was fine with a friends-with-

occasional-benefits relationship with Trevor—
for the time being, anyway—it bothered her that
he'd been so reserved after they'd shared such
intimacy. Despite his current smile, she had the
sense the emotional barriers were still up. She
needed no promises from Trevor, but she did in-
sist on candor, just as she'd always been open
with him.

She sighed. "As tempting as the offer is, perhaps I should just collect Bella's socks and be on
my way. I know you have things to do."

"I have time for tea with you. I'd enjoy it, actually. It'll give us a chance to catch up."

Which sounded exactly like something Mary
Pat would say.

Jade shook her head. Oh, no. He was not going
to just pretend nothing had happened between
them in that hotel room. She knew when a man's
teeth had been rattled—and Trevor's most definitely had, no matter how hard he'd been trying
since to convince her—or himself?—that their
lovemaking had been no big deal. A woman had
her pride, after all.

Stepping up boldly in front of him, she walked
her fingers up his chest. "Actually, I don't think
I want tea, after all."

He went very still in response to her touch, his
expression studiedly blank. But before he could
mask it, she saw just enough in his eyes to be re-

assured that he was no more impervious to her now than he'd been that night in Fayetteville.

"I have a couple of hours free this afternoon," she added meditatively. "I could go home and do laundry. Or do a bit more organizing in my kitchen. Maybe catch up on some TV. Or…"

She ran a fingertip along his lower lip, remembering just how clever he could be with that nicely shaped mouth. "I could stay a while and we could have that tea. If that's what you want, of course."

"Oh, hell, no." Seemingly losing all resistance, Trevor tugged her into his arms, his mouth covering hers in a kiss that rocked her to her toes, effectively evaporating any lingering teasing.

The wooden door was hard against her back. Trevor was hard against her front as he wrapped himself around her, diving so deeply into the kiss that she shuddered in his arms. She welcomed him, strained against him, moaned with need for more, the low sound smothered in his mouth.

Her loose top proved no barrier to his hands when they slipped beneath it, and her bra snaps cooperated willingly with his skilled fingers. His hands cupped her, lifted her, his thumbs circling to draw a gasp from her.

As though he'd waited only for that, Trevor drew back and took her hand to walk with her to his suite.

TREVOR SAT ON the side of his tousled bed, wearing nothing but his jeans as he watched Jade dress to leave. It seemed as though she'd only just appeared at his door. Time buzzed past when he was alone with Jade—whether sitting by his pool talking and laughing, or entwined in bed with no words at all. Being with Jade—making love with Jade—well, it was something special. That was all he was willing to label it for now.

And then all too soon it was time to go their separate ways, she to her children, he to his guests.

Flipping her hair out of the neckline of her top, she turned to find him watching her. "I can't say I was expecting to spend the afternoon this way."

Amused by her tone, he replied, "Can't say I was expecting this, either."

"It was nice."

Why did that statement make him inwardly recoil? There was nothing at all wrong with *nice*. *Nice* was good. Like *pleasant*. And *fine*. What had he expected? *Earth-shaking?*

"Yeah," he said. "It was nice."

He pushed himself to his feet and reached for his shirt. "Sounds as if the rain has stopped."

She tilted her head to listen, then nodded. "I think it has. Finally. Let's hope it stays away for a while. The kids really need to get outside soon."

"A touch of cabin fever?"

"More than a touch. They've all been cranky as bears."

"I find it hard to believe your kids ever misbehave."

She laughed lightly and reached up to pat his cheek. "Hold on to that fantasy. They're good kids, but they definitely have their moments."

Catching her hand, he planted a kiss in her palm before releasing her. "Why don't you bring them over here after school? They can hang out in the rec room, play games and stuff. Maybe I'll have a few minutes to shoot some pool with them or play a video game with Caleb before I have to cut out."

What might have been a frown flashed across her face before she shook her head, her smile perhaps a bit too firmly in place. "Thank you, Trevor, but not tonight."

Had he said something wrong? It had been an impulsive offer, nothing more. Maybe he was reading too much into her response. "You have to rush off? I could still make that tea."

Glancing at the clock, she shook her head. "No, I'd better be on my way. I don't want to be late picking up the kids. I was five minutes late once and got the Bella lecture for it."

He laughed, picturing young Bella with her hands on her hips and her lower lip poked out gravely. "You don't want to risk that."

"Oh, goodness, no." Rising on tiptoes, she brushed her lips over his, then stepped back before he could wrap his arms around her and deepen the kiss. "Have a good dinner with your guests this evening. And please tell Mary Pat I hope her sister gets well soon."

"I will." He shifted his bare feet on the floor and pushed a hand through his tumbled hair, feeling suddenly, unaccountably awkward.

"No need to see me out. I'm sure you need to get ready for your motorcycle gang thing." Even as he chuckled at her wording, she was already moving toward the bedroom doorway. Glancing back, she looked distracted, as if her thoughts had already moved on to the next part of her day. "See you later, Trevor."

"Yeah. See you—"

But she was already gone, leaving him feeling bemused and vaguely unsatisfied. Not physically—she'd more than taken care of him in that respect. But as if there was something else he should have said, or that she should have said. Something other than a breezy "it was nice."

Shaking his head in exasperation with himself, he headed for the shower. He should be relieved that Jade expected nothing more from him than the occasional intimate encounter, a little fun in the sheets as a break from responsibility and commotion. To be honest, he hadn't really

even had this hour to spare in the schedule he'd
set for himself that morning.

But maybe it would have been nice if she'd at
least acted as though she'd have liked to stay longer.

CHAPTER NINE

THE FORMAL GRAND opening of the Shorty's Landing Family Medical Clinic was held on the second Friday afternoon in October, a month after they'd officially started seeing patients. Starting at three in the afternoon, two hours after the last patient was seen for the day, the event featured welcoming speeches by the mayor and the president of the chamber of commerce. Tables had been set up in the reception area to hold coffee, lemonade and finger foods, and shiny metallic balloons floated cheerily above them. All very festive and welcoming, and the nice-sized crowd in attendance was gratifying for the doctors and staff, including Jade.

The staff had all agreed to remain in their official clinic scrubs, making them easier to identify for guests, though Jade wasn't the only one who'd freshened up after closing. Amy and Lincoln circulated comfortably in their white coats, shaking hands and chatting, looking confident, professional and friendly. Jade watched her cousin rather closely, trying to assess the sin-

cerity of Amy's bright smile. Amy had been in an
odd mood for the past couple of days. Not a bad
mood, exactly, just distracted and more serious
than usual between patients. Jade hoped nothing
serious was troubling her, but she had decided to
give it a day or two before asking.

Jade wasn't sure how much her cousin's distraction was affecting her own mood this week,
which even she was having trouble defining.
Things were definitely better at home, so that
was good. She credited the weather for much of
that; the sun had returned and temperatures had
been ideal for a fun weekend spent at the beach
and the local amusement park with her children.
The kids delighted in the outings.

Caleb eagerly boogie boarded at the beach and
braved every gravity-defying ride at the amusement park. It was only when they returned home
that he retreated into grouchiness again. Jade was
still unable to find out if it was only adolescent
moodiness or if something specific was bothering
him. He growled at her whenever she asked, and
subtly questioning Erin hadn't provided any more
details, as he hadn't confided in his sister, either.
The scores he brought home from school were
still good, he was staying involved in after-school
activities and he seemed to have made a few new
friends. All she could do at this point was make it

clear to him that he could talk with her anytime and she would always be there for him.

As for herself—she'd thought about last Friday afternoon with Trevor quite a bit. She was well aware that once again she'd been the initiator, though Trevor had been a fully involved participant. She remembered every erotic detail.

She had focused deliberately on the physical memories, pushing aside potentially thorny emotional connections. Maybe there'd been a few moments of raw vulnerability during their lovemaking that would trouble her if she examined them too closely. She thought she'd done a decent job of putting on a breezy, sophisticated front afterward—her "social mask" as Trevor probably would have labeled it. The fact that she'd felt the need to do so—and that he so often retreated behind his own mask even with her—was only one of the reasons she thought they should go back to being merely friends. She was aware of the irony of that decision considering she'd initiated the "with benefits" part thus far.

"Hi, Jade."

Realizing abruptly that a public reception was totally the wrong time and place to think about relationships—friends or otherwise—she was grateful for the distraction. She nodded in greeting to Elle, who approached with her new husband. "Elle. Shane. It's good to see you. How was the honeymoon?"

Elle took both of Jade's hands and squeezed, her face beaming. "Oh, it was heavenly. Five days away was much too short, of course. Still, we missed Charlotte and couldn't wait to get back to her. She missed us, too, though she had a wonderful time with my mom and with Shane's family."

"I've been trying to find time to come by The Perkery for coffee and to hear all about your trip, but it's been pretty crazy both here and at home the past couple of weeks. The only downside to having children who are interested in learning about everything is that they keep me busy chauffeuring them from one activity to another."

Elle laughed. "Trust me, Charlotte's only three and I get that. And still, Shane and I are hoping to adopt at least one more child. When we do, you'll have to give us tips about juggling siblings."

"I'd be happy to." Jade doubted it would be necessary. Elle seemed to be very skilled already at balancing family and work, and she would have Shane to support and encourage her.

The blissful newlyweds moved on to visit with other attendees, leaving Jade to mingle with other guests, a few of whom she'd already met as patients. When a hand touched her arm, she turned with a smile that she managed to hold in place as she said, "Hi, Trevor."

Dressed in his Wind Shadow polo and khakis, Trevor stood beside the identically clad resort manager he'd introduced her to the day she and the kids had visited there. In her most brightly social voice, Jade welcomed them, pointed out the refreshments and invited them to help themselves. The manager drifted that way, though Trevor lingered with Jade.

"Good turnout," he said, glancing around the bustling room.

"Amy and Lincoln are delighted. We've all been pleased by how warmly we've been welcomed into the community." She glanced across the room to where Elle chatted cordially with Verita.

"How's your family?"

"So much happier now that the sun's been out. We had a nice weekend. A picnic at a beach park we hadn't visited before, and several hours Sunday afternoon at Thrill World."

His nod acknowledged that he was familiar with the amusement park. "I'm sure they had fun there."

"Oh, very much. Caleb and Erin experienced everything, even the crazy roller coaster that flips upside down. Bella wanted nothing to do with that, of course, so she and I spun around in teacups and then she and Erin rode the carousel a couple of times. We ate corn dogs and cotton candy and played some carnival games. Caleb won a stuffed floppy-eared puppy, which he gave to Bella, and Erin brought home a purple teddy bear. Everyone was smiling when we headed home and they've been getting along amazingly well since—though I don't expect that to last indefinitely," she added with a laugh.

"I'm glad you had a good time."

"Yes, we did." Did Trevor actually look a bit envious? Surely not. She had to be projecting. She couldn't envision him spinning in a teacup. He'd probably do so only with his phone in his hand while checking to see if the park was profitable and for sale. Smiling in response to the amusing image, she asked, "What about you? Did you work all weekend?"

"Pretty much."

"I talked with Mary Pat Wednesday. She said her sister is much better."

"Yes. She told me you invited her to Sunday lunch with you and the kids this weekend."

"I did. You'd be more than welcome to join us, of course, but she said you'll be out of town again."

"I'm afraid so."

"Trevor. I hope I'm not interrupting?"

Trevor turned smoothly to greet the woman who'd approached them. "Not at all, Mayor Stanfield. You've met my friend Jade Evans?"

The woman nodded cordially at Jade. "Yes, we were introduced earlier."

"I'm sorry I missed your opening speech," Trevor said. "I was running a little late. How are you?"

"Very well, thank you. I wonder if I could talk with you for a moment about an idea I've had that would involve several of the largest local tourist venues. I'll have my assistant call Tamar to set up a meeting, but it—"

Excusing herself, Jade stepped away to leave the mayor and the business mogul to discuss their plans. She joined her coworkers to mingle among the guests during the next twenty minutes until the gathering was scheduled to end. As that time grew closer, she was approached by a tall, auburn-haired man she'd spotted in the crowd a time or two but hadn't yet had the chance to meet.

"Hi," he said. "I don't think we've been introduced. I'm Kevin Rainey."

She shook his hand, thinking that he was an interesting-looking man with his blue-green eyes, slightly crooked nose and cleft chin. Not traditionally handsome, perhaps, but appealing. "Jade Evans. It's nice to meet you."

His broad grin revealed an overbite that could only be described as cute. "I have to confess, I already know who you are. Melissa Jackson is my sister."

Melissa was a phlebotomist in the clinic lab, so Jade had gotten to know her during the past month of working together. "Now I see the resemblance," she said, thinking that Melissa had that same chin cleft. "I've enjoyed working with her. She keeps us laughing."

"She's always been a cutup. She loves working here, too. She's told me about all her coworkers. She said you have three children?"

Melissa was the mother of a teenage girl, and had already humorously prepared Jade for what was to come with Erin and Bella—not to mention Caleb. "I do, yes."

"I'm a single dad, myself," he confided. "Two boys, eleven and eight. Quite a challenge, isn't it?"

"Yes, it is."

Jade remembered that Melissa had mentioned her brother had full custody of his sons after an ugly divorce. Melissa had also hinted strongly that she thought Jade and Kevin would make a cute couple, a suggestion Jade had laughed off as too *Brady Bunch*. She'd thought she'd put a damper on that idea, yet here he was. Friendly, cute, obviously intrigued. Seemed nice.

She wasn't feeling sparks from their handshake, and still wasn't interested in getting involved in a serious relationship nor looking for a father substitute for her children. But, she supposed it never hurt to make a new friend, especially one who understood the struggles of single parenting.

"Tell me about your boys."

RATHER TO TREVOR'S RELIEF, the mayor was rushed away by a member of her staff as the event drew to a conclusion. He liked the enthusiastic and gung ho mayor quite a bit, actually, but when she got off on a tangent, it could sometimes be difficult to break away from her. He glanced around for Jade, but didn't immediately spot her. Instead, he shook hands again with the two doctors and the remaining clinic staff around him and moved toward the door.

He spotted Jade then. She stood half hidden by a decorative column, her expression warm as she looked up to speak with someone. Following her glance, he felt his shoulders tighten. He couldn't place the man with her, though he looked familiar—tall with reddish hair and obvious appreciation for the shapely woman in front of him. They seemed to be getting along famously; as Trevor watched, Jade tossed her head and laughed in a way he had come to know very well. Not flirtatious. Just genuinely engaged and amused. Straightforward. One of the things he had always liked most about her.

Which meant that it made no sense at all that seeing her like this now made him scowl.

Smoothing his face, he stepped forward to catch her attention. "Jade. I didn't want to leave without saying goodbye."

She turned to him without any sign of irritation that her conversation had been interrupted. "Trevor Farrell, have you met Kevin Rainey?"

The name triggered his memory. He held out his hand to the other man. "You work at the DMV, don't you? I think you helped me with some licensing issues recently."

The other man looked pleased to have been recognized. "I did, indeed. And you own Wind Shadow Resort. I've had dinner there a time or two. Great place. Your chef is savage, as my older son would say. At least, I think that's high praise. And as a member of the National Guard, I appreciate the support you give to our military."

Trevor's resort-host response came easily after so much practice. "Thanks. I'll pass along the compliment to my chef."

"If you'll excuse me, my sister's motioning for me. I should probably go see what she wants." Kevin turned to Jade. "It was a pleasure to meet you, Jade. Maybe we'll see each other again sometime. We can share a cup of coffee and commiserate over the trials and triumphs of being single parents."

"That would be nice." Jade looked at Trevor again when the other man wandered off. Trevor noticed that Kevin glanced back once over his shoulder, the look focused only on Jade.

"You said you're leaving?" she asked. "Thanks for coming by, Trevor. I know Amy and Lincoln and the other staff appreciate your support."

With so few people remaining in the clinic, he was aware that they could be the subject of some attention, so he kept both his expression and body language neutral when he spoke again. "So, I guess I'll talk to you later?"

"Of course. Have a good business trip, Trevor."

"Thanks. Do you and the kids have plans for tomorrow?"

"I think the kids want to go back to the beach tomorrow."

"I'll repeat that they're welcome to play at the resort, if they like. I won't be there this weekend, but as I've said, I've left word that your family is always to be treated as our guests."

"Thank you, Trevor. I'll see what the kids want to do."

"Okay, then." He should leave. He needed to get back to the resort, had a dozen more things to do before calling it a day. Nadia would be waiting on the tarmac early in the morning to haul him off to his next business destination. And Jade had to pick up her children soon. "So, I'll call you sometime to see how things are going."

"Call any time."

It occurred to him that her expression with that invitation was the same as it had been when she'd breezily agreed that she would meet sometime for coffee and parent talk with Kevin. Made perfect sense, of course. Kevin seemed like a nice guy, was apparently settled down with kids of his own. Worked at the DMV—which probably meant he got nice perks and rarely if ever left town on business trips. Probably more flexible when it came to kids and their extracurricular activities. And judging by the way Kevin had looked at Jade as he'd asked her out without worrying about who might hear or how it might be interpreted, he was looking for a permanent match, a combining of households and kids.

On the surface, it seemed like a no-brainer of a match. Yet he couldn't really see Stephen Evans's widow settling down with a pleasant guy from the DMV, he thought. Then he chided himself for that unwarranted comparison. It cheered him a bit to remember that Jade had firmly asserted that she enjoyed her independent single state— but seriously, why should that matter to him? He was filled with both discomfort and shame that he could possibly resent Jade seeing anyone else when he'd made no commitments to her, himself, and wasn't looking to do so.

Because they were in public, surrounded by her friends and colleagues, he knew better than to offer a kiss in parting, not even on the cheek. Instead, he touched her arm in what he hoped appeared to be nothing more than a friendly gesture. It was immensely gratifying to feel what might have been the faintest shiver go through her in response to that contact between them. Maybe they didn't have commitments, but they definitely had chemistry, and Jade had never seemed to have an issue with that. In fact, she'd been very open with her enjoyment of their intimate time together.

Even though she'd called it nice, he thought fleetingly before smiling down at her.

"I'll call you, Jade."

Her response was unrevealingly cheery. "See you later, Trevor."

TUESDAY WAS A somewhat slower day at the clinic, busy in the morning but less so as the afternoon wore on. A couple of patients canceled, leaving extra time for Amy and Jade to focus on notes and other paperwork. It was nice to have that chance to catch a breath.

As she prepared to leave a few minutes early,

Jade glanced into Amy's open office doorway to see Amy sitting at her desk, staring out the window beside her with a faraway expression. Amy rubbed at her temple in a gesture Jade knew well from a lifetime of familiarity; something was troubling her cousin. Had been for at least a week. Maybe it was time for family concern to supersede professional discretion.

She stepped into the office and closed the door behind her. "Okay, Amy, let's have it. What's been bothering you lately? Is everything okay with you and Lincoln?"

That had been the first concern to pop into her head because Lincoln, too, had been unusually distracted lately, according to Verita. Jade would hate to see trouble crop up between the long-time couple for so many reasons. Mostly because she knew Amy loved Lincoln deeply and would be devastated if they broke up. Not to mention how awkward it would be businesswise, having opened their clinic so recently.

Amy blinked, started to speak, probably to brush the question aside, then stopped and made a face. "Can you sit down for a minute?"

Jade glanced at her watch. "Bella has a performance at school in forty-five minutes, so I can't stay long. But if you need to talk, we can get together after—"

"Jade, I'm pregnant."

Jade sank into a chair, stunned. "You're pregnant?"

For the first time in memory, Jade saw her usually confident, virtually fearless older cousin looking daunted when she nodded slowly. "Yes. Seven weeks. We were going to wait a few more weeks to say anything, but I guess I should have known I couldn't hide my emotions from you."

"I hate to tell you this, Amy, but everyone in the clinic knows something is going on with you and Lincoln," Jade responded dryly. "Apparently, neither of you is as good at hiding something this big as you thought."

"Oh."

Jade searched her cousin's face. "So—are you happy? Was this planned?"

"Ish. I mean," Amy elaborated, "Lincoln and I have talked about having a kid someday, but this timing was a little unexpected. But, well, yeah. We're happy. Just…sort of scared, you know?"

"I was fifteen years younger than you when I had my first child," Jade reminded her sympathetically. "I know exactly how scary it is. But you and Lincoln are going to be great at this."

"You think?"

"I know."

"So, anyway, Lincoln and I are thinking maybe

we'll head over to the courthouse one afternoon and just do the marriage thing, you know?"

Jade had to laugh at the wording from her typically non-sentimental cousin. "Aunt Loretta will pout for a month if you do that."

Amy winked, looking somewhat more cheery now that she'd shared her secret. "Not once she finds out she's going to be a grandmother again. She's been hinting forever that she wishes I'd join my brothers in giving her babies to spoil, so this will make her overjoyed."

"Well, yes, it will." Knowing her aunt, Jade didn't consider Amy's statement an exaggeration. "But if you want a witness and moral support for that afternoon at the courthouse, I'm there."

"Oh, you'll be there. Maybe next Friday afternoon after closing?"

"Of course. But no honeymoon?"

Amy waved a hand to dismiss the suggestion. "No time for that now. We'll take a little time off to relax after the baby gets here."

Oh, honey. Jade bit back the ironic words, but couldn't resist shaking her head with a low laugh. Amy still had so much to learn.

She glanced at her watch again. "I really should go. Bella's class is singing for the PTA meeting this afternoon."

"PTA. Oh, my God."

Laughing again, Jade stood. "You can do this, Amy."

"Yeah, okay. I know."

They met at the end of the desk for a tight hug. They weren't employer-employee at the moment but friends. Family. And that bond would always be there between them.

Jade drew back to move toward the door again. "I won't say anything about this, of course, until after you've made your announcement."

"Thanks. I knew you wouldn't."

Jade was reaching for the doorknob when Amy spoke again. "So, have you heard from Trevor since the grand opening reception last Friday?"

"No. He's been out of town. Mary Pat had lunch with us Sunday, and she said he's not expected back until Thursday."

"He hasn't called you, hmm?"

"Amy—"

Her cousin held up both hands, palms outward. "Just asking. He sure seemed to watch you a lot at the reception."

"I'm leaving now."

"So, how about Melissa's brother?" Amy asked before Jade could stalk out. "Has he called you? He sure seemed intrigued by you."

"Would you stop trying to fix me up? Just because you're planning to tie the knot doesn't mean I'm looking to do so right now. See you in the morning, Amy."

She escaped before her cousin could respond.

The truth was, Jade hadn't heard from Trevor, but she had from Kevin. She tried not to be disappointed by the former, and she wished she could be a touch more enthusiastic about the latter.

She'd put off Kevin's invitation to have dinner with him sometime this week, telling him it was a particularly busy week for her and the kids—which was true—but she hadn't yet closed the door to seeing him in the near future. There was no reason not to—except that she didn't want to mislead him into thinking anything could develop between them. Melissa had confided that her brother was looking for a serious relationship, and that he hoped to marry again soon. If that were the case, he didn't need to be wasting his time with her, Jade thought somberly.

She wasn't entirely opposed to marrying again, but neither was she in a hurry to do so—especially not just for the sake of being married. Having spent so much time on her own from the beginning of her marriage to Stephen, she'd simply grown accustomed to taking care of herself and her household without needing to consult anyone, at least not often. She had the final say with her schedule, her children, her finances, any major purchases—and she didn't need anyone to take care of her. Cinderella had never been her role model.

There were times when she missed Stephen very much. She deeply regretted the laughter he hadn't heard, the hugs he hadn't received and the father-to-child talks he hadn't had. She would spend the rest of her life making sure her children remembered their dad, even Bella, who'd been too young to form memories of him. But the family had carried on since they'd lost him, and would continue to do so.

Still, there were times when she thought wistfully that it would be nice to have someone to talk to after the kids were in bed. Someone with whom to discuss literature and politics, theater and religion, anything but school and video games and kids' sports. Someone to share her love of moonlight, to laugh with her in the daytime and make love with her in the night. Someone who'd be there with her after her children had struck out on their own.

That person, if he ever appeared, wasn't going to be Kevin Rainey, she thought with a gut-deep certainty.

JADE'S DAUGHTERS WANTED to eat out after Bella's class's performance. Because she wasn't really in the mood to cook that night, Jade agreed, even though it would be an earlier-than-usual dinner.

"Where would everyone like to go?" she asked as they buckled themselves into the car.

"Chinese!" Erin replied loudly. "I want to eat with chopsticks."

"Fried shrimp," Bella said at the same time. "Or ice cream."

Erin sighed heavily. "We don't eat ice cream for dinner, silly."

"I'm not silly! I meant ice cream for dessert."

"Girls," Jade warned, starting the car. "If you start fighting, we're just going home and I'll choose the menu."

"Okay, Mom." Erin held up her hands. "I'm fine with whatever Bella and Caleb want. Though Chinese sounds especially good today," she couldn't resist adding.

Jade glanced toward the front passenger seat. "What about you, Caleb? Is there anything in particular you'd like for dinner?"

He shrugged. "Doesn't matter. Anything's okay with me."

He pushed at his glasses, drawing her attention back to the scrape high on his cheek. He'd told her it had happened in PE class when he'd fallen while running sprints. It looked painful, though he'd brushed off her concern. She wondered if he was embarrassed that he'd fallen in front of his classmates, but she wouldn't discuss it with him in front of his sisters. That would just embarrass him further.

"They have good shrimp at Wind Shadow," Bella said wistfully. "We could eat at that place by the lake. The lights are so pretty."

"Honey, we're not driving out to Wind Shadow today. That's a weekend place." And not one Jade had been in a hurry to revisit with the kids, she had to admit.

"How about that Chinese place near the grocery store we go to? They have fried shrimp on the buffet, and Erin can use chopsticks. And they have an ice cream machine for dessert," she added, thinking she'd covered all the bases with the suggestion. At least she could make sure the kids had vegetables on their plates from the extensive buffet.

Caleb nodded his approval, and the girls agreed that it was an acceptable compromise—though Bella muttered that she'd have rather gone to Wind Shadow. The child didn't mention Trevor, but Jade wasn't fooled. Bella missed him.

Much to her discomfort, Jade knew the feeling.

She looked at her phone screen for several moments later that evening before taking Trevor's call. It wasn't that she was considering not answering. She was simply gathering her thoughts before speaking with him.

"How was your day?" he asked after exchanging greetings.

She shared a couple of amusing anecdotes from the PTA performance, making him laugh as she described the tall first grader who'd tried to hide behind shorter Bella to mask his discomfort at being on stage and about the utterly mangled high note the class had gamely and rather painfully attempted at the end of their performance.

"I have to admit, I'm not sorry I missed hearing that," he said with a laugh.

Though he was teasing, she suspected there was a grain of truth to his comment. She doubted that Trevor would choose to spend an afternoon sitting through a PTA meeting. She couldn't help remembering when she'd once dragged Stephen to a particularly long, drawn-out meeting filled with procedural discussions and a kindergarten musical production back when Caleb had been in first grade. Stephen had said afterward that he'd rather go back into battle any time than to do that again. He'd been joking, too—and yet completely serious at the same time.

"Did Caleb and Erin join you for the performance?" he asked.

"Yes, Caleb and Erin were there. The kids like to support each other—even if Erin makes wisecracks later."

Trevor chuckled deeply. Jade's bare toes curled

on the patio lounger in reaction. The night air was cool, but that wasn't what caused her sudden shiver.

"Erin always makes me laugh," he said.

"Yes, well, sometimes I have to rein in that smart mouth of hers. But I have to admit, she makes me laugh very often, too."

There was a moment of silence. She thought maybe Trevor was about to end the call, but then he said almost abruptly, "There's a charity thing at the resort Saturday night, a fundraiser for the local animal shelter. I wasn't sure I'd be back in town in time to attend, but now I know I'll be home Thursday night. So, would you like to go with me?"

She blinked in surprise at the unexpected invitation. Did he see this as another "date of convenience"? Had he asked *her* because he knew she wouldn't read anything into it or expect more from him?

Was she playing with fire to keep seeing him? As much as she'd told herself she wasn't looking to further complicate her life and risk more disruption in her tight little family, she did find herself thinking about Trevor an awful lot these days. And while she believed a single woman had every right to enjoy sex and adult companionship without a ring or a promise, she remembered somewhat nervously how hard she'd fallen for the last larger-than-life man in her life.

"Unless you already have plans for Saturday evening?" Trevor asked.

Was he giving her a cordial out? "Well, actually, my mother is coming Saturday morning to spend a few days with us."

"I see. Well, I'm sure you want to spend that time with her, so maybe some other time. It looks like I'm going to be in town for several weeks, barring any unforeseen emergencies, so—"

"Actually, Mom would love to have the kids to herself Saturday evening. There's no reason I can't attend the fund-raiser with you." Jade's acceptance had come on a sudden impulse, perhaps like his invitation. Whatever the motivation, they owned it now.

"Yeah? That's great, if you're sure she won't mind."

"To be honest, I'm more concerned that she'll be a little too approving," Jade said.

"Ah. That matchmaking thing again."

"She'll probably be on the phone to your mom at the first opportunity gloating about how well their scheme is working out."

"No doubt. But let's not worry about that. Let's just have a nice evening with some of our good-hearted neighbors, shall we?"

He seemed so genuinely unconcerned about

their mothers' opinions, and so casual about the purpose of the outing that she told herself she should just relax and go with it. Nothing had changed on his end of their friendship, apparently, and she would take care to protect her heart, as well. "It sounds like fun. And definitely a worthy cause. I'd love to go."

"Great. So, I'll look forward to seeing you Saturday. I'll let you know what time I'll pick you up."

"I can meet you at the resort," she said quickly. "That would probably be less awkward." Much less like an actual "date," she added silently.

"If that's what you'd prefer."

"I think it would be best."

"Then I'll send you the details about when and where."

Trevor really was a good man, generous to a fault in contributing to making his community a better place. A good friend to have on one's side, Jade mused as she put down the phone a few minutes later.

She was probably being foolish to worry that the special friendship they'd developed would cause either of them heartache, she told herself with a sigh that drifted softly into the night.

CHAPTER TEN

"Wow, Mom. You look great!"

"Thank you, Erin."

"You're beautiful, Mommy," Bella echoed with sweet sincerity.

"Thank you, Bella."

Jade couldn't help preening a bit in response to her daughters' heartfelt compliments as she joined her family in the living room early Saturday evening. She was glad her girls approved of her effort, she thought as she smoothed her royal blue dress with one hand. She'd kept her look simple with the classically tailored cocktail dress and minimal jewelry. Heeled sandals in a vibrant fuchsia gave an unexpected pop of color, just for fun.

She did a slow turn for the family. "What do you think, Mom?"

Sitting on the sofa with Bella and a book they'd been reading, her mother smiled. "You look lovely, dear. Maybe a touch more lipstick?"

With a laugh, Jade promised to freshen her lipstick when she arrived at the resort.

Caleb looked up from the graphic novel he was reading while sprawled on the floor. "You sure spend a lot of time with Trevor."

Taken aback by what might have been an undertone of disapproval in the observation, Jade looked at her son in question. "I've only seen Trevor once since the wedding I attended with him, and that was only for a few minutes at the clinic. That's hardly a lot of time."

He shrugged and looked at his book again.

"Don't you like Trevor, Caleb?" his grandmother asked, looking surprised.

"He's okay," the boy muttered. "I just don't see any need for him to hang around so much now that we're in our own house. I like our house better than his, anyway."

"Dude." It was Erin's turn to study her brother in open bewilderment. "Did you forget about the rec room? And that monster pool?"

"They're okay. Anybody with money can buy that stuff, though."

Bella's bottom lip quivered now. "Mr. Trevor is nice. I wish we could see him soon."

Jade was beginning to second-guess her decision to meet Trevor at the fund-raiser rather than have him pick her up here and greet the family. Perhaps Caleb felt that Trevor was deliberately avoiding them, unaware that it was Jade who'd been keeping them apart. Was she really trying to protect them from disappointment—or to make it easier for her to keep these two parts of her life tidily compartmentalized?

"I'm sure you'll see him again soon, Bella. He asks about all of you often," she assured her youngest child, then glanced at her oldest. "Caleb, I have to leave soon, but if you want to talk about anything, I can—"

He shook his head. "No. Just saying. You can go."

She hesitated, exchanging a troubled glance with her mother. But then she told herself there was little more she could do at the moment. She would try later to figure out what was going on with Caleb in many areas, not just his sudden antipathy toward Trevor. "I should go. Have fun with Nanna, kids. Be good. Mom, I'll have my phone with me all evening if you need anything."

"We'll be fine, Jade. Go, and don't feel that you have to rush back."

Definitely a mixed-message sendoff, Jade thought with a shake of her head as she settled into her car. Her mother was pushing her to take her time, her son apparently sulking because she was going at all. And then there were her own confused emotions. She'd been second-guessing her decision to appear in public with Trevor again and all the resulting gossip that could ensue, but at the same time she was excited to see him and wondered if they would have a chance to be alone that evening. And now she had the added worry about how she was handling all of this with regard to her children.

As they'd arranged, she met Trevor in his office fifteen minutes before the event began so that they could enter the ballroom together. The management offices were empty at this hour on a Saturday, though the reception desk downstairs had been fully staffed for the convenience of the guests. Trevor sat at his computer when she peeked in through his open door. Though she was relatively sure she'd made no sound, he looked up, anyway, as if sensing her arrival. His grin took her breath away, making her remember why she'd accepted this opportunity to see him again despite the complications.

Standing, he rounded his desk and held out his hands to her. "You look particularly lovely this evening," he said.

Her pulse gave a little flutter that rather annoyed her for some reason, but she hid the silly reaction behind a bright smile as she rested her hands in his for a warm squeeze of greeting. "Thank you."

"How are you and the kids enjoying your mother's visit?" he asked, reaching for the dark suit coat he'd draped over a nearby chair while he'd waited for her. She'd already figured out that

Trevor didn't care to wear jackets and ties more than necessary, though his job required him to do so fairly often. Most days found him in the resort uniform of a branded polo shirt and khakis, which seemed to suit him much better.

"We're having a great time. We took her for a sightseeing tour earlier and stopped by The Perkery to introduce her to Elle and Janet. She and Elle's mom hit it right off. Not such a surprise since Janet seems to charm everyone she meets."

"She does, yes," Trevor agreed with a laugh. "Has she read your palm yet?"

"No, but I've heard she has a talent for it."

"Well, perhaps 'talent' is overstating it a bit. She's almost never right but she has fun with it, anyway."

"Fun is good."

"Yes." He touched her face, his thumb tracing her jawline. "Fun is definitely good."

Her smile trembled. She reached up to touch his hand. "We should probably go to the party. Before we get distracted."

"And we do tend to get distracted," he murmured in agreement, his gaze hungrily on her lips.

Drawing a deep breath, she stepped back. "Party."

"Party," he repeated regretfully and offered her his arm.

Jade didn't recognize as many people at this event as she had at Elle's wedding. Trevor knew only some of them, though he was very good at working a room full of strangers and making them all feel as though they'd held his full attention for the duration of their conversation, no matter how brief. Though Jade interacted comfortably enough in both her work and social life, she still envied the effortlessness with which Trevor set people at ease despite his wealth and status.

Speeches were made, toasts offered, funds solicited, all to the backdrop of polite conversation and unobtrusive music. Jade had a very nice time, not in the least because Trevor stayed so considerately close to her. As independent and modern as she liked to think herself, she could definitely appreciate the attentions of a handsome, charismatic man by her side.

The highlight of the event came toward the end, when a bevy of young shelter volunteers brought in several puppies and kittens currently available for adoption. Oohs and aahs greeted the furry little charmers, all of which Jade suspected had been deliberately chosen for their calm natures and cute faces.

"It's a good thing the kids aren't here," she said with a laugh as she and Trevor admired the animals. "We'd be going home with all of them."

"They are hard to resist." Smiling at a blushing young volunteer, Trevor rubbed the head of a curly haired puppy with floppy ears and suspiciously large feet. Jade figured this was going to be a big dog, about the size of her mother's JoJo, whom she had often postulated must be part horse.

She turned away from him and found herself looking straight into a pair of huge brown eyes in one of the most homely cute little canine faces she'd ever seen. She hadn't a clue what breed the pup was, but it was utterly endearing with one ear up and one slightly down, a chubby little brown body supported on stubby legs and a tail that never seemed to stop wagging. "Oh, my gosh."

Following her gaze, Trevor grinned. "That's an interesting-looking dog."

"He's adorable." Jade had to pet the pup, who rewarded her with wiggles and licks in return. "What's his name?" she asked the young man assigned to this one.

"She's a girl, ma'am. We call her Zoe. She's three months old, spayed and mostly house-trained, and she's had all her shots."

Jade laughed as Zoe kissed her on the cheek with a friendly swipe of the tongue. "Oh, my goodness, my kids would love this one."

"She's looking for her forever home," the volunteer said promptly. "Couldn't ask for a sweeter-tempered pet. She's one of my favorites at the shelter. If you want her, she could go home with you Monday, after you stop by the shelter to fill out the adoption paperwork."

Jade figured she could leave work a little early Monday. She had been considering getting the kids a dog, even though she hadn't expected to find one quite so soon. But it would be good for them to learn the responsibility—and, she had to admit, she hoped a puppy would lift Caleb's spirits again.

"I want her," she said, needing no more time to think about it.

Heedless of dog hair on her dark dress, she gathered the blissful puppy up for a happily squirmy hug that made her laugh. "Oh, you are going to be so spoiled with love, Zoe."

She looked up sheepishly at Trevor as she realized how impulsive she must appear to him to have met and claimed a pup within approximately ten minutes. Especially after all her speeches about not being ready to bring a dog into her household. And even after that "mostly house-broken" description.

Rather than looking surprised or judgmental, the expression in Trevor's eyes made a deep shiver run through her. Her arms tightened instinctively around the puppy, who wagged even more enthusiastically and licked her chin.

Making herself look away from Trevor, she hoped her flushed cheeks and sudden breathlessness were attributed to her interactions with the dog when she spoke again with the volunteer.

A few minutes later, the animals were gathered up to be taken back to the shelter. Jade patted Zoe one last time before turning back to Trevor. She swiped futilely at the dog hair on her dress, not that she really cared that it was there.

"The kids have been begging for a dog," she reminded him, even though he hadn't said anything.

"Yes. I'm sure they'll love that one. She seemed like a sweetheart. Energetic, though. She'll probably keep you all busy."

Jade thought of Caleb. "That's not necessarily a bad thing."

The event ended soon afterward with a final appeal for volunteers and for continued financial support of the animal shelter. The ballroom cleared out quickly, leaving only the staff to clean up. Trevor spoke to each of them as he and Jade left the room, praising their work during the evening and thanking them for their efficiency.

The last time she'd visited the resort with the children, it had still been light when they left. Now, with the days markedly shorter, darkness had fallen while they were in the ballroom and Jade saw the resort lit up for the evening. It was truly beautiful with subtly illuminated walkways threading through the tropical foliage, multicolored beams glowing on the fountain in the lake, fairy lights draped overhead, the moonglittered ocean as a backdrop.

"Do you need to leave right away?" Trevor asked.

"No. It's still relatively early and Mom said she has everything under control at home. If I don't get home until after they're all asleep, that's not a problem."

She could tell her answer pleased him.

He motioned toward the bustling outdoor bar visible from where they stood. Strains of cheery reggae music drifted toward them, inviting them to join the party. "We could have a drink, maybe dance a bit. Or go into Torchlight for desserts and coffee."

She considered, for a moment, suggesting they have that coffee in his suite, knowing what would likely happen if they did. Yet, as appealing as that sounded, she didn't think it was a good idea tonight, given how volatile her emotions had been in recent days. Perhaps it was best—safest—for now to focus on the just-friends part of her relationship with Trevor.

"Maybe we could walk on the beach and talk for a while," she suggested. "It's such a lovely night."

"And we both know how much you love the

nighttime," he commented. Then, motioning toward one of the paths that led to the beach with his right hand, he held out his left to her. She placed hers in it, telling herself it was perfectly natural for two friends to hold hands while sharing a moonlight stroll on the beach.

THEY WALKED IN silence for a time, passing only a few other people on the beach at this hour. The fingers of her right hand laced loosely with Trevor's left, Jade carried her shoes in her other hand, letting them swing from her fingers by the strap. Moonlight glittered on the endlessly moving water, and the breaking waves lapped hungrily just out of reach of their bare toes. She wouldn't call the silence companionable, exactly—she was too aware of Trevor physically for that innocuous term—but it was still nice.

She glanced up at him, finding him smiling down at her. "I've never seen anyone love the moonlight as much as you do," he commented. "You soak it up the way some people bake in the sun."

She shrugged lightly. "Just a little quirk, I guess. I love sunny days as much as anyone, but there's just something about the night."

Trevor stopped walking and turned to cup her face in his free hand. "It looks damned good on you," he said, his voice suddenly husky.

She tilted her head to meet his lips for a kiss that made her heart pound in rhythm with the surf. She could keep telling herself they were nothing more than friends, she thought as her eyelids drifted closed, but that would never explain the electricity that sparked between them whenever they touched. She could blame it on the moonlight—but the sensations were just as explosive in daylight. She couldn't even remember when, exactly, she'd become aware of them. It seemed that one day they'd been casual acquaintances and the next they'd been tearing up the sheets in a hotel suite. Crazy. Reckless. And so unlike her.

Smoothing her hair away from her face, he smiled back, though his eyes were more serious. "I hope you know that I enjoy spending time with you, even if we don't end up in bed. That wasn't why I asked you to join me this evening."

With the uncomfortable feeling that he'd somehow read her thoughts, she had to swallow before answering with a soft laugh. "You haven't forgotten which of us made the first move both times we ended up in bed, have you?"

His smile broadened. "No. I haven't forgotten that."

Releasing his hand, she took a step backward on the damp sand. "I'm not complaining, Trevor. Just the opposite. I've enjoyed the time I've spent with you very much. Both in bed and out. It's good for my mental health to have the occasional night out with a friend."

Not smiling now, Trevor looked as though he was trying to choose words carefully before speaking again. She studied him curiously, wondering what he wanted to say.

"So, that guy at the reception last week," he said after a moment.

She felt her left eyebrow rise. "Which…do you mean Kevin?"

"Yeah. The guy from the DMV. He practically asked you out in front of me. Well, actually, he did ask you out in front of me. I mean, he probably didn't know that you and I are…that we see each other."

She had to admit she was startled. It was completely unlike Trevor to stumble so awkwardly over his words. He always seemed so confident and articulate.

"To be fair, you and I haven't actually been seeing each other," she pointed out carefully. "We said that wasn't a path we wanted to take."

He agreed a bit too quickly. "True." He caught a wind-tossed strand of her hair and wrapped it around one of his fingers, seemingly concentrating almost fully on that task as he said, "Kevin seems like a decent guy."

"Yes, very nice. His sister works at the clinic with me."

"And he's a single dad?"

"Yes."

"So, you have quite a lot in common."

Once again, Jade was done with subtext. "Trevor, is this your way of asking me if I'm interested in Kevin? Because if you are—and this is a rather odd time to do so—the answer is no. Kevin is looking for a wife and a stepmother for his boys. I'm not looking to be either of those things."

He cleared his throat, and had the grace to look sheepish. "That was about as subtle as a Sherman tank, wasn't it?"

"Somewhere along those lines," she agreed dryly.

Trevor sighed. "I'm sorry, Jade. That was both clumsy and inappropriate. My only excuse is that I'm just rusty at this."

She eyed him skeptically. This was definitely a man who knew how to turn a woman's knees to jelly. "I find that hard to believe."

He barked out a laugh. "I meant, I'm rusty at trying to have any sort of relationship, even a noncommitted one."

Relationship? She went very still, her eyebrows dipping into a frown. "I'm not sure where you're going with this, Trevor."

He sighed heavily. "In my strangely clumsy and inappropriately timed manner, I'm just trying to say that I enjoy being with you, Jade. I know neither of us are looking for anything serious, but there's no reason we can't attend some parties together, maybe have dinner occasionally, just have some fun together. Is there?"

Have fun together. The advice her cousin had given her, the advice she'd given herself. She thought she understood what Trevor was suggesting. A breezy, no-strings affair while he was in town and not expecting to be overly busy for a few weeks. And when, not if, they drifted apart, that would be no more than expected.

Having heard stories about Trevor for years, she was well aware she wouldn't be the first woman who'd filled that role in his life during the past decade. Though he'd just admitted it had been a while. Perhaps that was because of his busy schedule or because he'd spent the past year recuperating from his accident. Maybe both.

The scenario he'd sketched out sounded rather ideal for them. Companionship when they wanted it, occasional physical release for two healthy adults with off-the-chart chemistry. Frankly, some of the best sex she'd ever had. She wasn't sure she had the willpower to resist when or if the opportunity arose in the future, especially since Trevor seemed to be going out of his way to remove any potential complications. So, there was no reason at all for her to feel a bit empty in response to this suggestion, right?

"Obviously, you can feel free to call me any time," she said, deciding to play it light. "If I'm not busy, I'd certainly be open to seeing you."

"That would be nice." He didn't sound particularly satisfied with her measured response, but perhaps they were both just tired.

And speaking of which…

She bent to scoop up her shoes, which she'd dropped at some point during their kiss. "I should probably go. It's getting late."

"It is, I guess." He pushed his hands into his pockets as if to remove them from temptation. "I guess your household will all be asleep when you get back."

"I expect so." She tucked her shoes beneath her arm and put up a hand to brush her breeze-tossed hair out of her face. "I'll have to tiptoe in so I don't wake them, though Caleb's the only light sleeper of my three."

She took a moment to study Trevor as he stood on the beach in the bright moonlight. He'd abandoned his jacket and tie at some point and loosened his shirt collar just enough to reveal a wedge of the tanned chest she'd explored so thoroughly with her hands and lips. His usually tidy hair had been rumpled by the wind and there was a smudge of lipstick on his chin.

"Damn, you look good," she said, making a show of fanning her cheek with one hand. "You could pose for a calendar like that."

"Thank you." Trevor laughed then and shook his head. "I never quite know what you're going to say next."

Which perhaps explained why she was able, occasionally, to coax him out from behind that social mask, she thought as she turned to walk back into the resort with him.

"You really don't have to walk me to my car," she said when they neared the main building. "I can't imagine a safer place at night than your resort."

"It is absolutely safe," Trevor agreed. "And I'm absolutely walking you to your car."

Smiling faintly, she abandoned futile arguments and dug in her bag for her keys.

"Are you going to tell the family about the pup you're getting Monday?" he asked.

"I'm considering surprising them with her. I think it would be fun to let Mom pick the kids up from school, and then I can show up with Zoe after they're all home." The plan was as spur-of-the-moment as her decision to adopt the dog had been.

"That should be fun," he agreed. "I'd love to see their faces when you walk in with her."

Though she knew it was only a rhetorical comment, she tilted her head thoughtfully. "Why don't you? You could meet me at the shelter, if you could take a couple hours away from work. You could see the kids get their puppy and say hello to Mom while she's in town."

He looked surprised by the suggestion. "You'd really want me there?"

"You'd be welcome. I don't want to give the appearance to my kids that I'm trying to hide our friendship or they'll definitely think it's something it's not. And Bella has been asking about you, so I'm sure she'd love for you to visit again."

Something passed across his face so quickly she wasn't sure what she'd seen. Had she said something that bothered him? Thinking back over her words, she couldn't think what it might have been.

"I could probably take a couple hours to visit your family Monday. Seems only polite to say hello to your mother while she's in town."

"Of course. She'd enjoy seeing you, too."

"Yeah, okay. Sure. That sounds like fun."

Maybe he was just tired. His limp was a bit more pronounced as they walked across the now-much-emptier parking lot toward her car. She told herself that weariness was just as valid an excuse for her own sudden change of mood. There was no other reason to feel slightly melancholy when she unlocked her car door.

She opened the door and looked up at him. "Good night, Trevor. Thank you for the lovely evening."

"Thank you for being here with me. Be safe driving home."

Yes, the polite veneer was definitely back in place. She saw nothing but an affable courtesy reflected now in his eyes. "I will. I'll send you a text about times for Monday, if you have a chance to stop by."

"I'll make time. Can't wait to see the kids meet Zoe."

She laughed. "Neither can I—though I may regret it and ask myself what was I thinking?"

"About the dog, of course," he murmured.

"Of course."

Trevor brushed a kiss across her cheek, then stepped back to let her get into her car. She waved as she drove away and saw in the rearview mirror that he lifted a hand in return.

He really had been in an odd mood after their walk, she mused, her eyes focused on the road ahead. Not a bad mood, just…well…odd.

She hadn't expected him to try to define what had started as a brief affair as a relationship, even an open-ended one.

Did it really have something to do with Kevin flirting with her at the clinic reception, as his comment had suggested? Could Trevor have been jealous?

An interesting possibility, if true. And one she didn't want to dwell on tonight.

CHAPTER ELEVEN

HAVING COORDINATED THEIR schedules by text, Jade and Trevor met in the parking lot outside the animal shelter Monday afternoon. He showed up with a backseat full of puppy supplies, including a carrier, dog bed, food and water bowls and even a few toys.

"Consider them adoption day gifts for Zoe," he said with a grin that made him look younger than his age. "And here's a collar and leash. I got them in purple to make Erin happy."

Jade studied the leash and collar, shaking her head in resignation that Trevor had been so typically generous. "She will most definitely approve. And Bella will like that the collar's got a touch of glitter to it."

"Think a glittery purple collar will be okay with Caleb?"

Tucking her hair behind her ear, Jade sighed. "Who knows? But I think he'll be okay with it, just to get the dog he's been asking for. He said he wanted a big dog like JoJo, but something tells me Zoe will win him over."

Trevor caught her arm when she started to move toward the shelter door. "Things are okay with Caleb, right?"

She supposed she shouldn't be surprised that Trevor had heard the undertone of worry in her tone. "I think so. Admittedly, it's hard to tell sometimes.

Trevor winced humorously. "Okay. I get it. Adolescence."

"Oh, yeah."

"The dog will be good for him," he assured her. "She'll give him something to focus on other than himself."

She gave him a quick look. "Experience?"

"Maybe. I had a couple dogs growing up. And a scrappy cat that could hold his own with both of them."

The nostalgic affection in his voice made her cock her head. "You obviously enjoyed having pets. When did you stop?"

He glanced away then. "Don't know, exactly. After I was in the service, I guess. When I got so busy and was gone so much it seemed unfair to commit to an animal."

After his wife died, she interpreted. She wondered if Lindsey had liked animals. If they'd had pets together. Other than that one night of bonding over the social expectations of widowhood, they hadn't talked much about their late spouses.

"Ready to collect your new family member?" he asked. "Unless you've talked yourself out of it?"

With a little laugh of anticipation, she shook her head. "I gave myself all day yesterday to change my mind, and I'm still confident this is the right decision for both Zoe and the kids."

"Then, lead the way."

If Jade had allowed any second thoughts to creep in since the shelter fundraiser, they were instantly put to rest when she saw Zoe again. She felt in love as quickly as she had before, unable to resist those sweet eyes and that wiggly body.

"I think she remembers me," she said to Trevor, laughing as the eager puppy tried to lick her face.

"How could anyone forget you?" he asked, watching her with that look again.

Clearing her throat, she patted the pup one more time, then focused on filling out adoption paperwork.

Finally done with formalities, she tried to lead the bouncy dog out of the shelter by the purple leash Trevor had provided. She ended up with the leash tangled around her ankles and the dog hopping around her like a hyperactive bunny. "Okay, maybe I'll carry her," she said ruefully.

"Not the way to start out," Trevor said with a shake of his head. "Mind if I give you a hand?"

"Please do."

"Zoe." Handing Jade the bag of food she'd purchased, Trevor took the leash in exchange and gave it a gentle tug to get the dog's attention. "Heel."

He repeated the word several times as he firmly positioned the dog at his left side. Keeping the leash short and taut, he walked her across the parking lot to the cars, where the dog crate waited in his backseat. Zoe still tried to jump and wander, but he kept her close to his side, speaking encouragingly to her. He stopped at the car, he pressed gently on her hindquarters, saying, "Sit." When she did, he praised her and rubbed her ears, at which time she jumped up and kissed him right on the mouth.

Jade couldn't say she blamed the dog one bit. Trevor was just too cute with the silly pup beside him. Sexy as all get out.

He grinned up at her and the attraction sizzled even hotter beneath her skin. "It's going to take time and a lot of practice, but she's a smart dog," he said, probably unaware that Jade was fighting a silly urge to jump on him much like Zoe was. "She'll learn. Caleb will probably enjoy training her."

Telling her hormones to behave themselves, she nodded. "I know he will."

They closed Zoe safely into the crate, which they decided to leave in Trevor's car. He followed her home. Each time she looked into the rearview mirror, he gave a thumbs-up to let her know all was well. She wasn't sure if her rapid heartbeat was due more to her anticipation of her children's excitement or knowing that Trevor would be back in her home.

Maybe spending more time with him in less intimate situations would ease some of her own fascination with him. Maybe her thoughts would stop drifting to him so often when she was alone in her patio chair or her bed. Maybe she'd stop automatically looking for him at the coffee shop or when her daily outings took her past his neighborhood. And maybe she'd conquer the nagging voice at the back of her mind that warned she was in danger of falling for him despite her better judgment.

When she walked through the front door of her house, her mother, who of course knew of the imminent surprise, looked up from a board game with Erin and Bella to smile a greeting. Caleb was nowhere in sight.

"Mommy!" Bella ran to hug her. "You're late getting home today."

"Yes, I had a few stops to make first. Where's your brother?"

"He's in his room doing homework or something. Nanna's making beef stew for dinner. Doesn't it smell good?"

"It smells delicious. Erin, would you ask Caleb to come out, please?"

"Are you sure you want him to?" her daughter asked with a roll of her eyes. "He's a grump again today."

"He hurt his lip at school today," Jade's mother explained. "I think it's sore. I had him put an ice pack on it."

Hurt again? When had Caleb become so accident prone? "How did he say it happened?"

Again, Erin answered, this time with a snort. "He said he opened his locker door into his face. Smooth, huh?"

Jade frowned. Something about that explanation seemed off to her, especially since it was the second injury to Caleb's face in a very short time. She was beginning to worry that there was more going on at school than her son had admitted, but she would have to talk with him later, in private. "Just go get him, Erin. Preferably without wisecracks."

"I'll try, Mom." Erin gave her a saucy wink that made Jade smile despite herself.

Thinking of Trevor waiting patiently outside with Zoe, Jade hoped Erin would hurry back with Caleb. Her mom grinned at her, clearly as keen as Jade for the children to be surprised by their new pet.

Jade's first glance at her son was not reassuring. His lower lip was swollen and scabbed and looked painful. "You've been keeping ice on it?" she asked after she'd examined it, to his embarrassment.

He nodded, his hair falling over his glasses with the movement. "Nanna gave me a cold pack. It's okay."

"Erin said you did this on your locker?"

"Yeah. Looked away when I opened it and hit myself in the face. Stupid."

She noted that he didn't meet her eyes when he answered in a mutter, which wasn't particularly reassuring. She was having trouble picturing the accident, but she was distracted when Erin said something she didn't quite catch and Caleb growled in response.

"Okay, guys," she said, deciding to investigate the accident further later. "Straighten up now. We have a visitor."

All three siblings frowned and looked around in question. "Someone's coming?" Bella asked. "Who?"

"Trevor."

Bella clapped her hands together and squealed in delight. Erin grinned. Caleb scowled even harder.

Once again, Jade wondered what on earth had changed her son's attitude toward Trevor, who he'd seemed to like well enough at the beginning. If it was because Trevor had been away so much and Caleb felt abandoned by the man he'd considered his new friend, perhaps today would bring him back around.

"When is he coming?" Erin asked.

Jade reached for the door. "He's here. And he's brought a friend."

Perhaps Trevor had been working with Zoe while he waited for the door to open, his signal to come in. The small dog walked at his left side when they entered, though the leash was still held firmly in Trevor's left hand.

"Hi, guys," he said, grinning at everyone in the room.

The reaction to seeing the dog beside him was comically belated.

"You have a dog, Mr. Trevor? Can we pet him?" Erin asked, surging toward them while Bella inched forward more cautiously, intrigued but wary.

Caleb didn't say anything, but Jade saw his face brighten incrementally when the eager puppy abandoned any attempt at obedience training in excitement at seeing potential new playmates. The pup yipped a couple of times and wagged so hard her whole hindquarters whipped back and forth, licking frantically when Erin knelt beside her. Jade heard her mom's phone snapping rapidly to record the event, photos Jade would definitely want sent to her.

"Oh, he's so sweet." Erin already had her arms around the dog while Caleb bent to get in his share of pats and rubs.

Standing half behind her brother, Bella put out a timid hand, then giggled when her fingers were swiped by an affectionate tongue. "He's friendly!"

"She's a girl," Trevor told them, having to speak up a bit over the clatter. "Her name is Zoe."

"Cool name," Erin pronounced. "And I like her purple collar and leash."

"We thought you would." Trevor shared a smiling glance with Jade before adding casually, "Caleb, I hope you don't mind too badly that your dog has a purple leash and a shiny purple collar."

The boy froze for a moment. "My dog?"

"Our dog," Jade corrected, stepping forward then. "I adopted her for us at the shelter this afternoon. She needed a home and a family to love her and you all said you wanted a pet, so it seemed like a good match. But," she added as her children whooped joyously, "I expect everyone to help take care of her. I'll pay her bills, but you three will feed her, walk her, scoop poop, clean up messes. Got that?"

A trio of crossed-heart promises almost drowned

out her mother's too-knowing laugh. Trevor only grinned again.

In her excitement at all the attention, the puppy started to crouch as if to wet the floor. Caleb scooped her up and dashed out to the backyard with her, followed by his sisters. The adults were left to look at each other and then burst out laughing.

"This," Linda said, "is going to be interesting."

"I know. And I'm probably crazy."

"No. Did you see how happy they are? They'll love having a pet. Heaven knows I've enjoyed my JoJo. I miss the silly guy, even though I know my neighbors are taking very good care of him this week."

"In all the excitement, I haven't actually said hello to you, Linda." Trevor brushed a light kiss on her cheek. "You look well."

"I am. Have you talked to your parents? Are they enjoying their cruise?"

"Mom's having a great time. Dad said the cabin's designed for elves, but other than that, it's tolerable."

Linda laughed. "That sounds just like your father."

Trevor turned to Jade then. "Want to help me bring in the dog supplies while the kids are out back with Zoe? You'll probably have to drag them in for dinner."

"Of course."

"You are staying for dinner, aren't you, Trevor? I made plenty," Linda said.

Jade noted his slight hesitation before he replied, probably mentally rearranging his evening's schedule. "I'd be delighted, thank you."

Looking satisfied, Linda went into the kitchen to finish preparations for the meal, leaving Jade and Trevor to fetch the dog supplies. At least she wouldn't have to worry about the conversation getting too awkward at dinner, Jade thought as she followed him outside. The kids would see to that as they raved about their new pet, probably arguing who would be in charge of which pet care chore. She could deal with that.

TREVOR OPENED HIS car door, then reached in to pull out a few supplies for Jade to carry, reserving the larger items for himself. "I think we can declare the surprise a great success. Your kids were beside themselves."

He saw her face light up with pleasure at the memory. "They were, weren't they? I'm glad I went through it, despite the extra trouble it will bring."

Tucking the dog bed beneath one arm, he asked carefully, "So, did you get a chance to ask Caleb about that lip before I came in?"

She told him the story she'd been given.

"Huh." He slid an arm through the handle of a large bag holding assorted grooming supplies. Should he say anything? None of his business—but then again, he'd been a teenage boy and Jade hadn't. "You're good with that explanation?"

"Actually, I'm wondering if I should have his eyes checked again. He fell in PE class and scraped his cheek, and now this. Maybe his lens prescription should be adjusted if he's having trouble with depth perception."

"Could be."

Though he'd kept his tone as neutral as possible, it was obvious he hadn't fooled her. She'd been half turned away from him toward the house with the bags he'd handed her, but she stopped and spun to look at him with narrowed eyes. "What are you trying to say, Trevor?"

He sighed, wondering if he should have just stayed out of it. But still, he liked the kid and hated to think he could be headed for trouble. And maybe Jade wasn't as experienced with the signs of a knuckle-induced split lip as he was. "Look, it's just a gut feeling, Jade, but that lip—well, I don't think it was a locker door that split it. My guess would be a fist."

Jade winced. "The thought crossed my mind, but I didn't want to believe it. Caleb in a fist-fight?"

"Like I said, I have no idea if that's true. Maybe

he did have a dust-up with a jerk of a locker door. I'm just suggesting that I had my share of split lips in junior high and I always had a good story to explain them when I got home. Some of the guys I went to school with took issue with my family background, the excellent grades I was required to get in every class—I don't know, just something about the way I walked, I guess. But yeah, I think it's something you should keep an eye on, especially if this is the second time it's happened."

Jade bit her lip. "Do you think it's possible he's being bullied at his new school?"

He shrugged, seeing no need to state the obvious reply.

After a moment, she pushed her hair out of her face in a weary gesture before asking, "Do you think I should say anything to him? Ask him about it…?

"It's your call, of course, but maybe don't push it just yet. Ask how things are going at school, ask if he's got any problems, listen closely when he denies it, which he probably will. And if it happens again, start pushing. I'm hardly qualified to give parenting advice," he added quickly, in case she took offense to a child-free bachelor giving her advice on dealing with her son, "but I think that approach would have worked best for me when I was Caleb's age."

Drawing a deep, shaky breath, she nodded, and to his relief, she didn't look annoyed by his suggestions. "I hope you're wrong," she said, most likely trying to convince herself as much as him. "I mean, I was skeptical about the locker door story, but Caleb has always been honest with me."

"He's about to be a teenager, Jade. You can expect a few bumps on the road ahead. But he's a good kid. I'm sure he'll turn out fine."

She groaned softly. "For tonight, maybe I'll just enjoy watching them play with their dog."

With the bag dangling from the crook of his arm, Trevor touched her arm in sympathy. "A very good plan."

She gazed up at him, and though her smile looked a bit strained around the edges, he was pleased to see that her frown had lifted. Man, this raising kids thing looked like a field full of landmines, especially to someone with no training for that particular mission!

The children expressed delight with the supplies Trevor had impulsively bought for the dog, unanimously approving his choices. Jade insisted the pup be closed into her crate with a blanket and a couple of chew toys during dinner. Zoe, she explained, would have to be trained not to beg for food or attention when the family sat down to eat.

With the dog put away, the kids turned their attention to Trevor—at least the girls did. He heard all about school and extracurriculars, about new friends and upcoming plans. Bella told him proudly that she'd drawn in her journal every day. Erin admitted she wasn't as faithful with hers, but still enjoyed it when she brought it out. Caleb didn't volunteer whether he made use of his.

Though Trevor chatted with the whole family, splitting his attention between the adults and children, he still studied Caleb surreptitiously during the meal. He saw the boy wince a few times while eating, as if the lip bothered him, but the kid shrugged off his mother's and grandmother's concern.

With each passing minute, Trevor became more convinced that the locker door story was bogus, but he wasn't overly worried. Yet. Maybe there'd been a tussle or two at school, the new kid finding his footing there, perhaps, but Trevor didn't get the sense that Caleb was trouble. Just the opposite, in fact. Despite his adolescent moodiness, the boy was innately polite and respectful to his mother and grandmother, patient with Bella—if not so much with Erin, rather understandably—and an absolute marshmallow with the dog. As much as the girls would enjoy Zoe, Trevor suspected the dog would ultimately be Caleb's.

Figuring the best way to communicate with the kid was through that soft spot, Trevor told him, "It's obvious that Zoe's a clever dog. I bet you can have her sitting and heeling in no time, Caleb. You can find training videos online, or there's a pretty good obedience school in Shorty's Landing."

"I want to train her, too," Erin said quickly.

Caleb frowned. "I've studied dog training videos. It's best if the early training is done by one person so the dog doesn't get confused by inconsistency. Once it's trained, the dog will respond to anyone who uses the right cues. Isn't that right, Trevor?"

"I believe that is the prevailing advice. Erin, you could probably teach Zoe some games apart from the basic training Caleb wants to do. I bet she'd love to play fetch with you or learn to catch a disc."

That suggestion brightened Erin's expression. "Cool. I like playing fetch with JoJo—Nanna's dog. He gets bored quick, but it's fun while he plays. Maybe Zoe will be better at it because she's younger."

"Wouldn't be surprised."

After dinner, he asked Caleb lightly, "Would you like me to show you how I've gotten Zoe to walk on lead so far? She's a long way from being trained, but she's made a good start."

Caleb looked momentarily torn between longing to accept the offer and wanting to keep his distance. Was he concerned that Trevor would be more likely than his mom or grandmother to see through his flimsy excuses? The former desire won out, though the boy tried to play it cool. "Sure, that would be okay. If you've got time."

"I'll make time." Or was this the kid's problem? Was he ticked because Trevor spent so much time working and so little time visiting this family? Because that wasn't going to change anytime soon. In fact, with the Florida project ramping up, it was likely to get worse. But he was here now, and he'd offer what friendship he could.

He glanced at Jade, and she nodded almost imperceptibly, signaling approval even though there was still a hint of worry in her eyes.

Caleb focused intently on following Trevor's suggestions as the boy made a trip around the backyard with Zoe on the leash. Zoe wasn't quite as cooperative with Caleb as she'd been with Trevor, wanting to tug and run and play, but they had a fairly successful first attempt. It helped somewhat that it was only the two of them outside now, keeping the puppy from being overly distracted by onlookers. Because it was a school night, Bella was in the bath getting ready for bed and Erin had homework to finish before turning in.

Completing his first route around the yard, Caleb pushed on Zoe's hindquarters and ordered her to sit when they stopped walking, as she would eventually learn to do. He took her on one more tugging tour around the fence before repeating the sit command at the end.

"Now praise her and say the word 'break' before unsnapping the leash," Trevor instructed. "That'll be her signal that she's free to do her own thing until you call her or give the next command."

The boy completed those steps, then unfastened the leash to allow Zoe to sniff around the yard unrestrained. Twisting the leash around one hand, Caleb looked at Trevor. It was almost dark now, and the yard lights reflected on the lenses of his glasses. "She did pretty good, huh?"

"Yes, you both did for a first lesson. You communicate well with her. No doubt you'll be walking her around the block on lead in no time."

Focusing on the leash laced through his fingers, Caleb asked, "So, how'd you know how to do that stuff when you don't even have a dog?"

"I had dogs when I was growing up. A cat, too, but I never trained him to walk on a leash."

That coaxed a faint smile. "I've heard cats are pretty hard to train."

"That one was, for sure. Great cat, though."

Caleb let the leash dangle from his wrist by the loop when he boasted, "My dad had a dog who knew lots of tricks. He fetched and rolled over and played dead and ran those obstacle course things. He was bigger than Zoe. A German Shepherd."

"Big dog," Trevor agreed casually. "Zoe won't get near that size. She's a more compact model."

"What breed do you think she is?"

"A mix. But I wouldn't be surprised if she's part Corgi."

"Dad's dog was named Bruiser, but Dad said he wasn't scary unless he was on guard duty. I thought maybe I'd like a big guard dog, but I like Zoe better. Besides, Bella would be scared of a big dog, at least at first. She likes JoJo and he's huge, but usually she's scared of dogs she doesn't know. Of course, she's sort of scared of lots of things."

Trevor wondered if buried in that commentary was a clue to Caleb's possible troubles at school. Was his comment about wanting a guard dog related to his split lip, or merely a coincidence?

"Bella's lucky to have her big brother to watch out for her until she's old enough to stand up for herself."

He saw Caleb square his shoulders, chin rising and bruised mouth firming as he pushed his glasses higher on his nose. "That's my job."

Interesting. But before he could pursue it, Jade appeared in the doorway. "How's the obedience lesson going?"

"Zoe did good, Mom." Caleb seemed almost relieved by the interruption. "We went twice around the yard with the leash and she didn't pull much. Not too bad, anyway."

"I'm sure she'll learn quickly."

"She will. Trevor and I agree she's a smart dog."

Trevor had noted what seemed to be the deliberate drop of the "Mr." title this evening, and figured Jade did, too, but he shook his head slightly at her in a covert warning not to say anything about it. He was fine with Caleb calling him by his first name. "Mr. Trevor" sounded sort of silly to him, anyway, though it was almost standard Southern kid protocol for adult family friends.

He glanced at his watch and winced. "I should go. As it is, I'm about two hours behind on today's agenda, though it was worth it to spend time with you guys."

"Thank you so much for everything you did for us today, Trevor," Jade said, glancing meaningfully at her son as she spoke. "It was very nice of you to help me pick up Zoe and to give us all those great supplies for her. And to give Caleb pointers on training her."

"Uh, yeah." Dutifully prodded, Caleb muttered, "Thanks, Trevor."

"You're welcome." On impulse, Trevor pulled out one of his cards and offered it to the kid.

"This is my private number. Use this one if you ever want to give me a call, Caleb. Feel free to ask for advice or anything else you might need," he added.

The boy took the card and looked at it curiously, though he didn't say anything. Trevor didn't expect to hear from the kid, and honestly didn't know what he'd do or say if the boy did call, but he'd been absolutely sincere in making the offer.

"Why don't you take Zoe inside to her water bowl," Jade suggested to Caleb. "I'm sure she's thirsty after her lesson."

Sliding Trevor's card into his pocket, Caleb nodded. "Can she sleep in my room tonight?"

"We'll talk about that."

"Okay. Come on, Zoe. Here, girl." Caleb clapped his hands and the pup came running, more eager for attention than because she was responding to command, Trevor speculated.

Rather than reattaching the leash, Caleb reached down to pick up the dog, preparing to carry her inside. He staggered a little when he discovered that the compact dog was heavier than she looked, as Trevor already knew, but he righted himself quickly and moved toward the door. He paused just before stepping inside, looking suspiciously from his mother to Trevor.

"Aren't you coming in?"

"We'll be right in," Jade assured him. "Close the door, please."

Though he didn't look particularly happy about it, Caleb followed her instruction.

Waiting until the door was securely closed, Jade turned to Trevor. "Well? Did he say anything to you?"

"He really likes his dog."

"Yes, that's great," she said, waving a hand impatiently, "but what did he say about school? Is everything okay? Was it a fight or was it really just an accident? Should I be worried?"

"It didn't come up and I didn't ask. Not my place."

"Oh. Of course."

Was she disappointed that he hadn't asked?

Feeling completely out of his field of expertise, and not liking his uncharacteristic lack of confidence, he glanced at his watch again. "I really do have to go, Jade."

"Of course." She laced her hands in front of her, as if she didn't know what else to do with them. "Thanks again for the help."

"Any time." He took a step toward her and lifted her chin with one hand. "You're a wonderful mother, Jade. Your kids are damned lucky to have you."

The compliment was impulsive, but sincere. He was glad he'd said it when he saw some of the worry leave her pretty face to be replaced by a gratified smile. "Thank you, Trevor. Most days I think I'm doing pretty well, but there are others when I honestly have no clue. Anyway, it's nice to hear a vote of confidence."

He would have liked to kiss her then, but he resisted "I'll just say my good-nights to your family and be on my way. Good luck with your first night with Zoe."

"I'll probably put her in her crate for tonight."

Trevor chuckled. "If you really think she won't end up in bed with Caleb, you're kidding yourself. He's hooked hard."

She sighed. "You're probably right."

Grinning, he chucked her chin lightly. "Haven't you heard? I'm always right."

With a humorous roll of her eyes, she opened the door and walked inside.

CHAPTER TWELVE

AMY AND LINCOLN were married at the courthouse Friday afternoon at two o'clock. Jade and Verita were the only witnesses, and they made several good-natured jokes about how they assisted their respective doctors in their personal lives as well as their practices. They had all changed into street clothes after the clinic closed for the afternoon and headed straight for the courthouse in separate vehicles. Verita was live streaming the brief but lovely ceremony for the benefit of family and friends—their virtual guest list, as Amy referred to it.

Despite the teasing, Jade was touched by how radiant the happy couple was to make this public confirmation of their commitment to each other and the child they were expecting. She found herself thinking again of how young and innocent she'd been when she and Stephen had exchanged vows. It was different for the two couples she'd seen married in the past month, she mused. They were older, more experienced, more clear-eyed than she'd been. Yet she saw in them hints of the same eagerness for this new adventure, the same optimism that they would weather any storms, the same sense of hope and promise she'd once experienced.

It was a nice feeling, she thought with just a touch of wistfulness. She couldn't help wondering if she would ever experience anything like it again. That connection with another person. That shared passion for each other and for the future. Did she even want to go through that with another man, especially considering the risk that something could again go tragically wrong?

A deep shiver went through her when a sudden image of Trevor popped into her head. Not just any random vision—a very specific picture of him leaning over her in bed, naked and damp and sharing low, intimate laughter. Unnerved by the heat that rushed through her at this most inappropriate time, she told herself to stop being so foolish and pay attention to the ceremony being conducted in front of her.

They all moved out to the courthouse steps for hugs and snapshots following the ceremony. Amy and Lincoln left straight from there for a weekend beach-cottage honeymoon, after which they'd be back at work Monday morning. Jade and Verita lingered on the steps for a few more minutes to chat before Jade heard her name called by a male voice from behind her. She looked around to find Walt Becker descending from the courthouse.

She supposed it was no surprise to find a local attorney at the courthouse. Still, it gave her an odd feeling to have him pop up right after she'd had more than a few lascivious thoughts about his best friend.

Saying she'd see Jade at the clinic Monday, Verita left then, leaving Jade to wait for Walt to approach.

"I thought that was you, Jade," Walt said jovially. "Nice to see you. I hope I didn't interrupt your conversation."

"No. My friend and I were just saying goodbye for the weekend. We're coworkers at the clinic and were here this afternoon as witnesses for a wedding between our bosses."

"You told me you work for one of the doctors at the clinic, right?"

She nodded. "Yes. Amy Ford, my boss who is also my cousin. She just married her partner, Dr. Lincoln Brindle. They've been together quite a long time, but they decided to make it formal today."

"Well, mazel tov to the lucky couple." He tilted his head to study her as if he'd had a sudden inspiration. "Do you have to hurry off now?"

She looked at her watch. "No. Mary Pat's picking up the kids after school to take them to a park this afternoon. I said I'd join them later for an early dinner out, but I don't have to rush."

"Want to have coffee?" He motioned toward a chain coffee shop across the street from the courthouse. "It's not as good as The Perkery, but they do serve a decent pumpkin bread."

Jade didn't want pumpkin bread, but she wouldn't turn down a pumpkin spice latte. After all, it was that time of year when pumpkin seemed to be in everything. She nodded. "That sounds nice."

A few minutes later, they sat at a little table by the window, she with her latte and Walt with his coffee and pumpkin bread. They chatted about the wedding she'd just attended, the clinic, her children, the new puppy who was settling in with only a few minor calamities.

Walt laughed in response to her anecdotes about the new family member. "Puppies have a way of turning a household upside down. The kids will love her, though."

"They're already besotted. And she loves them back—though to be honest, she's bonded most closely with Caleb."

Jade had been heartened by how much happier Caleb had seemed that week, ever since she'd brought Zoe home. He seemed more open and smiling, more like his former self. He'd come home from school each day with no fresh injuries, thank goodness, so maybe he really had just been clumsy. He'd spent hours watching dog training videos and then trying to apply the instructions to Zoe.

"A boy and his dog," Walt commented. "Can't beat it."

"So, how is Maddie? I really enjoyed meeting her at Elle's wedding."

"She likes you, too. She said you and Elle are planning a girls' night when Trev and Shane and I go on our fishing trip sometime after the busy holiday season."

"I'm looking forward to it."

"So's Maddie. I'm sure she'll want to talk about the wedding. Frankly, I envy your friends with their no-fuss courthouse wedding, but Mads wants a little more ceremony. It's a first for her. Second for me," he admitted ruefully, "but this one's going to be the last for both of us."

"I believe you." And she did.

"Trev told me about helping you surprise the kids with the dog," Walt said casually. "Said he got a real kick out of it."

"Yes, he was very helpful. I was happy to have his assistance. It would have been a bit harder for me to juggle everything on my own, though of course I'd have managed."

"No doubt," Walt commented into his coffee cup. "Trevor enjoys helping people. Laps it up."

The words arrowed straight to her pride, making her frown. "I know he supports a lot of charities, but I hope he doesn't see my family as one of them."

"He sees your family as his friends," Walt corrected her gently. "He likes to help his friends, too."

Somewhat mollified, she tilted her head to study him from across the table. "Does he ever let his friends help him in return?"

"Not often. He's sort of compulsive about being the one rushing to the rescue rather than being rescued."

"Why do you suppose he's so resistant to accepting help?" she asked, figuring Walt knew Trevor better than just about anyone. "Do you think it's because his parents expected so much from him growing up? He just never got in the habit of depending on anyone else?"

"That probably has a lot to do with it. But—"

She lifted her eyebrows, sensing that *but* led to something important. "You think there's something else?"

After a moment, Walt grimaced. "I don't like gossiping about my friends, but—well, Trev's obviously very fond of you, and you seem to like him a lot, too. So, I'll just say that I think Trevor struggles with some survivor's guilt. He's mentioned to me several times that he wasn't even serving in a battle zone when his wife died. He was chained to an admin desk. The army gets a guy with an MBA, they're going to put all that education to good use. Still, he went through boot camp, and he trained with guys who died in battle or came back with lifelong reminders, both physical and mental."

He touched his prosthetic arm as if in illustration. "I'm no shrink, but I think Trev subconsciously feels that he has to compensate for having come home physically unscathed when so many didn't, even though his talent with numbers and logistics were more useful in other areas. I think that partially explains his insistence on doing everything he possibly can to help veterans and, though not to the same extent, other worthwhile causes."

It was an interesting hypothesis—and one Jade found to have merit, considering what she knew of Trevor. Trevor probably wouldn't like hearing it, of course. Wouldn't like being analyzed, his psyche summarized so tidily. Who would?

So why was Walt, who was Trevor's best friend, and a lawyer who understood better than most the value of discretion, saying these things to her now? Did he think her relationship with Trevor was more serious than it was, or that she didn't know Trevor as well as she should?

"I'm sure there are a lot of reasons for what

Trevor does, but it all comes down to him being a compassionate man with a generous nature," she said, picking up her coffee cup. "He's a good friend."

"The best," Walt agreed. "And as much a true hero as anyone I've ever known."

"I can tell he feels the same about you. Maybe his pride makes him resist your offers of help, as I understand very well—but deep down, he appreciates them very much, don't you think?"

With a shrug, Walt replied, "Yeah. I do. And maybe you're really getting to know him, after all."

Had this whole conversation been his way of determining that? Suddenly uncomfortable, due more to her own conflicted emotions than to Walt's probably well-intentioned fishing, she swallowed the last of her coffee and then reached for her purse. "I really should be going. Thank you for the coffee, Walt. Tell Maddie hello for me, and that I'm looking forward to seeing her again."

"I will." He rose and walked with her across the street to where she'd parked her car.

She had her driver's door open and was just about to get in when Walt spoke. "You're good for Trevor, Jade. You challenge him. You get behind the facade. There aren't many of us who can accomplish that."

She was startled by his words for reasons she didn't entirely understand. Perhaps because Walt was attributing too much importance to her in Trevor's life. Or maybe it was the reference to the facade, corroborating her own observation that Trevor kept a great deal hidden behind that charming demeanor. Though she'd suspected she had a somewhat rare knack for getting behind the veneer to the real Trevor, it shook her to hear his longtime friend's confirmation.

"I have enough matchmakers in my life, Walt," she warned him, trying to keep her tone light though she meant every word. "I wouldn't expect you to be one."

He scowled comically. "Hell, no, I'm not a matchmaker. Just saying, that's all."

"Yes, well, let's just leave it at that, m'kay?"

A reluctant smile tugged at his lips. "You got it."

Satisfied that she'd made her point, she left to collect her kids, but she knew she would think about her conversation with Walt when she was alone again that night. She'd wonder if he was right about what drove Trevor's almost compulsive charitable participation. And then she would question again why Walt had seemed so intent on sharing those details with her.

"How was the wedding?"

"It was nice. Very intimate, with just the four of us there, but several of their family and friends watched Verita's streaming video, so they were able to share the moment. My aunt and my mom and Lincoln's parents and sisters all watched live."

"Modern technology is great, right?"

Jade smiled into the smartphone at her ear as she chatted with Trevor from the quiet privacy of her patio later that night. "Yes, it is."

She pulled her sweater a little tighter against the coolish night air before asking, "Did you talk to Walt this afternoon?"

"No. Why?"

"I ran into him at the courthouse after the wedding. He and I had a cup of coffee together and chatted for a few minutes."

"Did you?" He sounded as if he didn't know what to think about that. "I thought my ears were burning this afternoon," he joked.

"Think a lot of yourself, don't you? What makes you think we talked about you?" she teased lightly, though she was sure he had no doubt. Perhaps that was why he sounded a bit wary.

"Ah. So my buddy was trying to move in on my…uh…friend, huh? You remember he has a fiancée, right?"

Even as she responded with the expected laugh, she wondered what word he'd almost said before he'd hastily swapped it for *friend*.

"I like Walt, Trevor."

"Of course you do. He's a great guy. One of the real-life heroes."

Maybe Walt was right that subconsciously Trevor compared himself to other veterans and wasn't sure he measured up.

He changed the subject rather abruptly. "So, anyway, Mary Pat has been hinting nonstop that she'd like to spend another evening with the kids, so it would be a good time for me to take you out to dinner or something. Apparently they talked about a movie they want to watch with her, and it's available now for streaming. So, how about it? Want to have dinner with me tomorrow night and leave them to their movie?"

Jade bit her lip, torn between accepting and finding an excuse to politely decline. Did he really keep asking her out because he was in town and at loose ends for an evening between work obligations? She found it hard to believe he was simply giving his housekeeper an excuse to spend an evening with the kids.

"As flattering as that offer was…"

He interrupted with a groan. "It was awful, wasn't it? Let me try again. I would very much enjoy spending an evening with you, Jade. I always enjoy being with you. There's a community theater production of *Driving Miss Daisy* tomorrow night and I have front-row tickets because

I'm a theater patron. Would you do me the honor of attending with me and letting Mary Pat spend an evening with your children?"

She was smiling before he finished, ruefully aware that her willpower was ridiculously weak where Trevor was concerned. The man was so damned charming. She had fun with him. With most of her life organized around responsibilities and family schedules, neither of which she resented at all, it was hard to resist a little extra fun. "Okay, I'll go," she said, "but only because I happen to adore that play, not because of your smooth invitation."

"Got it. I won't let your acceptance go to my head."

She chuckled softly. "Good."

He laughed, too, and she wished she could see his smile. Trevor had such a nice smile.

"So, I'll see you tomorrow."

"Yes." Whatever this was between them, she wasn't yet ready to see it end, though she hoped she was emotionally prepared for that eventuality when Trevor's lull between business trips ended and his overtaxed attentions turned elsewhere.

DRESSED IN A simple black sheath for the play Saturday evening, Jade tapped on Caleb's closed bedroom door. She heard a muffled sound she took to be "Come in" and opened the door to poke in her head. Caleb sat on his bed with an open textbook, Zoe curled up and snoring beside him. Jade had given up early on banning the dog from her son's bed. She chose her battles more shrewdly.

"Mary Pat will be here in a few minutes. She's looking forward to seeing you, so don't spend the whole evening in your room, okay?"

He nodded. "I don't know why you and Trevor can't stay here with the rest of us," he said.

"I told you, he has tickets to a play and he asked me to go as his guest."

"Just seems like he'd rather be alone with you than spending time with all of us," Caleb grumbled.

Jade winced. Was Caleb resentful of the time Jade spent with Trevor? Had she worried too much about Bella getting overly attached to Trevor when Caleb was the one most likely to bond with the man, perhaps most prone to missing a father in his life?

Or—she gulped—was her almost-teenage son beginning to wonder about her sex life? That subject would most definitely make him surly, as most teenagers preferred to see their parents as asexual beings selflessly—and unobtrusively—dedicated to the service of their children. She didn't have time to discuss such things with him now, and wasn't prepared for that talk. Not that she would confirm to him when she did whether she and Trevor had been intimate, but perhaps she should make it clear that there were certain parts of her adult life that just weren't open to negotiation.

"Trevor enjoys spending time with the whole family," she insisted. "Like I said, he already had these tickets, so maybe we'll have him over for dinner or something soon if he has the time. I know I don't have to say this, but please be nice to Mary Pat and help her if she needs anything this evening. She loves you and your sisters very much."

"I know. And I'm always nice to Mary Pat, Mom."

She patted his shoulder. "You are. Because you love her, too. And I love you, Caleb. Never forget that."

Wondering if there was something more she should say, she hesitated a moment longer until she heard Erin yelling from the living room, "Mom, they're here!"

Zoe lifted her head, then jumped down off the bed and lit out for the other room, probably aware that new people had entered and eager to find out who it was and if they'd brought treats or belly rubs with them. Putting his school book aside, Caleb stood to follow, so that Jade had no real choice but to fall in behind him to greet their guests.

Because there was nothing she could do about Caleb for now, Jade focused on enjoying her evening with Trevor. They made it to the theater just in time to take their seats before the curtains rose. As they were escorted in by a deferential usher, Jade was uncomfortably aware that many sets of eyes were on them. She didn't usually worry about what other people thought of her, but still she felt the weight of that attention as she and this prominent business leader settled into the front row for the play.

The production was quite good for a rather small theater company. The sets looked professional, the actors were talented and there were very few glitches in the performance of the play Jade knew almost by heart. And even as familiar as the lines were to her, she still laughed at the funny ones and sniffled a little during the heart-wrenching scenes. She tried to hide the latter from Trevor but apparently failed at that. He reached over and took her hand, giving her fingers a squeeze. He didn't immediately release her. For the next few minutes her attention was evenly divided between the stage and the strong hand laced warmly with hers.

After quite a few curtain calls to enthusiastic applause, the curtains lowered for the final time and the house lights came up. It took Trevor and Jade several minutes to exit because they were stopped so often by people who knew one or the other of them—okay, mostly Trevor—but eventually they were strapped in his car and on their way.

"I know we have to get back to your house soon, but maybe we could take time for another walk on the beach first?" Trevor suggested. "It's such a nice night."

"I think we could make a little time for that," she said.

He promptly turned the car toward the coastline. She didn't know the road he took, but it led to a beautiful stretch of moonlit sand that was completely deserted. She kicked off her shoes when she slid out of Trevor's car. It took him a bit longer to shed shoes and socks and roll up his pants legs, but then he joined her as she walked toward the water, stopping on the wet sand where the breakers almost lapped at her toes. The breeze was cool, but the thin black cardigan she'd donned over her dress kept her comfortable enough.

They didn't speak for several long minutes. Jade appreciated that Trevor gave her room to unwind without filling that space with words. Eventually, he took her hand and smiled down at her. "Do you want to walk, or are you good standing here?"

"I'm very good here," she said, sliding her hands up his chest and offering her mouth to him. She blamed the impulse on the moonlight.

He accepted the invitation instantly and eagerly.

The kiss lasted a very long time, then led into another. And another. They pressed so tightly together that not even a breeze could slip between them. There was no way for her to miss that Trevor was fully aroused, hard and hungry against her. In return, he had to feel her racing heart, her accelerated breathing making her breasts rise and fall against him.

Bliss.

His hands tangled in her hair, holding her head at the perfect angle to accommodate his mouth. She had her arms around him, her palms sweeping over planes and angles, lingering at the places where she knew just how to draw a groan from him.

When they stopped eventually to breathe and cool off a bit, he rested his forehead on hers with a deep sigh. "If we didn't have to get back to your house…"

Regretfully, she nodded against him. "But we do."

"Maybe we could slip away for a weekend

sometime. I'd like to show you my place in Texas. Or the site in Florida. Mary Pat would be glad to—"

"Trevor." Frowning, she stepped back, giving him a look that caused him to stop right there. "We should go. It's getting late."

Nodding, he turned in silence to walk with her to the car. She brushed off her feet before sliding in, then looked out her window at the peaceful scenery while Trevor put on his socks and shoes. She heard the snap of his seatbelt and then the car started, but he didn't put it into gear.

"Jade, I wasn't suggesting we go off every weekend. Not even next weekend, for that matter. It was just wishful thinking that maybe sometime in the future, we could get away for a couple of days."

She thought of her son, sulking in his room. Of Bella, who rarely let a day go by without mention of Trevor and still drew in her journal for him every night. Of family and friends who had become increasingly less subtle about nudging her and Trevor closer together. Of the lifted eyebrows and curious gazes that greeted them every time they were seen as a couple in public, attention that perturbed her despite her attempts to brush off gossip as inconsequential.

She remembered her own restless nights and the moments she found herself aimlessly daydreaming in the middle of a busy day. And the undeniable fact that she had been tempted, if only for a moment, to forget the reasons she needed to get home and instead find a private place to make passionate love to Trevor for the remainder of this perfect night.

She thought of Trevor's admission that he didn't think of himself as father material, and of her own reluctance to bring anyone new into her family. Especially a man with commitment issue and a predilection for frequent travel and dangerous sports. So just where did he see this no-strings affair heading?

"We should go, Trevor," she said, keeping her tone gentle. "It's time."

He looked disgruntled as he put the car into gear and drove away from the beach. She couldn't say whether it was because they were having to bring their evening to a close or because he wasn't satisfied with her non-answers to his questions. Probably a combination of both.

They didn't say much on the way back to her house. She deliberately kept what little conversation they shared centered around the play they'd seen. As they pulled into her driveway she thought the night would end on that note, but Trevor put out a hand when she reached for her door handle.

"Whatever is bothering you, we'll work it out,"

he said quietly. "I'm not trying to interfere in your life."

Seeing the gravity in his eyes, she tried to keep her tone reassuring. "I know, Trevor. You've been nothing but kind to me and to my family."

The words didn't seem to notably appease him, but it was the best she could do at the moment.

"Let's go in," she said, opening her door this time before he could detain her again. She thought he might have liked to kiss her good-night. As much as her lips ached for that kiss, she decided it best to avoid it this time.

Perhaps because she feared it would feel too much like a kiss goodbye rather than good-night.

"IS THERE ANYTHING else I can do for you now, Trevor?" Tamar asked, pausing in the doorway of his office. "If not, I'm going to go grab some lunch with Patty and Selena while Jay mans the desk downstairs."

"Mmm? Oh, yeah, sure. Have lunch. Take your time, I'm good here." He didn't even look around from his computer as he spoke.

Tamar hesitated so long that he finally looked around at her in question. "Something else?"

"No. But—well, is everything okay, Trevor? You've been awfully quiet this week since you got back from Florida. You said everything's okay there, right?"

"Yeah. Sure." For the first time in months, he could say that everything was right on track in Florida, at least according to the most recent job estimates. "It's going great down there."

"And Texas?"

"Yeah. All good now that the new assistant manager is on board. Seems efficient and personable, so I think that situation will work out fine. Everything's good, Tamar. Hell, you'll know probably before me if any problems crop up at any of our properties."

"True," she acknowledged with only a trace of smugness that faded when she asked, "What about your family? Everyone well?"

Had he really been so difficult recently that even his fearlessly straightforward assistant seemed to be tiptoeing around him? He smiled when he replied, "Everyone's fine, Tamar, thanks. I had lunch with my parents Sunday and all Mom could talk about was how much she'd enjoyed their cruise."

"And what about Jade's family?" She looked even more studiedly nonchalant, if possible. "They're all well, too? Have you seen them lately?"

"Not in a while." He turned back to his computer. "We've all been very busy, but I've heard they're fine, too. Enjoy your lunch, Tamar."

The hint hadn't been at all subtle, and she conceded with a sigh. "I will. Can I bring you anything?"

"No, I'm good, thanks. Late breakfast."

"Okay. Well, see you in an hour or so."

"Mmm." He hit Save and watched as the file he'd been studying disappeared from the screen in front of him. He quickly called up another. Staying busy was pretty much his modus operandi these days, even more than in the past. It kept him from letting his thoughts wander to uncomfortable places. As they were doing now, despite his efforts.

He hadn't seen Jade since the night they'd attended the play together, almost two weeks ago. Granted, he'd been swamped with work here for a good percentage of that time, but on the evenings he'd have been able to see her, she'd always had other plans with her kids. She hadn't invited him to join them.

She was avoiding him. She took his calls when he checked in with her, but kept the conversations as airy as Elle's meringues. When he tried to talk about seeing her again, or even hinted at the intimacies they'd shared thus far, she deflected the conversation with the skill of an escape artist.

He didn't know what he'd done to spook the normally unflappable Jade this way. One minute they'd been kissing on the beach, the next minute she'd shut him down and hadn't opened back up since. The only thing he'd said was that someday he'd like to spend a weekend with her. Considering their history, he hadn't thought that was such an outlandish comment.

So what was going on with her?

Had she taken his suggestion as an attempt to take their loosely defined relationship to the next level? It hadn't been; he'd been content with the way things were going between them. Amusing phone calls late at night, time spent with her when they could arrange it.

Okay, maybe he'd have liked to be able to schedule that private time even more often than they had—after all, he was a healthy male with a normal sex drive and Jade was…Jade. Honestly, there was no one else he wanted to be with just now. Which didn't mean he was trying to force her into a commitment. He knew she wasn't interested in anything more than they had. She'd made that clear. Abundantly clear, he thought with a scowl he forced himself to smooth.

Should he try to convince her not to call it quits just yet, or should he just let it go?

His personal phone rang in his pocket, and he stretched to reach for it. He frowned when he saw the number on the screen, one he didn't recognize. He didn't usually answer such calls, but something made him take this one. "Trevor Farrell."

"Trevor?"

The voice was young, shaky and—frightened? Still, he identified it immediately. "Caleb? Is that you?"

"Yes. You said I could call you if I need anything."

"I did. What's wrong, Caleb?" Trevor felt his heart give a thump in response to the kid's obvious distress. "Is it something with your mother? Your sisters?"

"No, nothing like that."

"It's not Zoe, is it?" Though Trevor would hate for anything to happen to the little dog, he couldn't help being relieved that Jade and the girls were apparently okay.

"No. It's—it's me, Trevor. I'm sort of in trouble and I…well, I didn't know who else to call. I mean, you could be in Florida or somewhere and I—well. I'll figure out something."

Trying to follow the disjointed words punctuated by unnerving sniffles, Trevor spoke firmly. "I'm not in Florida. I'm at Wind Shadow and I can drop everything and come to wherever you are right now if you need me."

"Really? 'Cause I kind of do. Need you, I mean. And please don't call my mom."

His stomach tightened again, but Trevor kept his tone even when he said, "Just tell me where you are, Caleb. I'm on my way."

CHAPTER THIRTEEN

IT WAS JUST BEFORE two in the afternoon when Jade rushed into her house, her heart pounding in her throat. She'd gotten a call at work from Caleb's school informing her that Caleb had gotten into a fight in the gym locker room and couldn't be found on the campus after he hadn't shown up for his next class. Her sympathetic coworkers had offered to fill in for her so she could go look for her son, and she'd already had her keys in hand when Trevor had called to let her know Caleb was with him. Trevor had promised they would be waiting at her house when she arrived.

Trevor had given her only the most basic details of what was going on with her son. Apparently, and inconceivably, Caleb had gotten lost wandering around town after running away from his school. He'd found Trevor's card in his backpack and had dialed him for help rather than calling his mother at work.

"He's bruised and scared, but he's not badly hurt," Trevor had assured her. "I haven't really talked with him about it yet. I thought it best if we wait until you get here."

Jade was utterly bewildered by her son's behavior, both at school and in calling Trevor. He had never been in trouble at school before, always a model student. And why on earth would he call Trevor instead of her?

Closing the front door behind her with more force than necessary, she tossed her purse and keys on the entryway table and called out, "Caleb?"

Trevor appeared from the living room, his expression solemn but calm. "Caleb's out in the backyard with Zoe. He needed a little time with her to prepare himself for talking with you, I think."

She pressed both of her unsteady hands to her aching temples. "Oh, my God, Trevor, what's going on? Why on earth did he feel the need to run away from school? Why didn't he call me?"

Trevor reached out to squeeze her forearm lightly. "I should warn you, his face looks worse than it is. I talked him into using an ice pack, but he's going to have a shiner. And his glasses will need to be replaced. I was able to straighten them enough for him to wear them for now, but they'll never be quite right again."

"Oh, my God," she moaned again. "Did he tell you what the fight was about? Who started it? Or why he ran away? Was he being bullied? Does he need to see a doctor?"

"No, I don't think so, though I'll leave that decision to you, obviously. I found him behind the shopping center on the west side of town, a good four miles from his school. He got in my car, looked out the side window and refused to say anything other than to mutter a thanks that I came to get him. To be honest, I think he regretted calling me after he did. I don't think he understands himself why he dialed me instead of you. Panic, I think."

"I have to talk to him."

She started to move toward the kitchen, but Trevor didn't let go of her arm. "Take a breath," he advised. "He's probably going to be surly and defiant with you at first, and that's going to make you even more upset, but inside he's scared and miserable."

"I know my son, Trevor," she snapped, then stopped herself with a sharply indrawn breath. What was she doing? "I'm sorry. It's unfair of me to take this out on you when you've only tried to help. I should be thanking you instead of sniping at you."

"I understand. This has got to be making you crazy. It's just that I've been in Caleb's shoes, and I remember what it was like. You're not nearly as scary as my parents—either of them," he added with a wry twist of his lips, "but I'm sure Caleb knows he messed up when he ran away, if not before."

Because Trevor did seem to understand, Jade gave herself a couple of beats to breathe deeply and try to calm down before talking to her son. When she determined her shaken emotions were under control, she nodded to him.

After searching her face and apparently reaching the same conclusion, he released her arm with a final, supportive squeeze. "Do you want me to call him in?"

"Yes, thank you." That would give her another minute to prepare herself, she decided.

She managed not to gasp when she saw her son, but it took an effort. The right side of Caleb's face was swollen and scraped, and an ugly bruise was definitely blooming around his eye behind his crooked glasses. He carried a medical cold pack from her freezer clenched in his left hand. She hoped he'd been using it while he was outside. Zoe bounced inside behind him, sniffing her shoes in greeting, then going straight to Trevor for pats and rubs.

"Let me see those scrapes." Jade was grateful her voice sounded relatively composed despite her state of mind. She opened the freezer and took out another of the cold packs she kept on hand for accidents. Swapping it for the one he'd held, she took his chin and turned his face to examine the darkening bruises.

"I don't see anything that needs medical attention," she said after a moment, relieved in that respect, at least. "The cold pack should help with the discomfort, though you're going to be very sore for a few days. Hold that pack to your face and sit down. We're going to talk."

"Maybe I should go," Trevor suggested, inching toward the doorway.

"No," Caleb said quickly, automatically reaching out toward him before jerking his hand back. "You can stay," he added in a mutter.

Jade narrowed her eyes at her son. Maybe it wouldn't be such a bad thing for Trevor to stay a while longer, she conceded. He did seem to have an understanding of the teenage male mind that eluded her at the moment.

She glanced at him. "I know you must be very busy, so if you have to go now, feel free. But maybe you'd like a glass of tea before you leave?"

Seemingly accepting the offer for what it was—her second of Caleb's request for him to stay—Trevor nodded. "That sounds good, thanks. I could use a cold drink before I go."

She pulled a pitcher of iced tea from the fridge and poured three glasses, setting them on the table. Trevor sat and reached for one of the glasses, looking prepared to sip quietly unless called on for his opinion. Showing no interest in his drink, Caleb slumped into another chair, hiding most of his face behind the cold pack. He'd removed his glasses and set them on the table, and the one eye not covered by the pack was half hidden now behind the fringe of hair he liked to wear shaggy.

Settling into her own seat, Jade wrapped her hands tightly around the tea she didn't really want and said, "Okay, let's have it. What happened? And why on earth did you leave the school without permission? Do you know how much trouble you're in?"

Caleb started off defensively, as Trevor had predicted. "It wasn't my fault. I wasn't the one who started it."

"What happened?" she insisted, keeping her gaze leveled on her son even though he was stubbornly avoiding her eyes.

He spoke in a mumble she strained to follow. "There's a bully at my school. Name is Theo. Jerk. He keeps picking on me and on some of the other kids. He pushes me down when we run the track, and he shoved my face into my locker when I was taking out some books. Today he and a couple of his friends jumped me in the locker room just because I tried to stick up for another kid they were picking on."

Sickened, Jade shook her head slowly, hating

the mental images called up by Caleb's account. "Why didn't you report to the principal or your teachers that this has been going on? Why didn't you tell *me*?"

"I thought I could handle it," he grumbled with a shrug. "I didn't want to be the new kid who ran to tattle."

"Why did you leave the school?" she persisted. She figured she needed to hear everything before she started lecturing him. "Were you afraid?"

If possible, his expression turned even more sullen. "The gym teacher came in just in time to see me throw a punch to defend myself. All the other guys said I started the fight. The kid I was trying to help rabbited and didn't stay around long enough to stick up for me. I didn't leave because I was scared. I was pi—uh, I was mad. I wasn't in the mood to go to class and have everyone staring at me."

"Did the teacher listen to your side of the story?" Jade would definitely be calling a meeting with the school administration, regardless of Caleb's answer. Reportedly this school had a zero-tolerance policy on bullying. She intended to make sure it was being applied. Caleb would accept whatever penalties he received for leaving the campus, but she expected the school leaders to make it clear that her son would not have to be afraid in school.

Caleb shrugged "I didn't say much. I was too mad. And, like I said, I didn't want to snitch. I wanted to show those assholes I can take care of myself."

"That's not the way to handle this, Caleb, and watch your language. You know very well how I feel about fighting. If you're being bullied, or even if you see it happening to someone else, you should tell a teacher or another adult. As for leaving school the way you did, that was dangerous and completely unacceptable. We'll discuss the consequences after I've had time to process all of this. But first, I want you to apologize to Trevor for dragging him into this. I'm sure he had important things to do this afternoon, and you interrupted his schedule."

"I told Caleb to call if he ever needed me," Trevor said with a shake of his head. "I meant every word of it. He owes apologies, to you, especially, but not to me."

Jade saw Caleb dart a quick look at Trevor, perhaps in gratitude. Between the cold pack and the hair in his face, it was hard to tell for certain. She thought she'd done a fairly good job of damping down her distress and shock, but her son knew her well enough to know that she wasn't going to just brush this off.

She looked at the clock over the stove, seeing that she had a little more than an hour before picking the girls up. Looking back at Caleb, she saw him wince when he shifted the cold pack.

"I'll get you an anti-inflammatory tablet from the medicine cabinet," she said, standing. "Don't move until I get back."

She glanced at Trevor, and he nodded. She sensed that he wanted a moment alone to talk with her son. It made her uncomfortable that her first instinct was to linger, to forestall that, and then to realize that the only reason for her resistance was knee-jerk territorialism.

It made her even more unnerved to realize how much she would have liked to just burrow into his strong arms and hide from all of this, if only for a brief respite.

She moved toward the door with a go-ahead gesture to Trevor to let him know that she'd sensed his hesitation and was giving her assent. Maybe it would help for him to talk to her son. After all, Caleb had called Trevor, even if he'd wanted to change his mind afterward.

She waited only until she was sure she was out of their sight before she allowed herself to bury her face in her hands and draw a shuddering breath.

IT WAS QUIET in the kitchen after Jade stepped out, with only the ticking of the decorative wall clock and Zoe munching at her kibble to fill the silence. Trevor looked steadily at Caleb, waiting for the boy to look up before he spoke.

Caleb was the first to crack. Drawing a sharp breath, he glared at Trevor from behind his screen of bangs. "Well? Are you going to yell at me, too?"

Jade hadn't actually raised her voice to her son, but Trevor decided not to argue the point now. He was sure Caleb felt yelled at, despite the technicalities. "No, Caleb. I'm not going to yell at you. I figure you already know you didn't make your best decisions today."

After a moment, Caleb nodded and said quietly, "I shouldn't have left school."

"No, you shouldn't have. And you should have reported the bullying when it first started, before it got to this point. You should have at least confided in your mom."

The boy straightened his shoulders then, lifting his chin in a proudly defiant stance. "My dad said a real man doesn't go looking for trouble, but he doesn't run from it, either. My dad said it's everyone's responsibility to stand up for what's right. That's why he was a marine. He wasn't afraid to fight. I didn't run to snitch and I didn't leave school because I was afraid. I was just mad."

Trevor grimaced slightly and glanced toward the kitchen doorway, hoping to see Jade entering again. He didn't know how he'd ended up in this position, but he felt utterly unqualified to be here, especially when it came to dealing with the boy's memories of his father, whom he'd obviously once idolized and had now idealized.

Because he was apparently on his own for the moment, Trevor weighed his words carefully. "I didn't say you should run away. And I applaud you for defending others. But you should always choose the smartest way to intervene. If there's absolutely no other option, sure, sometimes you have to risk physically fighting back. But if there are authorities nearby to deal with the situation— teachers or police officers or other adults—the best thing is to report to them, then step back. It's not the cowardly way, Caleb. Don't think of it as being a snitch. Think of it as following protocol and making sure proper steps are taken."

Caleb frowned, obviously not yet convinced.

Trevor cleared his throat. "Your dad was a hero, Caleb, there's no doubt about that. He paid the ultimate price fighting for what he believed in."

That brought the boy's chin up again, though his lower lip quivered just for a moment. "Yeah. He did."

"But," Trevor added quietly, "your father was first a soldier. And soldiers have a chain of command that they follow without question, isn't that right?"

"Well—"

"Your dad saluted those above him in rank and followed their orders because that was the right thing for him to do. He wouldn't have disrespected his ranking officers, right? Nor refused to follow their commands? Just as the men who served under him obeyed the instructions he gave them."

"Well, yeah."

"The chain of command at your school means that you report to your teachers and your administration," Trevor pressed on. "If you think rules are being ignored or applied unfairly, you should discuss it with your mom, who will always take your side when you approach it the right way. Always."

"*You* were never in combat," Caleb muttered beneath his breath.

Telling himself it was only a final, defensive jab because the kid knew he'd lost this battle, Trevor tried not to let it sting. Though it did sting, having hit the vulnerable spot Trevor was always aware of even while he did everything he could as a civilian to support those who'd sacrificed so much more than he.

"No, I never saw combat," he agreed. "I trained for it, and I was prepared for it, but my superiors thought my talents were better utilized in other ways. I wasn't a hero like your dad, but like him, I followed my orders."

Caleb didn't seem to have an answer to that. He twisted the cold pack in his hands on the table, his head bent to hide his bruised face.

Taking pity on the kid, Trevor reached out to lay a hand on Caleb's forearm. "Caleb, I know what it's like to try to live up to a father's legacy. I've spent my whole life living in the shadow of several generations of successful businessmen who not only expected but demanded that I follow in their footsteps. I made more than a few dumb mistakes trying to prove I was my own man and not just a reflection of them. Joining the army wasn't one of those mistakes. I'm proud of my service."

He cleared his throat before adding, "My family set a great example for me in leadership and hard work and integrity. Your dad did the same for you, and you should take his lessons to heart. But you have to forge your own path, too. Find your own way. You're a great guy, Caleb, with a good heart. Your dad would be proud of you, just like your mom is."

"Just as your mother will always be." Jade stepped into the room as she reiterated Trevor's assurance to her son. Trevor wasn't sure how much she'd heard before she came in, but her eyes glittered as if with unshed tears. "I love you,

Caleb, and I will always be proud of you. I know you thought you were doing the right thing, but we'll discuss better ways of handling those situations in the future while we're dealing with the repercussions of this one."

Judging it was time to leave mother and son to that discussion, Trevor looked at his watch. "I should go. I'm glad you called me, Caleb. Feel free to do so again if you ever need anything."

The boy nodded. Trevor stood and placed a hand on the boy's hunched shoulder, leaning over to say quietly, "Does Theo have a black eye, too?"

"Trevor," Jade said with a sigh and shake of her head.

Caleb's swollen lips twitched. "Yeah. Maybe."

"That's a real shame," Trevor said gravely, giving the boy's shoulder a little squeeze. "See you later, kid."

Zoe whined at the back door, wanting to go out now that she'd eaten. Caleb stood quickly. "I'll let her out."

"I'll walk Trevor to the front door," his mother said. "And then you and I will talk until I have to go get the girls."

"Yes, ma'am." The unenthusiastic response was barely audible as the boy opened the door and hurried out with the dog.

Tugging at the hem of her blue scrubs top in an uncharacteristically nervous gesture, Jade turned to Trevor then. "Thank you again, Trevor. And again, I'm sorry you got dragged into this."

"Stop apologizing. Friends help each other out. You'd have shown up for me if I'd called."

"I would, yes," she conceded, then grimaced. "It just seems like I'm the one who always calls on you for help. I have to admit that's getting a little hard to swallow."

"I wish you wouldn't feel that way. I'm convinced you're quite capable of handling any problems in your family without help from me—or anyone else, for that matter. It makes me feel good to help my friends when I can, and I wouldn't hesitate to call you if I needed you, if that makes you feel any better about it."

That made her wrinkle her nose. "As if you'd ever need to call me for help when you have a whole staff at your beck and call."

Something about that comment, teasing as it had sounded, bothered him for reasons he couldn't quite put his finger on. Still, he knew she was anxious to get back to her son, and he understood that. He'd helped as much as he could, but he felt that he was only in her way now.

"I'll clear out now so you can spend time with Caleb. I just want to repeat that you don't owe me apologies or gratitude, and I'll always be here for you if you need anything, even if it's just a sympathetic ear. And if you find a free hour to sit under the stars with me sometime—well, all the better."

She moved closer to him and rose on tiptoe to kiss his cheek. "Thank you, Trevor."

He'd have given anything to sweep her into his arms then, to give her a proper kiss. But because this was both the wrong time and the wrong place—again—he contented himself, for the most part, with just a quick hug.

Telling himself to be satisfied with that, he left. During the drive back to the resort, he thought back over the past couple of hours, shaking his head in bemusement. This, he thought, was why he'd avoided getting involved with single mothers in the past. Too many complications and pitfalls. Too many innocent bystanders. Too few hours to divide between too many people. And with Jade, especially, too heavy a shadow of the hero she'd once loved.

If he had any sense at all, he'd have pulled back from Jade as soon as he'd realized he was getting too attached. To her. To her kids. To the damned dog, for that matter. Instead, he'd kept being drawn back to the warmth that was Jade's sweet smile in the moonlight. And now he feared that she and her kids would be the ones who were burned—and that he would somehow be the one who'd let them down, despite his best efforts to protect them.

JADE SMILED AS she watched Trevor and Caleb trying to wrestle a plastic flying disc from Zoe on the beach at Wind Shadow. A week and a half had passed since Caleb's fight, and this was the first time they'd seen Trevor since.

This Saturday afternoon picnic at the resort beach had been Bella's idea, and she'd begged until Jade had given in. Though Jade had reminded the kids that it would be too cool for swimming, they hadn't cared. Wearing jeans and windbreakers against a cool but comfortable breeze for mid-November, they ran barefoot on the sand with Trevor and Zoe while Jade and Mary Pat sat on a blanket and watched indulgently.

It had been Erin's suggestion to ask Mary Pat to join them, an invitation their friend had accepted happily. Jade had been a bit surprised that Trevor had shown up to greet them when they arrived and had accepted their offer to join them for lunch. She couldn't help wondering if Mary Pat had guilted him into this. He'd been so busy and distant since that fateful afternoon with Caleb that Jade had figured he'd make a polite excuse if asked. He was welcome, of course, and he seemed to be enjoying the afternoon, spreading his attention evenly among the three kids, but he was most definitely wearing his resort host's expression.

No one had mentioned Caleb's recent troubles, focusing, instead, on the food and cheery small talk. Jade wouldn't attest that her son's actions on that fateful afternoon had been a positive thing, but certain changes had developed afterward that were definitely for the better. His attitude hadn't really changed overnight—he was, after all, still an adolescent boy—but he did seem to open up a bit more with her. She had the sense that he was somewhat more relaxed. Less driven to prove himself, perhaps, now that he'd been reminded that it was okay to ask for help.

She'd overheard part of Trevor's talk with him—enough to confirm Walt's theory that Trevor was driven to an extent by both survivor's guilt and family pressure. As she watched Trevor show the boy how to flip the disc underhand to better guide its trajectory, she mused that perhaps Caleb had taken to heart Trevor's advice not to try so hard to live up to his father's legacy—a legend that had only grown in scope since Stephen's death.

Jade had been aware that her son felt the responsibility of being "man of the house" in his family of women, despite her efforts to raise him in a less gender-defined atmosphere. She was, of course, proud of his courage and his kind heart, even though she hoped he saw now that he couldn't be a real-life superhero and take on all the bullies himself. Maybe Trevor had helped him reach that conclusion with his analogy to military structure. Or maybe, she thought with some reluctance, the boy had simply needed a sympathetic adult male to give him permission not to try taking on the world alone.

She had been to the school and met with the principal, teachers and other parents. Now a new, beefed-up policy against bullying had been instituted, along with new counseling measures for students deemed at risk of resorting to that behavior. To reinforce her commitment to the cause, Jade had agreed to sit on a committee to oversee the policy. She'd figured she'd find a way to make time for the monthly meetings because the policy was so important to her and her son, and to the other vulnerable children in the school.

Under penalty of dire consequences, Erin generally kept her mouth shut about the fight, at least within Jade's hearing. Bella had shown little interest, seemingly happy with her teacher and friends. Jade felt as though she should knock wood when the thought crossed her mind, but so far things were going very well for her family.

As for Trevor…

"Trevor's going to have to sit in his chair with an ice pack and a drink this evening," Mary Pat observed with an indulgent shake of her head, watching the antics. "He's really pushing that leg."

"He knows better than to injure himself again," Jade replied, though she frowned as she saw him limp a bit when he turned to glide the retrieved disc to Caleb, who swooped it to Bella. Perhaps they should eat soon to give Trevor a chance to rest his leg, even though he seemed to be having a good time. Jade wouldn't have minded being out there playing with them, but it had seemed rude to leave Mary Pat alone to watch.

"I know he does," the older woman agreed. "He just gets carried away sometimes. Hates admitting there's anything he can't do."

Watching Trevor pick a happily shrieking Bella up and spin her on the sand, Jade sighed. "Maybe we should get out the food."

"That's an excellent suggestion," Mary Pat agreed eagerly. "Have to admit I'm hungry."

They spent the next half hour dining on cold fried chicken, potato salad and coleslaw, all prepared by Mary Pat, with Jade's pecan fudge brownies for dessert. There was much laughter and teasing during the meal, especially when Zoe tried her best to help herself to Erin's lunch. Trevor solved that by tying Zoe's leash to a post and giving her a bit of chicken stripped from the bone to enjoy.

With Trevor sitting so closely beside her on the blanket that their thighs brushed whenever they moved, Jade thought that this picnic would go down as one of her happiest memories despite any misgivings. The children were all smiling and having such a good time—even Caleb—and their much-loved pet had settled down for a satiated snooze after her snack. Mary Pat's smile was almost as bright as the afternoon sun, and Trevor looked utterly relaxed. As if there were nowhere else he'd rather be…

It was all almost too perfect—a thought that annoyed her because she'd never been the superstitious type.

Yet when Trevor's phone rang in his pocket, she couldn't help grimacing with a sudden premonition. Minutes later, that bad feeling proved justified.

"I'm so sorry, everyone," he began.

"No!" Erin picked up instantly on where this was leading. "You said you'd show me how to serve a volleyball."

"You're going to look at tide pools with me, aren't you, Mr. Trevor?" Bella implored.

Caleb didn't say anything, but Jade could see that he looked resigned.

"I'm sorry," Trevor repeated, resting a hand lightly on Bella's shoulder. "Something's come up that I should look into. I don't know how long it will take, but there's no reason the rest of you shouldn't keep having fun. I'm sure your mom knows how to serve a volleyball, Erin."

"I do," Jade replied evenly, hating the disappointment on her children's faces. "And I used to hit a mean spike."

"I'll bet you did." Trevor looked at her in regret. "I really am sorry, Jade."

"Go," she said, waving a hand. "We're good here."

Bella was still pouting. "I'll make it up to you, Little Bit," Trevor promised. "I'll have your mom bring you early one morning when we can find the coolest shells and tide pools."

"Can we find a starfish?"

"There's a definite possibility."

"Okay. But I wish you didn't have to go now."

He leaned over to kiss a soft cheek, murmuring, "So do I, Bella."

Jade thought he looked genuinely regretful when he gathered his shoes and headed off toward his office. Which didn't lessen her children's disappointment—or her own.

Determined that the memory of the outing would not be ruined by this interruption, she reached for her phone so she could snap photos of the picnic lunch. When they'd finished eating, she organized a game for who could find the tiniest unbroken shell, knowing that would keep them busy scrutinizing the sand for a good while. She and Mary Pat put away the picnic supplies while the kids ran off on their hunt, getting distracted a few times by finding something else. Freed from the post now that the food was put away, Zoe bounced around them, yipping occasionally and whipping her tail like a spinning fan blade.

They were still having a great time, she thought with a sigh. And she was, too. They didn't need Trevor there to complete their family fun.

But it had been nice while it lasted.

TREVOR STOOD ALONE on a crowded beach during a lunch break from a hospitality-business conference, his hands in his pockets as he stared out at the breaking waves. This wasn't his usual Atlantic Ocean or Gulf of Mexico view; he'd been in Hawaii for the past two days at a conference that had been on his schedule for months. He'd made a speech that morning that had seemed well received, and he always made a few valuable new contacts at these gatherings. So, why was he feeling so restless and unsettled?

He glanced automatically at his watch, noting that it was just before six in the evening back home in South Carolina. Six hours later than here. Tamar was probably headed home, the day staff had ceded duties to the night staff, the resort restaurants would be busy with the first wave of the dinner crowd. Mary Pat had finished whatever household chores she'd scheduled for the day and was probably settled in her cottage. Jade would be feeding the kids dinner, getting them ready for homework and bath time and whatever other evening rituals they followed on a Thursday night. There would be lots of conversation and laughter and a few squabbles, and he knew Jade wouldn't trade a minute of that time with her children for a life of travel and schmoozing and deal making.

A tourist with a cheap faux-grass skirt tied over her bikini bottom dashed past him, giggling as she was followed by an eager young suitor holding an umbrella-topped plastic coconut shell sloshing with a drink he was imbibing in rather too early in the day. Stepping out of the way to avoid being showered by rum, Trevor drew out his phone, deciding to check in with Mary Pat. It wasn't that he was homesick, of course. He traveled too much to be prone to that particular malady. He just thought he should make sure everything was okay back at his house.

"Oh, everything is fine here," his housekeeper assured him a couple of minutes later. "The pool guy came today to get the pool ready for winter, and the plumber came by to fix that little leak in the upstairs bathroom I told you about yesterday. He said it's all good now."

"Good to hear. Thanks for taking care of that."

"Just doing my job, hon. Have you talked to Jade this evening, by any chance?"

He hadn't spoken with Jade since the picnic last weekend. The picnic Mary Pat had all but strong-armed him into attending, though he'd wondered at the time if he should just let the family have their fun without intruding. Seeing Bella's disappointment when he'd been called away before exploring tide pools with her, as he'd said he would, had convinced him his hesitation had been justified. He'd hated letting the child down, but he'd felt obligated to run when he'd been summoned by his staff—even though maybe, just maybe, it would have worked out fine without his actual presence. But still, that was his life.

"No, I haven't," he said lightly to Mary Pat, who he knew spoke with Jade often. "How are they doing?"

"They had quite a scare today when an elderly man pulled out of a parking lot without paying attention and hit their car with his pickup truck. Got 'em in the back right quarter panel, hard enough to maybe bend the frame. Jade's not sure how long it will take to be repaired."

Trevor's hand had tightened so hard around his phone that he heard the plastic case creak in protest. He deliberately loosened his fingers, though it wasn't as easy to loosen the invisible vise that seemed to have tightened around his chest, interfering with his breathing. "Were the kids in the car when it happened?"

"Yes, they all were. Jade had just picked them up from school and was headed home. But don't worry, hon, no one was hurt. The kids were all buckled in, of course, and the old man wasn't going very fast, though his big ol' truck did a number on Jade's fender. Jade said they were shaken up, but they're all fine, thank heaven. I don't want to even think about what could have happened."

All those alternatives had already occurred to him, leaving him tense and slightly nauseated. "I, uh, I'm being called in to a meeting," he said, uncharacteristically resorting to an outright lie because he needed a minute. "I'll talk to you later, Mary Pat."

"Okay, hon. Have a good time there in Hawaii."

Not likely, he thought as he disconnected the call and rubbed his forehead, dismayed to find his hand unsteady. Not likely at all now.

JADE'S KIDS HAD reacted to the startling car accident with predictable differences matching their disparate personalities. Bella had been shaken and scared, sniffling quietly while Jade spoke with responding police officers and the tow truck driver. Erin, after the first shock of the impact, had decided it was all a grand adventure. Caleb, as usual, had been solicitous, hovering around his mother and sisters to make sure they were all okay, telling Bella repeatedly that everything would be fine.

It took their favorite meal, followed by scoops of ice cream, to settle them down that evening. Jade let Bella take a long, lavender-scented bubble bath, then read her two stories, finally getting her to sleep half an hour later than usual. Bella made her promise to come running in case of bad dreams, which Jade reminded her she would have done, anyway.

Leaving Bella's room, she checked on Erin, who had just finished her own bath and was getting ready for bed, and on Caleb, who sprawled on his bed with his dog and his homework. Both assured her they were fine, with Erin adding that she couldn't wait to tell her friends at school the next day about their "smash-up."

Hoping there would be no bad dreams or sore muscles during the night, Jade wandered downstairs with a long, low sigh, her mind whirling with all the things on her agenda now. A busy time at work, the holidays fast approaching, shopping to be done, arrangements to be made with Mary Pat for the school breaks, and now the addition of dealing with insurance companies. Her car would either have to be repaired or she'd have to find a replacement if the insurance company deemed it totaled, which was possible if the frame was bent. Rubbing her temples, she told herself she could make it all work out. Somehow.

The strain of the afternoon was catching up to her now, and she could feel her mood rapidly deteriorating into weary crankiness. She needed to get outside with an herbal tea and the stars, though she wasn't sure even that usually soothing routine would help much tonight.

She was in the kitchen making her tea when her phone rang. She looked around for it, then realized she'd left it in the living room. Hurrying to answer, she wondered if it was Amy. She'd left a voice mail on her cousin's service earlier to tell her about the incident, and she wouldn't be surprised if Amy wanted all the details. She'd already told her mother and Mary Pat, who'd called coincidentally not long after Jade and the kids got home. She wasn't really in the mood for another recap, but she would reassure her cousin that she and the kids were fine and she'd tell her more tomorrow.

Seeing Trevor's number on the screen rather than Amy's made her already jangled nerves trip again. She knew he was at a conference in Maui, and hadn't expected him to call. Though she'd thought wistfully of him each night when she'd sat outside before bed, all too aware of the empty chair beside her. Had he spoken with Mary Pat that evening as she had, or was this merely a random call to say hello?

She lifted her phone and tried to speak casually, hoping she'd masked her stress. "Aloha, Trevor."

His answering chuckle sounded a bit forced but the deep sound still reverberated through her, making her wish futilely again that he wasn't so very far away. "Aloha, Jade. Is this a bad time? Are you taking care of the kids?"

"No, it's fine." She let herself out the back door and settled into a patio chair to talk in private. "Bella just fell asleep and Erin and Caleb are getting ready for bed, so I can talk for a few minutes. How was your day in paradise?"

"Better than your day, apparently."

So he had talked to Mary Pat. "I take it you heard about my accident?"

"I did. Everyone's okay?"

Sensing that he was genuinely concerned, she spoke reassuringly. "We're all fine. The kids were buckled in snugly and no one was hurt, not even the dear old man who hit us. My poor car was the only victim, and I've got a decent rental for as long as I need it. I actually like it so well I might replace mine with the same model. Bella's booster seat fits nicely into the rental."

"Was Bella frightened by the accident?"

His voice sounded tight, as if he were imagining the scene and hating the images he conjured. "She was shaken up," she replied honestly, "but I was able to calm her down. She's sleeping peacefully now. Erin and Caleb handled it great. None of them are sore or bruised, so we were very lucky."

She didn't want to describe—or even think about—that moment of terror she'd had when she'd felt the impact of the collision and heard the stomach-churning sound of crunching metal. Her first thought, of course, had been of her children behind her, especially Erin on the side of the crash. Slamming the car into Park, she had turned in dread, and had gone almost weak with relief when she'd assured herself that her daughters were startled but unharmed. Bella had cried until she'd been unbuckled and gathered into her mother's reassuring arms, but she wasn't injured.

"Trevor?" she said after a long silence. "Is our connection breaking up? Are you there?"

"I'm here. Just—is there anything you need, Jade? I have some people there I can call to give you a hand, if you need it."

She told herself he meant well, as he always did, but also as always, she found herself resenting any suggestion of him taking care of her. Perhaps he hadn't meant to imply that she wasn't capable of dealing with her own problems, but she was in no mood tonight to be patronized, even unintentionally.

"Thanks, but I can deal with the insurance stuff. It won't be the first time. And I've bought cars on my own before, if mine can't be repaired, or if I decide I'd like a new one now."

"I guess you're good, then."

Why did he sound so grouchy about that? "I'm good."

"Okay. That's great. So, I should go. I have more meetings to attend and then a dinner tonight."

"Of course. Enjoy your mahi-mahi or poi or whatever you're having at your luau."

He didn't chuckle. "Sure. You be careful, Jade. You'll be driving an unfamiliar car for the next few days."

Maybe because she was already grumpy, those words, too, hit her the wrong way. "I give you credit for being capable of taking care of yourself, Trevor, despite the risks you seem to enjoy. I'd appreciate if you give me the same courtesy about looking out for myself and my children."

"Okay, fine. You've made it clear enough that you neither want nor need my concern."

Already regretting her response, she sighed. "I didn't mean—"

"I'm sure you're tired. I'll let you get some rest. Good night, Jade."

"Good night." Frowning, she lowered the phone and looked at it as if searching the now-dark screen for clues as to Trevor's mood. She understood why hers was so dark, considering the day's mishap, but what was with him?

Obviously, hearing about the accident had bothered him rather badly. But why? She'd assured him no one was hurt and that she had all the details handled. His odd reaction had left her even more unsettled than she'd been before talking to him.

Or was it the fact that she found herself aching to have him sitting outside with her tonight, especially, that shook her so deeply?

Shoving herself from the chair, she pushed back her hair and went into the house to check on her children.

IT HAD BEEN years since Trevor'd had the nightmare. He rarely remembered his dreams at all these days, so it was rare indeed for him to wake gasping and sweating, his heartbeat pounding in his ears, his breathing ragged and harsh. He swung his legs to the side of the bed and reached for the water glass on his nightstand, gulping the soothing liquid down almost desperately.

The dream had started as it had in the past, with Lindsey waving goodbye as he'd disappeared into a Jetway, duffel bag gripped in one hand. It had continued with him a disembodied observer as she'd climbed behind the wheel of her car, singing along to one of her favorite songs on the radio as she'd driven with the windows open, her long red hair tossing in the breeze. All too painfully familiar elements of the nightmare that had haunted him during the first three years after her death, cropping up only occasionally since.

But this time something was different. Horrifyingly different. This time there were others in the car that was suddenly mangled and smoldering. Four others. He saw them all, one by one.

Lindsey.

Caleb.

Erin.

Sweet little Bella.

Jade.

And even in the dream, he was too far away to help them as they called out to him. While his consciousness was there with them, helpless and impotent, his body stood on a beach far away, surrounded by faceless people clamoring for his attention.

He moved to the window, staring blankly out at the Pacific Ocean. And then he opened the French door and stepped outside, sinking into a chair on the balcony to lift his face to the moon and soak in its soothing beams.

CHAPTER FOURTEEN

SOMETHING WAS DEFINITELY going on with Trevor. Ever since he'd gotten back from Hawaii several days ago, he'd been acting downright strange.

She'd neither seen nor spoken with him since his return, though he'd sent gifts for the children from Hawaii through Mary Pat a couple days after he'd gotten back.

Mary Pat had relayed Trevor's apologies that he wasn't delivering the gifts, himself, claiming he was extremely busy with work. The words had rung hollow to Jade, and something in Mary Pat's expression at the time had told her the house-keeper also suspected something more was going on, though they hadn't discussed it.

The kids were elated by their gifts. Bella had received a gorgeous doll with glossy long black hair, dark eyes, a lei, bikini top and hula skirt, even a delicate flower anklet. Erin and Caleb got ukuleles—Erin's with painted purple flowers, Caleb's in a glossy two-toned wood. Trevor had sent Jade a gift, too, a hand-carved box of curly koa wood with delicate mother-of-pearl inlays.

She wondered if he'd purchased these things before their tiff on the phone. Or—she swallowed painfully—were the gifts his way of saying goodbye? At least metaphorically. She was sure they'd still run into him occasionally, and of course Mary Pat was a part of their family now, but had that prickly exchange ended the more intimate friendship between her and Trevor?

Had he come to the conclusion that there was really no reason to continue as they had been? Attempting to analyze her own feelings about that possibility, she tried to convince herself that it was probably best for both of them to stop pretending they could be lighthearted lovers without emotional complications.

She missed him, damn it. Each time she'd looked at that little box during the past week, she'd felt her throat tighten. She'd shared her body and her thoughts with him, but she'd kept her scarred heart protected—or so she'd believed. This disappointment she felt because he'd been so distant—after she'd looked forward to seeing him ever since he'd left—suggested that maybe she hadn't been quite as careful as she'd thought. Somehow she'd let Trevor slip into her life and perhaps into that not-so-well-guarded heart.

She'd been deluding herself to think that for her there could be any other outcome.

"He misses you."

Startled, she looked across the kitchen table at Mary Pat, wondering for a moment if mind-reading was among the woman's many talents. Mary Pat had dropped by for tea and a visit on this Saturday afternoon, and though she'd arrived almost an hour ago, this was the first chance she and Jade had been alone while the children played outside with Zoe.

"Trevor misses you," Mary Pat repeated firmly. "He's been moping around the house like a love-sick schoolboy for the past week and a half since he got back from Hawaii. Every time I mention you and the kids, he grumps, but I can see in his eyes that he misses you all like crazy—especially you, I'm thinking."

Jade's chest tightened. She shook her head. "He has my number. He hasn't even bothered to call since he got back."

The older woman sighed lightly. "He's scared, hon. You both are, I think. You both know what it's like to lose someone who means the world to you—I've been there, myself, when I lost my Charlie. It's hard to put yourself out there again. But maybe sometimes it's worth the risk? Especially for two people like you and my Trevor, who both have so much love to give."

"Mary Pat—"

Her friend held up both hands. "That's all I'm going to say about it. I'm not one to meddle—

well, not much, anyway," she conceded with a laugh. "Just give it some thought, Jade. One of you is going to have to make the first move—and I think he considers himself doing you a favor to step aside. Knowing Trevor, deep down he isn't sure he's good enough for you. I think he believes he failed Lindsey by not being here to protect her. He never has dealt well with failure. A Farrell trait, I believe."

The children burst through the door then with their happily wagging pet, all of them thirsty. True to her word, Mary Pat said no more about the situation between Jade and Trevor, though she gave Jade a rather pointed look when she left a short while later.

Jade came to a decision that evening while sitting out beneath the stars in her backyard. She and Trevor couldn't go on this way, hot and cold, advancing and retreating. She hoped they could stay friends, regardless of what happened next, but if they were to be lovers, they had to be honest with each other. With themselves. She was going to have to confront Trevor before much more time had passed. One way or another, she would peel away the self-protective facade he had cultivated for so long and find out what he truly wanted from her, if anything at all. But first, perhaps it was time she looked more deeply into herself, to find out what she wanted. What she was willing to risk again for love.

TREVOR HAD TOLD Mary Pat he'd be home earlier than usual Friday evening, so he was a bit surprised to find the kitchen dark and unoccupied when he walked in. He could see that the den lights were out, too, so it was obvious Mary Pat had left for the night. Usually when she knew he'd be home before eight she waited to have tea with him, catch up on any personal news and discuss their schedules for the upcoming days. He didn't expect her to hang around and never asked it of her, but he enjoyed those rare kitchen-table chats and had gotten rather spoiled by them.

He tossed his keys on the counter and fancied the resulting clatter echoed through the empty house. Foolish. He really was in a melancholy mood tonight apparently. Must just be tired. It had been a long week. A long month, for that matter.

Opening the refrigerator, he pulled out a cold beer, deciding he might as well try to relax and enjoy the alone time. He closed the fridge door and then stood staring at the artwork attached to it by a sunflower magnet. Bella must have given this drawing to Mary Pat. The humorously executed crayon people crowded on the sheet of yellow construction paper were carefully labeled in Bella's shaky block letters. Bella. Caleb. Erin. Mary Pat. Zoe. Mr. Trevor. Mommy.

He pictured what it must be like at Jade's house right now. The kids would likely still be up on this Friday night, though Bella was probably getting ready for bed. Maybe they were playing a board game or watching a family-friendly movie together, talking and laughing while the silly dog gamboled between them for pats and rubs. Whatever they were doing, it probably wasn't quiet there. The sound of falling keys wouldn't echo through empty rooms in their home.

Groaning, he shook his head, calling himself a mopey idiot. What the hell was with him tonight? Maybe he was letting the upcoming holiday season get to him. Decorations were already going up everywhere, including at Wind Shadow, which would be lit up in an annual gala for charity next week. He'd have to make sure the kids visited one evening soon. Bella, especially, would be thrilled by the thousands of tiny lights covering nearly every static surface of the resort for the holidays, not to mention the huge lighted tree erected on a dock in the middle of the lake, the central fountain covered with a wooden platform for now.

In his role as official host of the glittering gala, Trevor never invited a date, telling himself that left him free to focus on his guests and staff. He wouldn't take anyone this year, either. For one thing, there was only one woman he would want at his side—the fallen hero's widow.

Great. Now add self-pity to the melancholy. Shaking his head in disgust, he gripped the beer bottle and turned away from the sweet drawing, deciding he could distract himself with work late into the night. There was always work to be done.

He saw a light coming from his suite when he headed that direction, and figured Mary Pat must have turned it on for him. Thoughtful of her. He really was lucky to have...

All rational thought left his mind when he stepped into his suite to find Jade sitting in his easy chair, her shoes on the floor beside her, her bare feet crossed on his ottoman, one of his mystery novels open in her hands. The golden light from the reading lamp beside the chair glittered in her blond hair and warmed her amber eyes when she smiled up at him as if it was not at all unusual for her to greet him like this.

"Hello, Trevor. Welcome home."

IT HAD BEEN Jade's intent to startle Trevor out of his usual equanimity—and she'd been completely successful. She saw his jaw literally drop in response to finding her in his bedroom suite at this hour.

Before he had a chance to recompose his features, she set the book aside and rose, automatically smoothing the thin black sweater she wore with slim black slacks. Stopping in front of him, she rose on tiptoe and brushed a kiss over his still-parted lips. "How was your day?"

She'd kept her tone light in what she thought was a fairly successful attempt to hide how fast her pulse was racing, how tightly her nerves were tangled. This stunt was either going to prove a delightful success or an embarrassing gaffe, but either way, she wasn't sorry she'd arranged it.

He still looked too stunned to return the quick kiss, but he reached out to catch her arm when she would have backed away. "Jade, what are you doing here? Where are the kids? Is Mary Pat with them?"

"My kids and their dog are spending the weekend with my mother, who decided this was the perfect time to decorate her house for Christmas. They wanted to help. Mary Pat, I assume, is in her cottage. That's where she said she was going after she let me into your house."

"Oh, well." He settled his face into the smile that was beginning to irritate her. "This is a nice surprise."

Because the only way to truly get through to

him seemed to be to catch him completely off guard, she retorted, "Liar."

His consummate-host aplomb faded. "Um… what?"

She slid both hands up his chest, moving toward him so that her breasts just brushed his chest. She was pretty sure she felt his heart leap in response, or was that her own?

"I'm not a stupid woman, Trevor."

Both his hands were on her arms now, though she couldn't say if he was trying to hold her in place or fend her off. "No, of course you aren't. Why would you—"

Deciding her strategy was working, she inched a little closer, their thighs brushing now. "I've gotten to know you fairly well during the past few months, wouldn't you say?"

"Well, sure." His voice was getting rougher, as if his throat had tightened. "But—"

One of her hands was behind his head now, her fingers toying with the silky hair at his nape. She felt him shiver in response and she smiled. "You," she accused him in a low voice, her face close to his, "have, for some reason, decided to pull away from me. And I think we should talk about that."

"I'm hardly pulling away," he pointed out, still rather hoarse, but sounding somewhat more composed as his hands moved from her arms to her hips.

"So I have to ask myself," she continued as if he hadn't spoken, "is it because you don't want me anymore?"

She nestled her pelvis more snugly into his, making them both aware of the answer to that question. "Or is it that you've decided that we'll never find time to be together? Obviously, we can, though perhaps not as often as you'd like?"

She cupped her hands around his face, forcing him to look at her. "Or is it something else, Trevor? Do I not know you as well as I thought? Am I misreading you entirely? Do you want me to leave now and keep my distance from now on? Because you know I will, and that I can put on a social mask just as easily as you do to pretend in future polite encounters that nothing ever happened between us."

He seemed to struggle for only a moment with how to respond to that. And then he groaned softly and rested his forehead against hers. "Damn it, Jade."

The hint of defeat in his voice gave her encouragement, but still she said, "You're going to have to give me more of an answer than that, I'm afraid."

His sigh was long and deep. "You deserve more."

She drew back then, satisfied that her methods had paid off. He was finally leveling with her. "In what way do I deserve more?" she asked evenly. "Especially as I haven't asked for one thing from you."

"That's just it." Shoving a hand through his hair, he half turned and moved a step away as if distancing himself from temptation. "Hell, Jade, you've gotten so accustomed to doing everything on your own that you don't even expect anyone to be there for you. The very few times I've been able to help you were because someone else asked on your behalf. My mom. Your son. You won't ask for yourself."

"Because I rarely need it," she said with a slight shrug. "I've been pretty much on my own since I graduated high school, and, to be honest, I'm good with that."

He turned toward her, and she could almost see him struggling to find the right words. "Your husband—"

"My husband was a larger-than-life hero," she cut in flatly. "That's how everyone will always remember him."

She knew from all her observations of Trevor that he couldn't help but compare himself to the legend, and she wanted to make it very clear that she, for one, would never compare them. Trevor and Stephen were very different men, though both were justifiably admired by everyone who knew or had known them. Both were honorable heroes in their own ways through their selfless service to others, though the description was one each would have respectfully rejected.

"Stephen saved lives, sacrificed his own, earned all the medals," she said. "I loved him very much when we married, in the passionate, all-consuming way only a starry-eyed teenager can love. I never stopped loving him, though I realized early in our marriage that his own true passion lay in his military career. As much as he loved me and the kids, he was never really happy unless he was among his brothers- and sisters-in-arms. I learned that I would be on my own for home and car repairs, for budgeting and bill paying, for changing diapers and wiping feverish brows. And I was okay with that."

She drew a deep breath and shook her head. "I didn't complain then, and I'm not complaining now. I did my part for this country, just as Stephen did his. Neither of us had second thoughts, though of course he was taken from us much too soon. I'll always regret that for his children's sake even more than my own."

Her words turned rueful. "I've been telling myself I didn't want to disrupt the comfortable routines my family has settled into since Stephen's death by bringing someone else in, but I've come to realize that was just an excuse. The truth was, I was afraid to love again. Afraid of having my heart broken again, either through tragedy or failure. And yet, you kept showing up with your sexy smile and your kind nature, sitting in the moonlight with me without making fun of my need to do so, walking with me on the beach, encouraging my kids, even helping me adopt a silly dog," she added, laughing softly. "And you made me fall for you even as I gave myself every excuse in the world not to."

Trevor shook his head, clinging doggedly to his own doubt. "You've seen my life. I work all the time. I've had to break promises to Bella, gotten called away unexpectedly, frequently missed my own family's events for an emergency meeting or situation."

"Some of which you could have left to your excellent staff and monitored from a distance, according to Mary Pat and Tamar. But no one is demanding that you stop rushing off to put out fires. Least of all me. Though it's probably best if you continue to say *I'll try* instead of *I promise* to Bella in the future, considering promises are sometimes difficult to guarantee."

He didn't return her smile. When he looked at her then, the expression in his eyes tore at her heart. It contained so much longing...and so much fear. Was he even aware of the latter?

She cocked her head as a sudden thought occurred to her. "You know, Trevor—I don't think you're really worried at all about not being the right man for me. You know I can take care of myself. You're well aware that I'll never ask more of you than you're able—or willing—to give. You know my own spare time is limited, and I can't make many more promises than you do since I never know if something might come up with the kids."

He eyed her warily. "Where are you going with this?"

Even more convinced now that she was onto something, she surged on. "I think you're the one who believes your commitments are an obstacle, not to protect me, but because you're afraid of adding more responsibilities to your own life. You know yourself well enough to suspect that if you and I get more involved, you'll automatically start trying to take care of me and the kids. You've already been trying, regardless of my assurances that we don't need it. You're trying to pull back now for your own sake, not for all these noble excuses you're supposedly making for me."

That brought his chin up, and she actually welcomed the spark of temper in his eyes. If he was letting himself show his annoyance toward her, it meant he was being honest, which was all she demanded from him.

"That's ridiculous," he snapped. "I'm not that selfish."

"I'm not calling you selfish. I'm calling you self-protective. There's a difference."

He was scowling now, more agitated than she'd seen him. "What the hell are you talking about?"

Rather than taking offense at his tone, she ached for him. It couldn't be easy for him to deal with emotions he'd been suppressing for so long that he'd hidden them even from himself. She stepped forward to lay a hand gently on his rigid arm.

"Have you ever asked yourself why you feel the need to directly supervise every problem within your company? Why you went so far as to build a house for Mary Pat so she'd have a close place to stay after her husband died, and so you could keep an eye out for her? Have you ever considered that maybe—just maybe—you feel the need to try to personally control every situation as a way of making sure nothing goes wrong for the people you consider your responsibility?"

"That's—"

"All this time, I've believed you were so hands-on and micromanaging with your company because you were trying to live up to your family's expectations. And while I'm sure that is part of it, I think even more you're trying to protect the people you care about. And in doing so, perhaps trying to protect yourself from feeling at fault if you didn't do everything within your power to personally prevent something bad from happening. The same guilt you felt when your wife died while you were sitting behind a desk in another country."

Even as she spoke, she knew she was taking a gamble. She would either drive Trevor away for good with this confrontation or force him to talk to her, to level with her—with himself—about whether her accusations held any merit.

He swallowed so hard she could hear it as well as see his throat work. Was there also a muffled grunt of pain in that swallow? Was he still angry, or had that emotion been crowded out by others that were even harder for him to accept?

"Why were you so upset when I told you about my car accident, Trevor?" she asked very quietly. "I assured you no one was hurt, and I told you I was taking care of it, but it obviously bothered you very badly. Was it because it made you feel like you needed to do something for us, yet you felt helpless because you were so far away?"

The look in his eyes broke her heart now. His shoulders sagged in surrender when he conceded. "Maybe you're right, at least in part. I have to admit it disturbed me to imagine how scared the kids must have been after the crash. How badly it could have turned out if the other car had been going faster or if the impact had been in a more damaging spot. It's only natural to think about things like that after an accident."

"Yes. But completely shutting down afterward isn't." She drew a deep breath and blurted, "Are you really so afraid of your feelings for my kids, Trevor? Of your feelings for me?"

"I'm freaking terrified," he answered simply, barely even hesitating this time.

It wasn't exactly the response she'd expected, but it was honest, at least. "Because of the possibility that something could happen to one of us?" she asked to clarify.

He cupped her face with one hand and she felt a hint of unsteadiness in his fingers. "Because I'm not sure I'd survive if anything did happen to any of you," he said, his face stark now. "And I don't know how to protect you or the kids when I've got so many other responsibilities pulling me in so many different directions."

She covered his hand with hers, her own trembling now. She was touched by his admission, but his obvious pain caused an answering hurt inside her.

"Once again, Trevor, I haven't asked you to protect us. That's *my* job, to the best of my ability, though I have to admit there are some things that are simply out of my control. I try not to dwell on those things. I try to just enjoy the present, instead, and to do all I can to ensure a safe and happy future for my children."

"How do you deal with the fear?" The question seemed almost ripped from him as he searched her face in open bewilderment. "After losing one person you loved, how do you not worry all the time about something happening to those kids you adore?"

"I just keep loving them through the worry," she said on a low sigh. "I do whatever I can to keep them safe, and then let myself accept that's all I can do."

She met his tormented gaze evenly. "Losing Stephen was hard—I won't lie. You and I share a fear of loving and losing again, and I think it's as hard for me to get past that as for you. But then I think about how grateful I am for the time I spent with Stephen and the memories I made with him—memories I've tried to keep alive for his children. Even had I known our time together would be so short, I wouldn't go back now to change the choice I made to start a family with him. And I've decided that I'm not going to let that fear harden my heart any longer against a new love. I'm scared, too, Trevor, especially considering you seem to enjoy testing your limits at every opportunity—but I'm willing to risk it, if you are."

It was the first time she'd even allowed herself to think the word *love* in relation to her feelings for Trevor, but she knew now that her complicated emotions toward him couldn't be defined in any other way. How could she not love this man?

He was still, silent for so long that she wondered if she really had scared him off for good this time. And then he released a low breath that sounded both weary and accepting. "You know what's really stupid?"

She lifted her eyebrows in silent question.

"All this panicking I've done wasn't because I was afraid of falling in love with you and your kids," he said, his sudden, faint smile embarrassed. "It was because I already have. Because no matter how hard I tried, I couldn't seem to stay away from you. I kept finding more excuses to be with you. And I didn't know what the hell to do about it."

Well, here he was, she thought in aching wonder, her gaze searching his face. The real Trevor. Vulnerable, uncertain, even a little scared—and yet still so incredibly special.

"You don't need to panic over that," she whispered as she stepped into his waiting arms. "All you have to do is to let us love you back. Because we do. *I* do."

As if he found it physically impossible to hold back any longer, he gathered her into a kiss that rocked her all the way down to her bare toes. And she threw herself wholeheartedly into the embrace. Neither of them was holding back now. Neither hiding behind a mask of any kind, social or self-protective.

Whatever may come, they would face it with their combined strengths and talents, she assured herself. And most powerfully of all, with love.

IT WAS WELL into the night, perhaps even very early morning when Jade roused enough to raise herself on one arm in Trevor's bed and look down at him. She didn't bother looking at the clock, because she didn't care what time it was. She wasn't sleepy. She didn't want to waste one moment of this night with sleep.

Judging by Trevor's glittering eyes and satiated expression, he felt much the same way.

She dragged a finger along his jaw, dipping the tip into the faintest hint of a dimple in his chin. "Tell me about her. Your wife, I mean."

It seemed to startle him only for a moment that she'd asked that now, while they lay naked, sweaty and entangled in his bed. Maybe he was getting used to her saying what was on her mind without regard to finesse, at least when it came to him. Rather than answering, he reached into the nightstand and drew out a small framed photograph.

Lindsey had been pretty, Jade thought, studying the smiling face in the photo with a twist of her soft heart. Rich red hair, dark eyes, a lovely smile. So young.

"She was sweet," Trevor said quietly. "Poised, self-confident, a talented singer. She was raised in the beauty pageant world—and that was obvious to anyone who met her—but she wasn't vain or pretentious. She dreamed of being a leading member of the social charitable circles, but she really did want to make a difference with those charities, not just be seen at the events. She wasn't thrilled that I wanted to serve a hitch in the army after I finished my degrees, but she considered that a fair trade-off for the life she envisioned for us afterward."

Jade gave him back the photo. "You loved her."

"Yes. I'm not sure it was the kind of love you described when you married—that crazy, passionate, starry-eyed teenage thing? But I admired and respected her and I thought we made a good couple. I was sure we'd have a good life. And then she died while I was off proving something to my dad."

"Something that could very well have happened even had you been here," she reminded him, but let it go at that. Trevor would have to work out his baggage in his own way, just as she had. He knew she was always here when he needed to talk, and that she would always understand.

He returned the frame to the nightstand and closed the drawer. It didn't bother her that he kept it there. She wouldn't put away her photos of Stephen, either.

Their pasts, joys, tears, mistakes and successes had brought her and Trevor to this place—and there was nowhere she would rather be.

"Jade?"

Her cheek on his shoulder now, she snuggled into him. "Mmm?"

"It's different, isn't it? Being in love after a few more years of experience, I mean. It's…deeper. Steadier. Richer."

"All of those," she agreed around a lump in her throat. "But still scary. Mostly in a good way."

"I'm going to make some changes," he announced, his arm tightening firmly around her. "I'll cut back on the travel, let my staff take on more of the responsibilities so I can spend more time with you and the kids. And I won't take any extraordinary risks with my safety in the future. I'm going to have to stay healthy to keep up with three active kids and their unpredictable mom," he added with a chuckle.

She lifted her head then to narrow her eyes at him. "I'll never ask you to give up the sports you enjoy—only that you'll take reasonable precautions while pursuing them. And while I think you should delegate a bit more just because I think it's better for your health and well-being, I still expect you to continue to fulfill your responsibilities to your work. I understand that involves quite a bit of travel. I'd love to accompany you occasionally, but between the kids' school and my job it won't be possible very often. So the deal is, when you're gone, we'll carry on as we always do, quite well. And when you're with us, be with us completely. Let us know when we're together that there's nowhere else you'd rather be."

He shifted his weight to loom over her, tumbling her into the already-wrinkled sheets. "That I can guarantee," he promised.

Leaning his head down, he kissed her thoroughly, then broke the kiss only long enough to murmur, "Maybe we should explore a few of the other benefits of experience."

"Mmm." Pulling him down to her, she smiled against his lips. "I'm absolutely positive that we should."

EPILOGUE

THEY WERE MARRIED on Valentine's Day in the Wind Shadow Resort ballroom. Erin and Bella, who were thrilled that Trevor was joining their family, had insisted on that date, though Jade had tried halfheartedly to convince them it was a bit of a cliché.

As many guests as would safely fit in the ballroom were in attendance for the celebration, and all of them smiled when Bella practically danced up the aisle in her pretty garnet-red flower girl dress. Bella had gained more confidence in the past months, and Jade conceded that Trevor had something to do with that. He loved all three of her kids, but he had always had a special bond with her youngest, and Bella thrived on the attention.

She wouldn't call him Daddy, Bella had pronounced after some consideration. That name was reserved for her late father. Instead, she had decided to call him Pop, a nickname Trevor had accepted graciously. It hadn't been long before both girls were chattering about their Pop, though Caleb had decided to stick with Trevor's given name.

Jade knew Caleb was having a bit more trouble accepting the changes than the girls. He remembered their father the most clearly of the siblings, and he hesitated at the thought of anyone taking his hero dad's place. Both Jade and Trevor had made it clear that Stephen and his legacy would never be forgotten, just as Lindsey's memory would always be respected.

Trevor was giving Caleb time and space to adjust. He'd told the now-teenage boy that he wasn't trying to replace Caleb's father but he would always be Caleb's friend. It had apparently been the right approach. Caleb seemed more relaxed lately, and was doing well in school. The bullying had been resolved for now and he was finding his place in the school social circles. He looked quite proud to stand up as groomsman for Trevor in front of their family and friends, along with best man Walt.

Amy and Erin served as matron and maid of honor, Amy quite large with pregnancy but lovely in her flowing garnet frock. Loving the audience attention, Erin preened with such pride that the wedding could have been totally in her honor. There had never been a stage Erin didn't want to perform on, Jade thought with an indulgent shake of her head.

Walking down the aisle behind Bella to formalize their new life, Jade couldn't help thinking that she simply adored everyone standing there waiting for her. When Trevor stepped up to take her hand with a tender, very real smile, she wondered if it were possible for a heart to get any fuller.

Family sat in the front rows of chairs for the ceremony. Jade's mother wiped her eyes copiously, while Trevor's parents smiled in approval. His mother, in particular, looked almost smug at this satisfactory result of her plotting. Mary Pat had a position of honor among the families, and she looked as thrilled as any biological grandmother when she beamed at the children.

Jade and Trevor had written their own vows, and they exchanged them with confidence. Jade had never been more certain that she was doing the right thing. When he'd proposed with a beautiful ring on Christmas Day, Trevor had told her he didn't want to wait any longer to get married and have everyone under one roof again. Jade suspected he'd have been quite happy with a courthouse wedding, though their respective families would have rebelled had they tried it. Especially Bella, who'd thrown herself wholeheartedly into the hastily arranged plans.

Fortunately, Trevor had resources—a venue, caterers, musicians and staff all at his disposal—

so it had come together smoothly enough. Jade had no complaints about her wedding. None at all, she thought when she and Trevor shared a kiss to seal their commitment to a backdrop of hearty applause.

Lifting his head from the kiss, Trevor murmured in a voice meant only for her ears, "It's going to be a grand adventure, Jade. I love you."

Smiling up at him, she replied, "It is, indeed. And I love you, too."

Turning with her children close behind them, they faced their future hand in hand, armed with love, optimism and a deep commitment to this family they would cherish for the rest of their lives. Together.

* * * * *

If you loved this romance by Gina Wilkins, be sure to check out her other books in the SOLDIERS AND SINGLE MOMS *trilogy,* THE SOLDIER'S FOREVER FAMILY *and* THE WAY TO A SOLDIER'S HEART

Available now from Harlequin Superromance!

Get 2 Free Books,
Plus 2 Free Gifts—
just for trying the Reader Service!

Get 2 Free Books,
Plus 2 Free Gifts—

just for trying the Reader Service!

READERSERVICE.COM

Manage your account online!

- Review your order history
- Manage your payments
- Update your address

> ### We've designed the Reader Service website just for you.

Enjoy all the features!

- Discover new series available to you, and read excerpts from any series.
- Respond to mailings and special monthly offers.
- Browse the Bonus Bucks catalog and online-only exculsives.
- Share your feedback.

Visit us at:

ReaderService.com

RS16R